Pregnant Pause

Pregnant Pause

HAN NOLAN

HARCOURT
Houghton Mifflin Harcourt
Boston   New York   2011

Harcourt is an imprint of
Houghton Mifflin Harcourt Publishing Company.
www.hmhbooks.com

Text set in 12.5-point Fournier MT
Design by Christine Kettner

LIBRARY OF CONGRESS CATALOGING-IN-PUBLICATION DATA
Nolan, Han.
Pregnant pause / Han Nolan.
p. cm.
Summary: Married, pregnant, and living at a "fat camp" in Maine,
sixteen-year-old Eleanor has many questions about her future, especially
whether the marriage will last and if she should keep the baby.
ISBN 978-0-15-206570-6
[1. Pregnancy—Fiction. 2. Marriage—Fiction. 3. Camps—Fiction. 4.
Overweight persons—Fiction. 5. Family life—Maine—Fiction. 6.
Maine—Fiction.] I. Title.   PZ7.N6783Pre 2011
[Fic]—dc22
2011009601

Manufactured in the United States of America
DOC 10 9 8 7 6 5 4 3 2 1
4500307548

For my husband, Brian,

and my sister, Lee Walker Doty,

with Love

O KAY, I'M PREGNANT, and so here's what I'm scared about. What if my kid turns out to be a mass murderer? You know, one of those kids who shoots half the school, then shoots himself? Or maybe a drug dealer, or really, just—just what if my kid lies to me, or sneaks out a window to go see her boyfriend, or gets pregnant at sixteen like me? I'd hate to have me for a kid.

I waited until I was five months pregnant to tell my parents. I guess I had sort of hoped the whole thing would go away. At first I thought maybe I wasn't pregnant, and I just tried to ignore the signs, like painful boobs and feeling sick all the time and, oh, yeah, a missing period or two. But then once I figured out that yes, I am pregnant, I thought that I would probably miscarry, because in those first weeks I had been drinking V-O's (vodka and OJ) and smoking my Camels, which, okay, I realize now was a bad idea. But like I said, I didn't know for sure I was pregnant, and I figured the baby wouldn't live, because my mother miscarried three times before she had my older sister and twice before she had me. My sister has already miscarried twice, and she's been trying to get pregnant with her husband for four years. It figures: my baby is alive and kicking.

I hate doctors. The whole reason I didn't have an abortion, besides the fact that I didn't believe I needed one because I figured I'd miscarry, is because I hate, hate, hate doctors. And, okay, my parents would more likely kill me if I had had an abortion than if I were just pregnant, because that's very against their religion. So now I've got to somehow get this baby out of me, and from what I've seen in health class and in the movies, I'm in for a night or two of complete and utter torture!

* * *

When I told my dad that I was pregnant, he stormed through the house yelling at me loud enough for the whole state of Maine and part of Canada to hear. Then when he finally calmed down enough to talk to me in one place, the cozy farmhouse kitchen of our cozy, most favorite house in the world, he stood in front of me with his fists on his hips, his graying hair standing up on end from raking his fingers through it while he raged—maybe pulling it some, too—and he smiled at me. It wasn't this friendly, "I love you, anyway," kind of smile. It was this victorious, self-satisfied smile, like he'd just pulled a fast one on me.

"Well, well, well," he said, still smiling. "I guess it's payback time. All the times you snuck out of this house and ran away with Lam and worried your mother and me—payback. All the times you lied to us, came home drunk and way past curfew—payback. You like staying up all hours of the night? You're in luck. Your baby will keep you up whether you like it or not. And all the griping and complaining you did in Africa, making everyone miserable, the rude and nasty things you've said to us—"

"I know, I know," I said. "Payback. I get it, I get it." And I do, which is why I'm so scared about this baby. I don't want me for a kid. I really, really don't. Worse, I don't want my boyfriend for a kid. Hell, I'm not sure I really even want him for a husband, but my parents and his parents kind of pushed me into it, so what can I do?

I tried to get a little sympathy. "I know I messed up again, Daddy, but can't you at least say something nice? Are you just going to lay curses on me every day for the rest of my life? Won't you feel sorry if you've cursed this baby?"

"Hah!" Dad threw back his head and grabbed at his hair again. He looked a little wild—crazy wild. "Eleanor, you've cursed your own baby by getting pregnant. You're only sixteen! What kind of life can it possibly have? You've got a C average at best in school, so what kind of job do you think you'll get? And that punk-o boyfriend of yours isn't any better." Then back to that ugly smile of his. "But you've made your bed, and you're going to lie in it. We've always done right by you and your sister. She turned out beautifully, and she got everything you got, and you were treated exactly the same, so I don't blame myself for any of this."

"Well, neither do I, Dad, if that's what's got you so steamed. I was just born wrong, I guess." I felt tears stinging my eyes. "I'm a total loser." I rubbed my belly. "And this baby's going to be a total loser, too, because it's going to have such losers for parents. But thanks for all your love and caring sympathy, Dad. I knew I could count on you." I ran out of the kitchen, hoping my dad would call me back, hug me, say everything's going to be all right, he'd take care of everything, save me from my fool self, but he didn't.

* * *

My mom's reaction wasn't much better. I know, I know; I should have told them both at the same time, but I was afraid of the way they would gang up on me—two voices shouting and ranting, the two of them feeding off of each other's anger. To tell the truth, there is no good way to tell your parents that you got knocked up.

Mom's big deal was to find out who did this to me. That's what she said right off the bat. "Who did this to you?" As if he'd splattered mud on my shirt or something. She was setting the table in the dining room, not even looking at me, not even pausing to digest what I'd told her. She just set the plates down one by one, carefully, gently, as if the plates were my baby, its fragile skull cradled in her hands. My mom's calm reaction hurt as much as my father's rage, maybe even more. I knew she had grown used to my terrible surprises, maybe even bored with them. Two times in juvie for stupid stuff like breaking and entering—my boyfriend's house—and stealing a car, my parents' car. All the drinking and drugs, sneaking out, and running away—it's been too much for her, so now she's just bored. She's so bored she doesn't even care anymore. I think she's so done with worrying about me, she's just cut me loose. She couldn't even bother to look at me. Not once. And she didn't once say anything about this being a sin. It used to be I got the sin word slapped in my face every time I did something wrong, but come on, when you live in a sin-free family with sin-free parents and a sin-free sister, well, you can't help but sin a little extra on their behalf.

Mom just kept setting the table—knife and spoon on the right, fork on the left, carefully folded napkins, those tidy triangles of hers, placed under the fork. "Who did this to you?" she asked, and I told her.

"Thanks a lot, Mom!" I said. "Who do you think? Lam Lothrop, who else? I mean, come on, Mom, what do you take me for?"

Lam's real name is Lamont, which is why he goes by Lam. Mom didn't even raise an eyebrow or indicate in any way that she'd heard his name. She poured ice water in the glasses from a 1950s pitcher she found in the cabinet under the sink one day and had used every day since. She loved that pitcher, with its bands of orange and yellow painted on it, more than me. That's what I thought, watching her: *She loves it more than she's ever loved me.*

Mom and Dad didn't say a word during dinner. The only sound was the clink and scrape of our forks and knives, the heavy swallowing of our food and ice water with lemon. I couldn't eat much. After a while I asked to be excused, and my mom nodded, still not looking at me. I grabbed my plate, knife, fork, spoon, napkin, and glass and headed for the kitchen. On the way I knocked into the side table behind my chair and elbowed that pitcher my mom loved so much. It fell off the table, hit the wooden floor, and broke into two thick pieces. I froze. Mom jumped up from her seat, looked right at me, and exploded. She cried and she yelled at the top of her lungs so that all of Maine and half of Canada could hear her. She screamed at me to go to my room and stay there. I nodded and left, taking my plate and stuff up there with me, forgetting that I had them in my hands.

For two months my parents barely spoke to me, and when they did, it was to argue about what to do with the baby. The more they wanted me to give it to my perfectly prim, older sister, Sarah—just hand it over like a sack of potatoes—the more firmly I said that I was keeping it. "It's my body and my baby, and I want to keep it," I said. I mean, what the hell was I saying? I was just mad at my parents. I didn't really plan to keep the baby, but I couldn't shut up. I couldn't save myself. I was just too furious with them.

They're missionaries—educators. We've been in the States three glorious years, but they're heading back to Kenya tomorrow for three, maybe four years! Along with their teaching and all their good works, like fundraising for AIDS, and running a soup kitchen, and being leaders in their church, they've been raising money so they could to go back to Kenya. It's their big dream to return to work with the AIDS babies in the orphanages there.

At first, they expected me to go with them. Just give birth, hand my baby over to my sister, and go back to Kenya with them and forget about everything else. They assumed I'd go back there, when I've got my whole life here in Maine. They act like I got pregnant on purpose just so I could stay here. Well, if I had thought of it I might have done that, but it didn't occur to me. So anyway, they said that I knew their life's work was in Kenya, and that hundreds of people were counting on them, and that my grandmother, who also does good works in Kenya with my grandfather, is quite ill and dying of cancer, so they can't exactly change *their* plans. Okay, I'm sorry about Grandma Lottie having cancer—I am, even though I never liked that self-righteous do-gooder and the way she was always tsk-tsking and shaking her finger at me and then smothering Sarah with kisses and praise. The last time I saw Grandma Lottie, she told me I was going straight to hell, her favorite topic, and I told her if heaven meant living for all eternity with her looking down her long, pious nose at me, then hell sounded like a much better deal. All right, so that was mean, and I'm sorry for what I said, now that she's dying and all, but I still didn't want to go to Kenya and watch over her sickbed. So I told my parents one day when we were arguing in the kitchen that if they thought I was ever going to leave Lam, the love of my life, and go back to Africa with them to be chased by hyenas and get dysentery again and live without electricity and a real toilet, or worse, go to that horrible boarding school they sent me to there, then they had another thing coming.

"And if you think you're going to stay here in Maine all by yourself, then *you've* got another thing coming!" my mother fired back at me. "Honestly, I'm just so fed up with you. I'm at my wits' end."

Since my mother was always telling me she was at her wits' end, I'm surprised she had any wits left.

"You have two choices," she said. "Pick one. Either you go with us to Kenya, or you go stay with Sarah and Robby in California."

My mother should have known by now that I wasn't about to let her have her way. I'm way too stubborn for my own good, and I know this, but I couldn't help opening my big fat mouth. "That's what you think," I said. "You can't *drag* me all the way to Kenya, or California, and even if you could, I'd only run away." I crossed my arms and stood pouting in the kitchen like a little kid. My dad jumped up from his chair. He looked like he was about to throw me over his shoulder and march all the way to Kenya right that second. I saw him start to open his mouth, but before he could yell at me, I shouted, "And anyway, Lam asked me to marry him and I said yes, so there, we're getting married."

My mom yanked her silky scarf from around her neck and I thought for a moment she was going to wrap it around mine, but she slammed it and her hand on the kitchen counter and looked purple-faced at my dad for help.

"Is that so? Well, you can't get married at sixteen without our consent," Dad said, his voice firm, as if to say, *So that's that—end of discussion.*

"Fine," I said. "Then we'll just live together, but I'm not going with you."

I knew this would get my missionary parents good. There's nothing like adding the sin of living together on top of the sin of sexual intercourse. Only in the end, my parents got *me* good, because they agreed to the marriage. They insisted on it even, and the way they insisted made me feel like they were tricking me somehow. I just couldn't figure out how. Maybe they and the Lothrops had decided to let us get married and all because they figured we'd mess it up so royally that we'd finally come to our senses and give up the baby and then go our separate ways. Oh, yeah, I could just see the four of them hatching up some kind of scheme like that. My parents had talked it over with the Lothrops before I even had a chance to tell Lam what I had said. And I needed to talk to Lam because the truth is, I lied. Lam had never asked me to marry him. Who knew my parents would actually go for that idea? Luckily Lam knows me pretty well, and he said he knew what was up as soon as his mother jumped on him about it.

"Don't worry. I was cool about the whole marriage thing," he said when I did call him. "I was like, yeah, I asked her, so what? We love each other and we're going to have a baby, so why not get married?"

* * *

So, it ends up Lam's parents and my parents decided marriage was the best solution if we were so hell-bent on keeping the child. They acted like the whole thing was their idea in the first place. They had it all reasoned out. A child should have both parents, and by getting married I'd have a home, because my parents are only renting the house we're in and the lease is up today, and both sets of parents agreed that this baby was Lam's responsibility, too, so it was the right thing to do. If I got married I'd live with Lam and his family. We didn't know what we wanted, me and Lam, but it sounded a lot better than either Kenya or California, so we agreed to get married.

Now I'm in court again, only this time it's not for stealing anything, it's to get married, and I'm seven months pregnant, but I look and feel like I'm nine and ready to give birth any minute. My sister, Sarah, flew in from California for a couple of weeks, more in support of my parents than me, and she's looking at me squeezed into this orange maternity dress that makes me look like a pumpkin, and she's shaking her head. I think she's still wondering how I, the loser/moron/geek/freak/coffee-addicted, cigarette-addicted, booze-addicted, food-addicted, shopping-addicted younger sister ended up in this family in the first place.

My mom is dressed in beige and she's got her soft brown hair all knotted in a bun, and both she and Dad are looking so calm, maybe even a little pleased, and I know they're probably just so relieved to be getting rid of me. No more playing police or grounding me for the rest of my life. No more court dates and juvie sentences. I'm someone else's headache now.

Lam's parents are here, too, and it's a good thing they love babies, because they hate me for supposedly ruining their precious son's life. Who do they think pressured me to have sex in the first place? Who do they think got me onto dope and shit? Oh, don't worry, I'm off of everything except food and water and vitamins for the baby's sake. And believe me, getting clean was no walk in the park. Anyway, the Lothrops think they're so noble 'cause they run a camp for fat kids, but what's so noble about starving children for a living? They charge extra for the camp because it's specialized, with nutritionists and weigh-ins and such, and then they feed them half as much as any other camp, so they've got to be making big bucks at this fat camp. Since they love babies, and since they had always wanted two children but had lost their first child before it was a year old, and since they love Lam, and since we're getting married, and since my parents are leaving for Kenya, they've offered to take the baby if things don't work out with me and Lam, and they've offered us one of the cabins at the camp.

The camp is another reason why the Lothrops agreed to us

getting married instead of just living together. We have to set a good example for the kids. I have to pretend I'm twenty (yeah, lying—what a great example), and we have to be married and pretend the marriage came before the baby, so that it doesn't look like I got knocked up by accident or anything. Also, I have to tell the campers not to take drugs, not to smoke or drink or have sex, should these topics come up, because they might think I'm cool, and that would be wrong. So—fun—I'm going to be living deep in the back of beyond, surrounded by pine trees and starving fat children, giving birth and raising my baby in a one-room cabin heated with wood, with the kitchen up the hill in the main house, and the bathroom a hornet-infested latrine six cabins away.

* * *

Now here I am, standing in front of the justice of the peace, trying really hard not to give birth right here on the courtroom floor, but really something feels like it's about to burst down below, and I'm trying to figure out if I really even love Lamont Lothrop—I mean, enough to live with him the rest of my life, forever and ever, amen. For two and a half years I thought I did. That's why we tried to run away together, that's why I climbed out of my bedroom window at three in the morning—to be with Lam, my soul mate, my prince of a guy, my knight in shining armor, only right now, dressed in jeans and a T-shirt, he looks more like a dude and nothing else.

I hear something about husband and wife, and Lam leans

over and kisses me—leans way over. He's six-two, and I'm five-two; he's a hundred and ninety-nine pounds, and I'm not quite ninety pounds (well, usually). He's all muscle, and I'm all bones. I don't know how this marriage is going to work, but I kiss him and shout, "Yahoo!" and my dried-up, laced-up, thin-lipped sister comes forward with her ramrod-straight, penny-loafered husband in tow and says, "Don't expect us to cheer about this, Eleanor."

"I don't expect anything from you," I say, rubbing my belly, wishing I could put my feet up somewhere.

Lam puts his arm around my shoulder and squeezes me, and I'm so proud of him for doing this in front of Sarah that I almost forgive him for showing up stoned.

"Well, I think once you see how hard it is to take care of that baby, you'll give our offer another thought. It still stands. We'll take your baby. We'll raise it as our own. Won't we, Robby?"

Robby, Sarah's husband, nods, but his sour expression tells me he doesn't want anything to do with anything coming from me, and that's another reason why I haven't agreed to Sarah taking the baby once it's born.

"Yeah, well"—I rub my stomach some more, because it comforts me and maybe comforts the baby and it definitely annoys Sarah—"it's my baby, mine and Lam's, so we'll see."

"Don't cut off your nose to spite your face," Robby says.

"Yeah, okay, whatever *that* means," I say. He talks like that all the time. He says things like "Don't beat a dead horse," and

"Don't kill the messenger," and "When pigs fly." I guess he's got to borrow someone else's expressions because his own don't amount to a hill of beans. Ha! Take that expression, Robby boy.

My new mother-in-law comes forward to join us while my parents and Lam's dad talk over "future plans." I hear the words "cabin" and "when the baby comes," but then Mrs. Lothrop is speaking to me, so I turn my attention to her.

"I guess some kind of congratulations are in order," she says, frowning, and I wonder what the hell I'm supposed to say to that. I look her up and down. She's tall, sturdy, and beautiful, in a rustic, country-woman sort of way, and she's got herself all dressed in black. Black pants, sleeveless black shirt, and black gardening clogs—you know, rubber clog things—a real funeral outfit, I figure.

"I guess so." I sorta smile.

"I'm so stoked, Ma," Lam says. "I can't believe I'm married."

"No, none of us can believe it," she says, and her sarcasm goes right over Lam's head.

He gives her a peck on the cheek. "Thanks for everything, Ma. I mean the cabin and furniture and junk."

We all jabber for twenty more minutes or so, but then my parents have to go because they have to finish packing and cleaning. They leave me their car, a hunk-a-junk they named Rambo, bought cheap and well used, and only to last them the three years they'd be in the States. I'm grateful for it, though, because

I can't drive Lam's stick-shift Jeep, and I need it for my days off from the camp. I'm grateful, too, for the baby stuff they bought—crib and car seat and baby carrier and stroller.

Mom hugs me and kisses my cheek, and I see tears in her eyes. "I do love you, Elly," she says. "Anytime you want to join us, we'll get you a flight and take care of everything. Remember that."

I nod and feel ashamed for the millionth time that I'm pregnant. Yeah, I admit it, I'm ashamed. I talk a good game and my big talk gets me into all kinds of messes, but I know I've been stupid, and I know, too, that most likely, after I've made my sister jealous long enough and she's suffered some as payback for always being better than I am, I'll give in and hand her the baby to raise.

Dad pats my back and kisses the top of my head. "You're still my li'l gal," he says. "We're gonna miss you."

I nod and feel queasy in my stomach. I can see they're so anxious to get going, to fly far, far away, and get back to feeding the bodies and souls of people who really need them. I want to say, "I need you, too. I need you, Mom and Dad. I just have a crappy way of telling you." But it's too late. When it comes to me and my timing, it's always too late. Too late to get an abortion, too late to say I'm sorry, too late to say I need you, and I'm scared, and I don't want to live in a cabin in the woods. It's just too late, or maybe too hard to admit that I don't want a husband and baby, and that I'm just so tired of being me.

CHAPTER TWO

Here's what I hate about all the pregnancy books I've been reading. They're meant for perfect people who are going to have perfect babies and live perfect lives with their perfect husbands. Everything sounds so simple and orderly—even emergencies like miscarriages and preeclampsia and terrible stuff like C-sections and edema and having to stay in bed for the whole nine months. The writers make it sound like this calm, easily managed, well-behaved problem that we will all handle rationally. And I hate all the parenting magazines with the beautiful people and children on the covers, and all the bright toys and pretty living rooms and baby bedrooms in the photos inside. I'm thinking I'm going to put out a teen pregnancy magazine. Why not? And it will be real. Real people on the covers, and stories about how real people are dealing with being pregnant, and working and going to school, and parents and friends who are no longer there for you because you just don't fit in anymore, or they're too busy—and so are you, but in a different way—and how it feels to be left out of everything. Yeah, I really ought to start that one up. Right now, though, I'm making my way through the throng of fat kids who are moving into camp today, climbing the steep mountain slope thick with pine trees that leads to my humble new home, while Lam's in front of me telling me to hurry up because it's not just his wedding day, it's his graduation day, and he's anxious to get to the parties. All I'm anxious to do is to sit down. I notice kids hugging their pillows and their parents dragging trunks and staring at me as I huff it up the slope, and I can see their little minds working: *Is she fat or is she pregnant? She looks pregnant. Am I/is my kid in the right place?*

The camp starts at the base of a mountain where there's a lake that smells like wet logs and ducks. Canoes are stacked on a rack at the edge of the water, two tall lifeguard chairs dug into the sand, a long dock with a ladder going down into the lake, and a rope with little plastic buoys marking off the shallow and deep parts. The dirt parking lot is down by the lake, and on the far side of the lake sit eight boys' cabins and four latrines dotted about the woods. The rest of the camp is tucked into the mountain itself, with the large red main cabin in the center, and the girls' cabins, latrines, activities huts, and the Lothrops' cabin/office scattered in the woods on either side. From the parking lot, most of the buildings are hidden by the trees, and by the fact that they're all made of logs so they just look like part of the mountain. The climb to the cabins is steep and rocky, and black flies are nipping at my calves. I'm trying to swat at them and walk at the same time.

"Come on, Eleanor," Lam calls to me, his voice sounding impatient. He's reached our cabin. It's set back a ways from the others and is slightly bigger, too. It once housed the older kids, but this camp now only goes up to age fifteen instead of nineteen, and the older kids have become the camp counselors. Even I'm supposed to be a counselor-in-training, or CIT, and I've got two jobs, one to help out in the crafts cabin, and the other to help out in a dance class. What I know about crafts can be said in one word—*nothing!* What I know about dance is next to nothing, but I had to fill out a CIT application just like any other counselor here, and when it asked what training or experience I had and gave me a list to choose from, dance and crafts seemed like they might be the most fun. So I lied and said I had taken dance for six years. Really I had only had dance lessons for two, when I was six and seven. I also lied and said my mother and I did crafts all the time, because I thought the Lothrops might like me better if I said I did something homey like crafts with my mom. I mean, really, what was I thinking? Oh, and I had to have an interview, too, only it wasn't with Mr. and Mrs. Lothrop. Mrs. Lothrop was in some meeting in Boston, so it was with Mr. Lothrop and this crazy old bat of a lady with a witch's nest of wiry gray hair who sat in her wheelchair like it was a throne and who, it turned out, used to own and run this camp way back in the dark ages. I could tell by the way her evil black eyes squinted at me, she didn't believe a word I said about knowing how to dance and do crafts. She saw *liar* written all over me, and I knew it, but she didn't let on to Mr. Lothrop, and the only question she asked me was, "What would you do if a camper came up to you and told you she was homesick?"

What the hell? I didn't know. "I'd talk to her," I said.

"Oh, would you?" she said back to me in this witch-like voice.

"Yes, I would." I glared right at her.

"And what would you say? How would you talk her out of her homesickness?"

Was this a trick question? You can't talk someone out of being homesick. Believe me; I know. I was homesick for America for years and nobody ever talked me out of it, not even for a second.

"I wouldn't talk her out of it," I said. "You can't do that. It doesn't work." I tried to think of what I would have wanted someone to do for me in Kenya, what would have made it better. "I would just let the camper know that I was her friend and that if she wanted to talk about being homesick for eight weeks straight that I'd be willing to listen to her. And if she wanted to talk about something else, I'd listen to that, too."

My answer must have been okay, 'cause the old bat got this

twinkle in her eye and nodded, and that was that. She let Mr. Lothrop do the rest of the interview while she conked out and snored and blew air out of the corner of her mouth throughout the rest of my interview. It was only later, when I told Lam about the old bat, that I found out she was Lam's grandmother and Mrs. Lothrop's mother, which explained a lot!

So now Lam stands in the doorway of our cabin, and when I catch up to him, he asks, "Want me to carry you over the threshold?" I look at his face. He looks worried. I can tell when he's worried because this deep line forms down the center of his forehead, and that's what I see.

"How about we just hold hands and go inside together."

He smiles, and the line disappears. "Yeah, perfect."

We hold hands, and he has to step inside before me a bit because no way can wide ol' me fit alongside his big self through the door at the exact same time.

Once inside, he shouts, "Yow! I'm through with school forever. Forever!" Then he reaches around me and grabs me from under my ass and lifts me. I hold on to his neck for dear life, not thrilled that he had no oomph to lift me when it was about us being married but suddenly he's feeling like Superman 'cause he remembers he's a high school graduate. I'm jealous of him, too, because I still have another year to go before I graduate—*if* I'm able to go back to school in the fall. Lam's eighteen, and I think the truth of how I got myself pregnant is that I was so flattered that a guy two years older liked me, and I was so scared that I'd lose him, that I finally broke down and said yes to having sex with him, even though I had had a bad feeling about it. It was the first time I ever had sex, and he wore a condom, and still I got pregnant, which is just my luck. Of course my parents, his parents, my sister, and everyone in school think I'm a whore now. Like just because I did drugs and crap, they think I must have been going around having sex with everyone, too, so I was bound to get pregnant sometime. No need trying to tell anyone the truth. Who cares, anyway?

"So, which party first?" Lam asks. "Matt's or Rolly's? I vote Matt's."

"Come on, Lam," I say. "It's our wedding day. Here we are alone together, and we have this cabin, and we're in the woods. Wouldn't it be nice to just be cozy together and forget about the rest of the world for a while?"

A bunch of kids yell, "Lake!" and there's a stampede outside our door as they run down the hill, past our cabin, and toward the lake.

I make my way over to the couch that sits in the middle of the cabin and start backing myself down into it. I am so looking forward to getting off my feet. I've been real good about eating well and keeping my weight up because I read that teens that don't gain enough weight can have low-weight babies with birth defects. But now I'm too big and I get tired too easily.

"If I stay, are we gonna have sex?" Lam asks.

I stop in mid-sit and push myself back off the couch. I

spread my arms out and glare down at my orange belly. "Do you think I could possibly want to make love? Give me a break." We haven't had sex in over two weeks, and I could see Lam was getting desperate about it, but I just can't do it anymore. I'm just too pregnant.

Lam puts on his camo hunting cap with the moose emblem on the front, salutes me, and clicks the heels of his hunting boots together. "Well, then, I'm going to Matt's. He's got the party of the century going on, and I don't want to miss it. You're not coming?"

"No, and I can't believe you'd just leave me here on our honeymoon night surrounded by a bunch of whiny kids and your parents and all those counselors. And, look around. We don't even have a TV or a refrigerator, so what am I supposed to do while you party?"

Instead of easing myself onto the couch as I had started to do earlier, I just let myself go and fall back onto the sofa cushions. The two cushions on either side of me puff up with a gasp, then settle back down. Lam's parents had given us the couch, and Lam acts like they were just so generous, but all it is is a shredded, cat-clawed, brown and tan plaid box that scratches your skin if you have any exposed. I put my feet up on the coffee table, which is really the trunk I used for my years in Kenya. I've covered it over with a pretty flowered scarf, but Lam has already burned a cigarette hole in it—the butthead. I feel tears starting to well up, and I blink several times to hold them back.

"Don't start acting like my ball and chain on our first day, El. Come on, I just graduated. No more school forever! Anyway, you love a good party. It'll do you good to get out and see the guys."

I sniff and wipe a stupid tear away. "They've always been more your friends than mine, and anyway, what am I gonna do while everyone gets stoned? Just stand there and watch? I can't do anything, Lam. I can't do anything ever again. We're going to have a baby—a kid, a responsibility."

"But not forever, right? You said we might give it to my parents, right? Or maybe your sister, right?" Lam edges toward the door. It's an old-fashioned latch-kind of door with no locks and so poorly sized for the opening that you can see the great outdoors through all the gaps. The cabin was built for summers, for young campers, not for pregnant girls, and not for year-round living.

I swat at a fly, then let my arms flop onto my belly. "Yeah, well, we haven't exactly made our final decision on that, have we?" Then I look at Lam, already standing with the door open and his hand on the screen door, hot to get going. He looks so good, even with his doofus-looking, too-big-for-his-head hunting hat on. I think that's what I fell for, his looks. He's got big round blue eyes the color of chicory, which is the stuff that grows all around here along the roadside, and he's got a flush to his cheeks, and he's tall with a cute butt, and sandy blond hair with bangs that slant down into his eyes. I know girls will be all over him at the party, even if he does kind of have big ears. Shit, he'll probably screw one of them—on our wedding night.

"Have you even thought about this baby?" I ask. "I mean, it's part yours. It's going to look like you and maybe talk like you and—"

"Yeah, I've thought about it." He huffs and pushes open the screen door. It groans. He stands halfway in and halfway out and scratches his chest through his very faded, deer-skull T-shirt. He glances outside, then inside at me. "So, you comin' or what?"

"I said no, already!" I pound the arm of the couch. "It's our wedding night, Lam. Don't you even love me? Why did you marry me?"

Okay, never mind that I don't know how I feel about him. I need him to tell me he loves me. I need this really badly.

"Yeah, I love you," he says. His voice softens. "You're pretty, Elly. Even seven months pregnant, you're so pretty. I mean, come on, half the guys in school were always after you. You're like this guy magnet."

"Yeah," I say, still wanting to feel sorry for myself. "But all the girls hate me—and for no good reason."

"Like I said, you're pretty—and you have this, I don't know, this cute way about you that guys like and girls are jealous of." Lam steps back into the cabin and tries again. "And—and—you look smart-pretty, too. Not like dumb-pretty—all boobs and bubbly-blonde pretty, but sexy-lawyer pretty. You know? 'Cause you're really smart. And, I—I like how your eyes have those golden flecks in the brown part and, uh, I like your hair in that ponytail thing you've always got, and I like how you pull the thingy out and shake out your hair and it's perfect, like you just brushed it. I like—I like your hair."

I feel embarrassed now because I've let him go on so long with his compliments. I try to flick them off. "So you married me for my mousy brown lawyer-lady hair?"

He rolls his eyes and shakes his head like he's just too fed up with me. "Come on, Elly, you know why I married you. You told your parents that I asked you to marry me. And anyway, we're pregnant. It's my duty. My parents made real sure I understood that." He raises his fist and sets it on the doorsill as though he needed it to prop him up. "A Lothrop always does his duty. A Lothrop always fixes his mistakes, and he *always* does the honorable thing."

I frown. "Yeah, uh-huh, so the honorable thing is to leave me here alone on our wedding night? Great! You know what Matt said? Matt said our marriage would only last six months, and he's our best friend!" I rest my head on the back of the couch and slouch down a little more. I'm so tired all of a sudden. I hate that about being pregnant—being tired.

"Oh, yeah?" Lam says. "Matt told *me* that he gave us two months, just long enough to have the baby, give it away, and split up." He studies his boots, picking one foot up to examine the sole and then the other, as if he's inspecting them for dog doo-doo.

"So, is that all this is?"

Lam shrugs. "I don't know, Elly. I don't know what it is. Shit, I'm just doing what I'm supposed to do—what everybody's telling me to do. You go off and tell everybody you want to keep the baby, so okay, we're keeping the baby—*maybe.* Then you tell everybody I asked you to marry me and then our parents say we *have* to get married, but Mom and Dad want me to graduate before we get married 'cause they figured I'd never graduate if I got married first, so okay, I graduate—just barely, but I do it. Then *your* parents want to be there for the wedding, so we do it today before they leave for Africa, *same* day as graduation. And tomorrow I start working here at the camp—like always. So, see? I'm doing my part." Lam slams his fist on the door. "I'm doing my part! And I don't know anymore how I feel about anything." He checks out how I'm taking what he's saying, and I'm not taking it too well because it sounds like it's all about doing his duty and nothing about loving me. More tears spill down my face. Mom and Dad are gone, and now Lam's mad at me and leaving me alone in this boring cabin, and he doesn't even love me anymore.

I don't say this out loud, but he reads my mind, which he can do sometimes. "Come on, El," he says. "You're just being weepy and cranky 'cause you're so pregnant. You know I love you. That hasn't changed." He leaves his position by the door and walks toward me. While he's walking he reaches into his pants pocket. He's wearing baggy camo pants. Everything is about hunting to Lam. If he isn't getting stoned, he's hunting—or, as one of his many bumper stickers proclaims, he'd rather be hunting.

"Okay," he says. "I was going to give you this tomorrow as a first-day-of-marriage kind of thing, but here, I got something for you." He pulls out a purple cloth pouch and hands it to me. It says Albert's Jewelers on the front. That's where my wedding ring came from. My ring is gold with a small pink tourmaline stone in it. Tourmaline is Maine's state mineral, so it's cool. I like it better than plain old diamonds any day.

"Lam! What's this?"

Lam gets this too-cute bashful look on his face—all blushing and staring down at his feet.

I pull open the pouch and empty the contents into my hand. "What . . . a bracelet! With another tourmaline—Lam!"

It's a gold chain with a gold heart dangling from it, and in the center is a tiny pink tourmaline. I get to my feet and reach over the coffee table/trunk for him and kiss him. "I love it! I can't believe you got me this. When did you . . . ?"

Lam's giggling like a girl, he's so proud of himself. "It matches your ring. See?" he says, coming around the table to me. "Let me put it on for you."

I hold out my arm while he places it on my wrist and messes with the clasp.

"How could you afford this? It must have cost more than the ring."

"Yeah, I used all my savings." The clasp locks, and he steps back. "I couldn't resist getting it for my girl—my wife," he says.

I lift my arm up and look at the bracelet. "Yeah, well it's beautiful." I smile at him. "Lam, you're so sweet. I love it." I say all this, even though my first thought is that maybe we could have used that money for us and the baby, but then my second thought is, I love how romantic he is sometimes. I love him so much. He's always surprising me with some sudden thoughtfulness. Always. And for a second or two, I'm really glad we got married.

CHAPTER THREE

I KNOW LAM is proud of himself about the bracelet. We stare at it together and we're standing so close that our heads touch and the moment feels so good, but it's only a moment because then Lam pats my arm and backs up. "Okay," he says. "Gotta party. I swear, I'm gonna go out and get piss-ass drunk. You comin'?"

"No! I already said, but hey, don't let me keep you. You gave me this bracelet—what more could I want? Go on, have a good time." I say this sarcastically, of course, but Lam has never been good at sarcasm. I've always loved that about him, but now it only irritates me.

"Yeah, great! So, I'll see you." He kisses me, his lips barely grazing mine, then he heads for the exit.

I watch Lam push open the wooden screen door, listen to it

slam behind him, and then through the screen I see him jog down the hill toward his Jeep. I stand in the middle of the cabin, turning the bracelet around and around on my wrist, and look about me. I see the full-size four-poster bed in one corner of the room that I made up with a cotton blue bedspread and a gray wool camp blanket folded at the bottom. There's a bookshelf next to it that's supposed to hold all our crap, but we've got too much crap. It all sits in a heap on the other side of the room. There's my clothes and shoes and books, and all the baby stuff my parents bought me—the car seat and crib and baby carrier and stroller—and then there's Lam's clothes and our computers and even a real stuffed moose head. The giant head sits lopsided, resting on the left side of its antlers, a souvenir of the first moose Lam ever shot. There's a card table with an old record player on top, and in the center of the room is the scratchy couch and trunk/coffee table. The room looks so depressing that I can't help it, a fresh batch of tears rolls down my face. I flop down on the couch and have myself a good long cry. While I'm crying I rub my belly and talk to my baby, which is something I've kind of gotten into the habit of doing—when nobody else is around.

"Don't you be sad," I tell it. "I don't even know why I'm crying, except I just feel so alone, except for you. Mom and Dad are gone, and I'm pregnant, and I'm married, and Lam's at a party, and I'm at a camp in the middle of nowhere, and I mean *nowhere*. This has to be the last place in the whole state of Maine where cell phones and computers don't work, you know? You know, baby cakes? Anyway"—I rub my belly some more and I feel it move—"what if I want to keep you? You're kind of growing on me—ha, ha. Well, if I did keep you, I wouldn't ever leave you to go off to Africa, or to some dumb party, that's for sure. And you wouldn't leave me, and I would never feel alone like this again." I sigh and feel the baby move, trying to get more comfortable inside me. "Maybe Lam really wants you, too. Maybe that's why he let me and our parents push him into getting married. Maybe—I don't know."

I cry some more, but after a while I hear kids outside yelling and counselors ordering everybody around, and then I hear the heavy clang of the dinner bell, and I figure I might as well go eat, although since I'll be eating at least twice as much as everybody else at the camp, I can't eat in the dining hall with the kids. I have to eat in the kitchen.

The dining hall is at one end of Moosehead Lodge, the camp's main cabin. Instead of being boxlike and made of unpainted logs or slats of wood like the campers' cabins, it looks more like a sturdy barn, with the two-story roof and dark red paint and these wide entry doors that slide open.

When I step inside the dining hall, I'm hit with the smell of something really sweet and something really sour at the same time. It makes the baby kick. One of the counselors hired to do kitchen duty—or, sorry, KP; that's what they call it—tells me to sit at the picnic table in the back of the room where the kitchen help eats. I waddle my way to the back, noticing the trays of dessert lined up on the stainless-steel counters—some kind of oatmeal/berry crunch brownie stuff. Only you can't call it a brownie, because it's not brown, but they're the size of brownies, and they smell really good. My stomach growls.

I struggle to fit myself between the bench and the table. Once I'm seated, I stare at the ketchup and mustard in front of me and listen to all the voices. There's the noise of all the kids on the other side of the wall, and the *tap-tap-tap* of someone patting a microphone. In the kitchen it's dishes clattering, and stainless-steel cabinets opening and closing, and orders being given, and laughter, and laughter, and laughter on both sides. I'm not a part of any of this. I'm just sitting like a rotting pumpkin one week after Halloween. Why, I wonder, did my mother ever buy me such a stupid dress? I hate being pregnant, I hate being married, and I hate this backwoods, fat-ass camp.

The campers on the other side of the wall are called to order, and after a welcome and the reading of some dining rules, Lam's dad says in a very serious and solemn voice, "Let us now say the camp prayer." Then the kids all shout at the top of their lungs, "Rub-a-dub-dub, thanks for the grub, yea God," and I guess it's all the new kids who laugh but maybe the old kids do, too. Some of the KP duty counselors smile to themselves and look at one another, but they keep on scrubbing gigantic pots or dumping mashed potatoes into serving bowls.

Kids come up to a wide window with a tray in their hands, and the KP counselors pass the bowls and platters of food out to them. It gets really noisy on the other side of the wall, but on our side it gets quieter.

I watch a guy load some dishes onto a tray and then head toward me. He stops in front of the table. *"Here, my lady, is your dinner. If there be anything else you are wanting, sing out. Sing out! Oh, sing out!"* He sings this to me. I swear on a stack of Bibles. He sings like a lady opera singer. Then he pauses, and it's like he's waiting for me to applaud him.

"Okay, first of all," I say, "don't *ever* sing to me again. Second of all, just put the tray down and go away."

The guy, tall like Lam but thinner, with a goatee, pierced ear with small hoop, dark brown hair in a ponytail, and gray eyes, sets the tray on the table and sits down across from me.

"I'm Ziggy," he says. "I'm the kitchen help and music counselor, and I already know that you're Eleanor Crowe, Lam's wife. Oh, or are you Eleanor Lothrop now that you're married?"

"No, it's still Crowe," I say. My last name is just about the only thing I like about myself, but I don't tell this Ziggy-person this. "Why should I take Lam's last name?" I say instead. "If there's going to be a name change, he can take mine. Crowe is better than Lothrop any old day."

"So then what name will you give the baby?" he asks, and picks up the bowl of mashed potatoes.

I shrug. "We're not sure yet," I say, as if this was something Lam and I had been discussing.

He hands me the bowl of potatoes and says, "Here, have some cauliflower."

"Uh—" I stare into the bowl.

He pulls it back, grabs an empty plate off the tray, and scoops some cauliflower onto it.

"Are you kidding me?"

He laughs. "You thought it was mashed potatoes, right?"

"Uh, yeah."

"Not at this camp." He gestures toward each item on the tray. "We've got mashed cauliflower with skim milk, parmesan cheese, and pepper; corn on the cob—no butter—and ham slabs with Diet Coke and raisin sauce."

I scoop up a blob of cauliflower and sniff. "What kind of hell is this? My baby's going to starve to death here. Diet Coke and raisin sauce?"

"It's not too bad." He takes a bite. "So, you don't like my singing?"

"I don't like you singing to *me*. That's so queer. Don't *ever* sing to me."

He holds one arm out toward me. *"Why ever not?"* he sings.

I get to my feet. "Rub-a-dub-dub and opera-singing counselors and fake mashed potatoes—I'm outta here!"

"Hey, where you going? Come on, sit down. I won't sing. I promise. Now, come on, sit. You need to eat." He reaches across the table and grabs my hand. I think he looks like he's proposing to me, and other kitchen workers are looking at us, so I sit down fast and take my hand out of his.

"So, where's Lam, anyway?" Ziggy glances around the kitchen like he might spot him rising from the sink or popping out of the toaster.

A girl carrying a small, single-size tray of food bustles up to the table and, after slamming her tray down, climbs over the bench and sits with a grunt. She's, well, I guess you could call her plump—not all that fat, but jiggly and pretty if you like that candy-coated look in a person.

"Ahh," she says. "It feels so good to sit down. I always forget how tiring the first week is. I get so out of shape during the winter." She looks at me. "You must be Lam's—uh—wife? I'm Jen." She tosses her over-highlighted, shoulder-length hair back with a jerk of her head, and smiles at me. She has the whitest, fakest-looking teeth I've ever seen. They're creepy looking.

"Yeah, hi," I say.

She stares at me a little too long, so I'm starting to feel squirmy. Finally she speaks. "So you're going to have a baby, huh? Like any minute, by the looks of things." She smiles after this comment, but it's one of those fake smiles that come out looking more snotty than friendly.

She keeps going. "Do you know if it's a boy or a girl? Where's Lam? Isn't this your wedding day? Did you wear that . . . dress . . . to your wedding? I like orange. It's so— bright and festive. Reminds me of a certain holiday—hmm, which one?" She turns to Ziggy. "Don't you like her dress?"

Ziggy shrugs. He's well dug into the ham and Diet Coke

crap. "She looks like a pumpkin. No offense." He blinks innocently at me.

"Ziggy . . ." I say to change the subject and go on the attack, since clearly that's what they plan to do to me. "So were you named after the bald comic-strip guy or what?"

"It's Siegfried, and I'm named after my grandfather, one of the greatest men to ever live. I'm proud to have his name."

"Then why don't you go by Siegfried instead of Ziggy, if you're so proud?"

"I take it you've never heard of Siegfried 'Ziggy' Grumbauer, the tenor."

"No, why would I? Is that you?"

Jen snickers.

"It was my grandfather. He sang with the Metropolitan Opera back in his day."

"So why the hell would I have ever heard of him? Opera? Who likes opera?" I take a bite of the cauliflower, still expecting mashed potatoes. I spit it back out onto my plate. "What the . . . ?"

Jen laughs out loud, and when I say out loud, I really mean *loud*. She's got a laugh like a foghorn—I mean!

"It's cauliflower. You ate it expecting it to taste like mashed potatoes—like fake mashed potatoes," Ziggy says.

I'm still spitting. "Well, aren't they?" I ask between spits.

"No. It's still just cauliflower. Just accept them as a veggie, not as a substitute for anything else."

I shove my plate away. "No, thanks. I'm not that hungry,

and the only veggies I like are real potatoes and green beans, and I don't like pig on a plate, just cow."

Jen laughs again. Gee, I'm so glad I can keep her in stitches.

"So how old are you? You look young—I mean younger than Lam," Jen says.

"I'm—uh—twenty. How old are you?"

"Right, uh-huh, sure you are." Jen nods and shakes her hair back out of her face again. She does this so often I think it's a nervous tic. "Well, I'm only sixteen. *Sweet* sixteen."

Sweet, my ass. The girl has horns coming out of her head.

Jen presses her lips together and shakes her head, not to get her hair out of her way this time but in preparation for zinging me one more time. "I'd hate it if I were knocked up. I mean you totally lose all your freedom. You can't go to parties or just hang out with friends. Lam must *hate* it. Everybody knows how he loves to play the field. And then there's college, and I want to be a pediatrician, which takes years and years. If I had a baby, my dreams would just go down the toilet."

She says all this with her head bent over her plate, digging into her food and stuffing her face with it. There's sauce on her chin and she dabs at it daintily with her napkin so the pounds of makeup she's wearing don't smear. Finally, she looks up and she has this gleam in her eyes, but she's doing this sweet, innocent-like smile act. "Did you *mean* to get pregnant," she asks, "or haven't you ever heard of birth control?" She shakes her hair out of the way again, and before I can answer, she adds, half under her breath and as if she's just meaning for Ziggy to hear and not me, "If she's gonna sleep around, you'd think she'd learn a little bit about birth control."

I check out Ziggy's expression, and his face says, "I'm staying out of this catfight."

"For your information," I say, "I only slept with one person, Lam, and I got pregnant the first time, and we did use birth control, not that it's any of your business, so just in case you think you're safe, you aren't. The first time I had sex. The first time, and with birth control, so—"

Jen pokes Ziggy with her elbow and giggles. "It helps if you actually know how to *use* the birth control, I guess. A condom goes *on* the—"

"Shut up," Ziggy says, not laughing, which makes me like him just the very, very slightest, teeniest, tiniest bit. "You're just being mean."

Jen opens her mouth wide with a look of innocent surprise. "Hah. Mean? I'm just trying to understand. What kind of example is she going to be setting for all these kids? She looks like she's twelve years old. I'm surprised it's even legal for her to work at the camp. And anyway, she's about to give birth any second. She shouldn't be here."

Ziggy brushes her comments away with his hand. "You're just jealous and being mean 'cause she's good-lookin' and she married Lam. Everyone knows you've had a thing for him for years." He looks at me. "Pay no attention to her."

Jen gives Ziggy a shove, and he just chuckles.

"Hah! You take that back. I am not jealous of that cow." She jerks her head back for the millionth time, and I can see her face is flushed. "And I could care less about Lam. He's already screwed just about every girl counselor here."

"Everyone except you," Ziggy says.

"Um, hello," I say. "I'm right here." I wave my hand in front of them. "Sitting right here across from you." I hate hearing what they've just said. Lam's been with me for two years. He's always denied that he's cheated on me.

"Believe me; we know," Jen says. "You're kinda hard to miss."

"Well, then, stop talking like I'm not," I say. "If you've got something to say to me, say it, and don't play games with me and pretend that you only meant Ziggy to hear, or that you're being nice when you're really not. What did I ever do to you, anyway? I hate girls like you. You give all decent girls a bad name. You're candy on the outside and tar on the inside. Be real, be straight, or stay outta my way. You got that, honey pie?"

I shove my tray at the two of them and stand up to leave. My exit would be great if I could just climb over the bench and sashay off, but I have to clamber over it, holding on to the table, taking it slowly, and then I have to waddle away. The effect I wanted is a total miss, but I had my say, and that at least feels good.

CHAPTER FOUR

I LEAVE BY the kitchen exit, grabbing a couple of those oatmeal-berry brownies on my way out. I take a bite and chew on it waiting for the big surprise, like they're really made out of beets and not berries, but it actually tastes pretty good—not too sweet, and kind of sour, and the oatmeal is crispy-crunchy. I come around the side of the building, and the wind serves up a nice warm gust of pine scent. I stop and just stand there on the side of the mountain, squinting out over all the pine trees, and I see the sun shining on the lake below. I take a deep breath. The water shines and glints like a million diamonds. I take another deep breath and mull over the conversation in the dining hall. *So that's what this place is going to be like, huh? Nasty counselors and bratty fat kids. Great. Well, they can all count me out. I'm going to do the bare minimum around here. The very barest of the bare. I'll*

get up late and quit early. I'm just a CIT, anyway. It's a nothing job.
It's like being a babysitter, and I hate baby-sitting.

I hear someone crying, but the sun is so bright and it's shining right in my eyes, so it takes me a while before I can find the person. It's a girl, maybe ten or so, sitting on the ground and leaning up against the side of a tree. She's got long wavy hair that looks like someone just poured it all over her.

"Hey, you," I say, sounding annoyed, because I am. "Shouldn't you be in the dining hall?"

The girl starts, and she looks so frightened of me. She jumps to her feet and begins to scramble away.

I sure didn't expect that. I can't go around scaring the kids to death, or the Lothrops will have my neck in a noose.

"Oh, come on, don't run off," I call to her. "I'm not going to do anything to you. Come on, don't make me run after you. I'm pregnant."

The girl stops and turns around, but she doesn't come any closer. She hangs her head.

"So what's wrong? You homesick?" I remember the old bat and how I said I'd talk it out with a kid if she were homesick.

She shakes her head. "No, I just hate it here." She says this with a squeaky-donkey-braying kind of whine in her voice.

"Yeah, tell me about it."

The girl looks at me, her head tilted, and I recognize her from when I first arrived. She was the scared little rabbit I saw walking between a man and woman who looked like they were straight out of Hollywood. They looked rich and glossy, with shiny skin and dressy shoes and tight-fitting clothing accentuating their thin bodies. The way they glided along, staring out from behind their sunglasses, it looked as if they very much wanted everyone to know *they* did not belong in a place like this.

"This camp's the pits, ain't it?" I say.

She shrugs. "I don't know. I guess the camp isn't so bad. It's just some of the people." She whines again when she says the word "people."

"Yeah, well, look at it from my point of view." I take a couple of steps closer, and so does she. "I'm seven months pregnant, living with my husband in one of these cabins with no bathroom, and I've gotta go like a hundred times a night at least, and there's no kitchen, and no TV or cell phone or anything fun but an old-timey record player with old-timey records."

The girl steps a little closer and wipes at her eyes. She peers up at me through her mass of hair. "Don't you like to swim? When my mom was pregnant with my little sister, she swam every day."

"Yeah, swimming's okay, I guess, but I can't do that all day. I'm supposed to help teach some kind of dance class and work in the crafts hut, and I can't dance and I don't even know how to glue two pieces of paper together. Lam claims the counselors will teach me all I need to know, but whoever they are, they haven't ever met a challenge like me, I'm sure of it."

The girl gives me a shy smile, and I take several more steps toward her.

"Everybody knows how to glue paper," she says, still whining. Could this be how she always talks? I wanna smack her. I do. But, okay, I feel sorry for her, too—a little. She looks so timid and pathetic, with her slouching shoulders and the way she tries to hide behind all that hair.

"Yeah, well, I don't. My art teacher used to get so frustrated because I could never glue a strip of construction paper together so the end pieces were straight. I was supposed to make a circle and link it with another circle and another to make a chain—a paper chain. What the he—What are we supposed to do with a chain, huh?"

The girl laughs a quiet little laugh and walks right up close to me.

I put my arm around her shoulder, because that's what I'd have wanted someone to do for me. "I mean, really," I say.

She brushes the hair out of her eyes. "It's for decoration. To hang in your room, or on a Christmas tree. You're supposed to do it in different colors so it looks pretty."

I shrug. "Yeah, well . . ."

We're silent for a few seconds, and I stare out over the pine trees to the lake again. It looks so peaceful. I picture Lam and myself in a canoe together, just lazily going along, but then I see my belly and remember Lam's probably doing it with some girl, and my happy little dream bubble bursts.

"The girls in my cabin pick on me," the girl blurts out with a sob in her voice.

"Oh, yeah? How come?"

"'Cause I'm fat."

"Say what?" I can't help it; I laugh. "But everybody here is—uh—struggling with a weight problem."

"Yeah, but I've got fat cheeks. They call me Chubby Cheeks and CC."

I look closely at the girl, who is again hiding her face behind all her hair. I brush it out of her face and lift her chin to get a good look. She blinks at me with worried eyes.

"Oh, I get it. Girl, they're jealous. You're real pretty. Yeah, you've got big cheeks, maybe the biggest, fattest cheeks I've ever seen, but somehow they make you look pretty. Honest, they do. You wouldn't look half so pretty if you were all pale with your cheeks sunken in. You've got nice rosy cheeks, and big wide blue eyes, and guy-magnet hair. Oh, yeah, they're *so* jealous. Believe me, I know."

Behind us we hear the kids in the dining hall cheer about something.

I look at the girl, who's smiling now. She really is pretty. She's the kind of girl that looks like she's just made for being fat, like she was probably born that way. I mean, does everybody in the world have to be skinny? Aren't we all shapes and sizes, and isn't one size fat? I know, sacrilege, right? People say, "But what about their health?" and blah, blah, blah, but my great-great-grandmother Ethel is huge, and she's ninety-nine years old and healthy as a horse, so there. The day she gets skinny is the day she's too ill to eat, and that's what'll kill her.

"So, I'm Eleanor Crowe, but you can call me Elly. What's your name?"

"Banner Sorensen," she says.

What a name!

"They call me 'Banny-bananny with the big fat fanny' at school."

Poor kid. I can just see her parents thinking their girl is going to be someone famous where a name like Banner won't matter, but don't they realize she's got to grow up first? She's got to get to the age of thirty before "Banner" won't be a curse. Banny-fanny—what a hex.

"Well, Banner," I say, trying not to show how sorry I feel for her, "your counselor's probably freaking 'cause you're not at the table. Doesn't she know you're missing?"

Banner shakes her head. "I'm supposed to be at the nurse's cabin. I told her I wasn't feeling well, and she let me go. I had my chum with me, and she knows where I am."

"Your chum?"

"You know, my buddy. They call them chums here. Everyone's got a chum that you have to be with if you go anywhere away from the group." Banner hangs her head, and her hair spills forward off her shoulders, hiding her face again. "I got Ashley—Ashley Wilson, not Ashley Ryan. I hate her. She's the one who started it."

"Started it? Calling you Chubby Cheeks?"

Banner nods and hangs her head again. She tears at a fingernail, which looks torn to the quick already. "She's not a real chum. I thought at least here, where everybody else is like me, I wouldn't get called any names. I hate the girls in my cabin."

"Well, we'll take care of her. Don't worry. She'll get hers. So come on, why don't we go hang out at my cabin till dinner's over? Would you like that?"

Banner lifts her head, and through her mass of hair I see her smile.

* * *

I open the door to the cabin and let Banner inside.

"Cool," she says, and her voice perks up. "It's like a house in here. Like a real house."

I look around and try to see it through her eyes: the four-poster bed made up in the corner with the empty bookshelf beside it, the couch and coffee table, the card table with the record player and the big moose head surrounded by all our junk. I don't know, maybe it looks more grown up in here than in her cabin with a bunch of bunk beds lining the walls, but still, it ain't pretty in here by a long shot.

Banner runs on tiptoe to the couch and sits down on it and rubs her hand on the scratchy armrest, and she has this look of awe on her face like it's made of rubies and satin.

"I'd love to live here."

"Believe me, no, you wouldn't."

"Yes, I would. I love the mountains and living in the woods. And swimming at the lake is my favorite thing to do in the whole world. I'd love to live here all by myself, in the dead of winter."

I go over to the record player that sits on top of the card table. "Sounds boring and lonely to me," I say.

"But I'd have a stack of books a mile high that I would read, and there would be deer and bears and moose and other animals to watch, and I'd skate on the lake and just sit and watch the snow fall during the day, and then watch all the stars at night. Have you noticed how big they are up here? And they twinkle. At home in New Jersey, the stars seem so far away, and they never twinkle." She crosses her ankles and leans back against the couch with a look of satisfaction, as if her living here were real.

"Yeah, I like to read, too," I say, while I look through the albums for something I recognize, but there's names here like Perry Como and Frank Sinatra. They're vaguely familiar, but judging by the way they look on the covers—clean-cut and wearing suits with ties—I don't think it's my kind of music. Then I find a Christmas album called *Holly Jolly Christmas*. I laugh and turn to face Banner. "You want to pretend it's winter here?"

She nods and clasps her hands together in her lap. "Sure!"

"Okay. Here goes something." I put the record on and set the needle in the first groove, and out comes "Rockin' Around the Christmas Tree."

"Come on," I say. "I need the practice. Let's dance."

She eases herself off the couch, looking uncertain, and

comes out to the center of the room, where I'm already dancing. She giggles and wipes at her eyes with the back of her hand. "You look funny dancing with your stomach big like that."

I grab her arms and twirl her around. She giggles again, and the two of us dance together.

She likes the twirling thing, so we do that a lot, and then we do some line-dancing stuff and just fool around, swinging and kicking and jumping, and I can tell she's having a great time, and so am I. If dance class could be like this, it wouldn't be half so bad to teach it. The entire album is full of fast, happy Christmas music, and we go through the whole thing, both sides, sometimes singing along when we know the song.

As the last song is dying down, we hear a siren outside, and it sounds kind of close. "What's that for?" I ask. "Are they calling everybody to the main cabin or something?" Lam's parents had given me a camp booklet with all the rules and camp business in it that I was supposed to read because I had skipped out on the sure-to-be-boring counselors' assembly by pretending that I had a doctor's appointment, but I hadn't finished reading it yet. The siren had to mean something big, like it's time for one of their camp-wide weight-loss pep talks they're supposed to give every day. Only I thought those were held in the morning. The two of us go to the door and step outside. We see people running around, coming in and out of the woods beyond the cabins, and I see Ziggy, and he's yelling something that I can't make out. Then I look out over the trees to the bottom of the hill at the parking lot, and I see a police car, and its lights are flashing. I'm about to say something when it hits me what everybody is saying, and it hits Banner at the same time, because she cries out, "It's me! They're all looking for me! Oh-oh. We're in so much trouble."

Before I can stop her, she jumps off the wooden steps and calls out, "Here I am. I'm here. Here I am."

CHAPTER FIVE

O KAY, TROUBLE ISN'T the word for it. I'm standing in Lam's parents' cabin after "lights out," getting an earful about how if I had read the rulebook, I would know that I'm never to have a camper alone with me in the cabin.

"Do you understand the worry and trouble you put us through? Do you realize the trouble you could be in if she decides to tell somebody you molested her?" Mrs. Lothrop asks.

"Wait a minute. Molested?" I fall backward and hit the doorframe. Are they freakin' kidding me?

"Yes! Molested. *M-O-L-E-S-T-E-D.*" Mrs. Lothrop spells it out. She's pacing, and her large, capable feet sound like blocks of wood being smacked together.

"Why would she do that? I didn't touch her—well hardly, but not like that! Give me a break!"

Mrs. Lothrop's face is so red hot I don't know why I don't see smoke rising off her head. Oh, wait—maybe I do.

"I just can't get over how stupid, how completely stupid and inconsiderate you were to take her to your cabin. You should have taken her right back to the dining hall. And *your* cabin of all places. From now on, no camper is allowed in that cabin, even if he or she is with a chum. It's unwholesome."

Right. I want to give the lady a whole shitload of unwholesome, but she's my new MIL—mother-in-law—so I bite down on my lower lip till I practically draw blood and say nothing. Meanwhile, Lam's screwing some bimbo at a party and will come home plastered and then some, maybe throw up or pass out right in full view of all the campers, but all he'll get is a "Clean yourself up before you come to work, will you my dearest, sweetest, most precious, darling perfection?"

How is it some parents can be so completely blind to their children's faults? Just because Lam is their one and only, they dote on him like he's God Almighty himself.

Mr. Lothrop, my FIL, looks too tired to say anything, so he just glares to show he's with her—the MIL. Lam has told me all about the first-night-of-camp after-dinner speech, so I know the FIL has spent the last couple of hours yammering to all the campers gathered in the main lodge about the rules—fifty rules that start with "Don't ever . . ." and a hundred that start with "You better not . . ." and another fifty of "If we ever catch you . . ." Then he talks about all the fun everybody is going to have, which to me seems to be a total contradiction of all the rules of starvation and exercise and "You're dead if you . . ." warnings, but who am I to say?

Finally they dismiss me, but not before the MIL calls me back from the doorway. "And Eleanor," she says, and I look back, "don't ever wear that dress again."

I don't say anything. I just leave, but you can bet your life that I'll be wearing this same dress tomorrow and maybe even the next day. I'm pregnant, lady! How many mother-to-be outfits does she think I have? And these tent dresses are the most comfortable. Of course I hadn't planned on dressing like a pumpkin again even if it is comfortable, but now that I've been challenged, I can't resist. What can she do to me, anyway? Ban me from the camp? Oh, boo-hoo!

* * *

Lam doesn't get back to our cabin until five the next morning. I didn't sleep much, anyway, because I had to keep getting up to go to the bathroom, which meant putting on some kind of shoes and a bathrobe because everyone must wear shoes and a bathrobe to go to the bathroom at night. It's rule number 5,987 in the camp fun book. Then I have to grab my flashlight and tiptoe around on piles of rocks and roots up the hill to the bathroom hut. It's a fifteen-minute ordeal at least, and I went through it some twelve times before I decided to just sit on the toilet and lean against the wall to get some sleep. That was the best sleep I got all night, but I didn't want to be found there and get into more trouble, so before daylight I got myself up again and trudged back to the cabin. I felt too hot and my butt was sore from where it had been sitting with the rim of the toilet seat wrapped around it. I could feel a deep ridge in my skin there that hurt to touch. I guess I won't be doing that again, but something has to change. Maybe I can find a pot to pee in and put it under my bed. I felt like I was the one who had been out all night drinking.

Lam wasn't home when I returned to the cabin, but about a half hour later he staggers in and when he sees me sitting on the couch fanning myself with our marriage certificate, he puts his finger to his mouth. "Shhh," he says. "Don't want to make up the missus—I mean, wake up the wissus." He laughs. "You know what I mean."

"Yeah, I sure do." I drop the certificate on the floor and sit with my arms crossed over my belly and my feet up on the trunk. Suddenly I see myself years from now, maybe I'm fifty years old, and Lam is still coming in at all hours, drunk and talking stupid, and I'm sitting just like this. The thought is so depressing I burst into tears, and Lam stumbles over and, half falling on the trunk and half on me, tries to comfort me. "Hey, baby, it's okay. Whassa matter? It's okay. Hey."

I lean away from him. He smells of B.O. and beer. "Lam, just go away. I'm too tired and too depressed for this," I cry.

"So go to bed. It's still earl—early." He pets my head and burps and laughs, and then he cries, too, and reaches out to me for some sympathy. I lean farther away from him, but not far enough, because then he throws up—not outside in front of the campers, not in front of his parents, but on me. His warm, stinkin' barf lands all over my arms, shirt, shorts, legs, and even my bathrobe, which I had taken off and Lam is half sitting on. I cry even harder and I think of my parents in Kenya, and I miss them, and I want them to come home and take care of me, and I wonder how and when life had gotten so complicated.

Lam is laughing and crying at the same time. He crawls off of me while I just sit there with my arms up in the air trying not to get any more vomit on me than necessary. I would have jumped up, only I'm *pregnant!* So I sit there while Lam in all his fog tries to figure out what to do.

I ever so slowly get myself to my feet. "Go get some wet paper towels from the bathroom or maybe the kitchen, Lam. Or wait, if the kitchen is open, get a wet cloth or a mop—yeah, a mop. Ask for a mop."

Lam nods and staggers to the door. I look at my watch. Just after five. "Wait. The kitchen won't be open. You've gotta go to your parents' cabin. Yeah, go there. They've got a bathroom and a kitchen—unlike us. Go there."

Lam blinks at me. "No way. No way. Come on. They—they'll kill me if they smee me like this—I mean smee lee like—I feel sick." He leans over like he's going to puke again.

"Lam! Do it! Just do it!" I yell this loud enough to wake up the whole camp, but I don't care.

Lam stumbles out the door, and I stare after him. I don't know what to do. I have nothing to clean the mess up with, but hiking all the way up to the bathroom without a robe on feels too risky, what with the MIL and FIL about to be wakened. All I can think to do is to go to the little square windows that run the length of two sides of the cabin and open them all up to air out the place. They're made of wood and I realize that they open from the outside, because window screens block me from getting at them on the inside. I think about getting into some other clothes but I have so few that fit me and I don't want to get any vomit on them. I figure going outside naked is out of the question, and although it's tempting to put on something of Lam's, I decide that's kind of mean, so I decide to risk it and go as I am to open the windows.

On the outside the windows are pretty high up so I have to find a rock or something to stand on to reach them. I find a log that's set up as one of the seats around a little campfire back behind one of the other cabins. It doesn't look too difficult to roll, and after a few false starts I get the thing moving and I roll it over to my cabin, stand on it, and raise the first window. It's easy to lift, and I find a six-inch hook that fits into a hole and holds the square piece of wood open. I move on to the next one and the next one, and while I open windows I think about Lam. Somehow, all the effort it took to find the log and roll it into place and get the windows open has softened my anger. It was his graduation day, after all, and his wedding day, which, I have to admit, is kind of a scary thing. Neither one of us knows how we ended up in this predicament. Okay, we do, but you know what I mean. Worse still, neither one of us knows what we're going to do about it or how this whole marriage/camp/baby situation is going to play out. So I don't blame him for getting plastered. If I could have, I would have gotten so blotto I wouldn't walk straight for a year.

I push the log along to the next window with my foot, and hurry to open it. I just have three windows left. All I need is for one of Lam's parents to catch me out here. I check behind me to make sure they're not coming, and yeah, you've guessed it. Here they come, charging down the hill, the MIL and the FIL, and behind them, Lam. The MIL has a mop in her hands and she looks like she went to bed still angry and the expression just froze on her face. The FIL is carrying a bucket and trying to keep up with the MIL without sloshing the water. I look down at my vomit-coated self outside without the requisite robe and shoes, and I groan. I know this whole thing is somehow going to get pinned on me. How dare I get vomited on, right? I mean, I should have had sense enough to move out of the way of their precious son's precious vomit. How dare I stand outside in men's underwear and a T-shirt and bare feet, too. I should have worn the robe, vomit and all.

"Eleanor Crowe, get inside the cabin, now!" the MIL says in this furious whisper when she gets close enough to be sure I'll hear her.

I let the window I held up but hadn't yet hooked slam back into place and step off the log. I remind myself that these are my in-laws and I'd better try to be respectful. I don't say anything. I just go inside and wait for them to follow. I step aside while the MIL marches in, her mop taking aim at the floor. Behind her comes the FIL and Lam, and Lam is whimpering, "I'm really sorry. I must have eaten something rotten."

Yeah, like a barrel of beer.

"You're drunk, son," the FIL says without emotion. He goes over to me, grabs one of my arms, and reaches into the bucket he's set at his feet. He wrings out a rag full of water and wipes me down. First one arm, and then the other. The water is cold and it makes me feel chilled down to my bones, but I don't say anything. I let him wash me off, and when, for a second, I look up from the floor where I've been staring and catch the FIL's eye, he winks at me, and my bones thaw and warm up toasty-cozy just like that. He winks, and suddenly it's all all right. I have a friend—maybe.

"I know, Dad, but hon—honest, I only had a couple of beers," Lam continues. He burps and giggles at himself but only for a second, 'cause his dad is watching him. "Someone must have spiked my Coke or something, 'cause I swear I only had a couple of beers. I swear, honest."

The MIL is mopping furiously. The mop *slap-slap-slaps* against the floor. She's in her bathrobe and slippers, of course. No emergency would keep her from following the rules. The woman is big and strong and she looks like she could crush me with one hand—and as if maybe she wants to do just that. I don't apologize, though. As far as I'm concerned, I don't see how I've done anything wrong. The MIL thinks otherwise.

"I hope this little drama is no indication of what this summer is going to be like. We've let you come live here out of the kindness of our hearts." She glares at me. "And because we know we have a duty to you and the child. But if you can't behave yourself and act in an adult manner, you can bet we'll ship you right off to Africa or California. No wonder your parents were so anxious to leave." *Slap-slap-slap!*

The woman is spitting mad, but what she says makes me even madder. "My parents wanted me," I say. "They wanted me in Kenya with them. I'm the one who wanted to stay behind with Lam. And I'm *not* the one who got piss-assed drunk and threw up. And what do you expect me to do? I'm pregnant! And in case you've forgotten, it takes two to make a baby. Besides that, I spent all night walking a mile to the bathroom and back, like a million times, so I got no sleep, and Lam left me alone here with you and this camp and . . ." By now I'm crying again, and I feel so miserable, and all I want are my parents. I can't talk anymore, I'm so upset, which is probably a good thing, because the venom in my heart has been making its way to the tip of my tongue, and who knows what I might say next?

Then Lam cries and he moves over to me and throws his arms around me while his dad is on his knees wiping his son's vomit off my legs. "Baby, I'm so sorry. I love you. I'm sorry. I'm sorry, everybody. I promise I'll straighten up."

"You're going to have to," the FIL says. "You've got to be down at the lake with the other lifeguards giving the kids their swimming test by nine."

"Right, I know. I'll be there. I'll get myself cleaned up and all, but I swear, I think I ate something bad. I feel—I feel—"

Lam turns green, and I think I'm going to get vomited on again, but he manages to turn away and run to the door before he explodes on the steps.

The MIL curses under her breath. I feel like laughing because it's more mess for her to mop up, which I know isn't a nice thought, but the woman hates me. Then Lam makes this funny shuddering noise—really funny—and then he honks or grunts like a pig, and I look around at the mad woman mopping away like crazy, and the FIL wiping down my feet, and the cabin with all the junk dumped on the floor, and the moose head staring at us, and silly, pregnant me, and it all seems too funny. I know if I laugh I'm going to make things worse, but knowing that only makes the whole scene funnier. Lam shudders and honks again, and that's the end for me. I burst out laughing. I laugh so hard it makes the baby kick. I know he/she is laughing, too. I hold the baby with my arms and the two of us laugh and laugh, and the angry glares from drunk Lam and my pissed-off MIL and the FIL only make everything funnier.

CHAPTER SIX

I'M STARVING by the time breakfast rolls around. It's eight o'clock, and Lam and I are sitting with Ziggy and Jen, a guy named Leonardo DeAngelis, and a shy girl named Gren Owens. I find out this morning that I'll be assisting Leonardo starting today in the crafts hut, but I don't have to assist in dance till next week, since there's just one class, taught once a day, and this first week Haley, the dance counselor, said she didn't need me.

I would have thought dance would be so popular that all the kids would want to take it and there would be classes every day all day long, but Lam said that the camp has never had good luck with the ballet classes, or its teachers, so they just do one class.

"Why don't they teach jazz or tap or something less stiff, then?" I had asked Lam, but he just shrugged. Well, as far as I was concerned, I hoped Haley wouldn't need me at all and I could just hide out in the back of the crafts hut till dinnertime every day.

Since I'm going to be helping Leonardo right away, I size him up. He looks nice enough, I suppose. I mean, he's got a decent-looking face, and he's tall, with really broad shoulders, but he's weird looking, too. He's got short hair, no jewelry or tattoos, and he's scrubbed so clean he looks like he uses pumice stone to wash his skin. He's wearing a Camp WeightAway shirt just like the rest of us, only on top of his he's wearing an unbuttoned Hawaiian shirt—you know, with flowers and bananas all over it—and beige shorts that come down to his knees. And he wears black dress socks pulled halfway up his muscular calves and the kind of shapeless, cheaply made running shoes that you could probably wear on either foot and it wouldn't matter. He looks like an American tourist in Europe, and he even has a camera, a small video camera that he set down beside his bowl of oatmeal. He's the camp photographer as well as the crafts counselor. He does these before-and-after pictures of the kids so they can see how much weight they've lost, and he goes around shooting everybody for a movie montage show at the end of camp, so we can be reminded of what a great time we've had. I feel kind of sorry for the guy, because he's got "nerd" written all over him. Before he eats he crosses himself and says a blessing after the camp blessing of rub-a-dub-dub. He tucks his napkin into the collar of his shirt and eats his oatmeal with a fork. I kid you not. He eats with his mouth open, which is so gross because the oatmeal in his mouth looks too much like you-know-what. I try not to look at him, but trying not to makes me look right at him. I try harder and stare at the spot between his eyes when he talks to me.

"I thought we'd start with something simple in crafts today," he says.

"Oh, yeah?" *Forehead, forehead, stare at the forehead.* "What's that?" I ask.

"Well . . ." He pauses and plows another forkful of oatmeal into his mouth. "Maybe the little ones can make sailboats to sail on the water. I've got all the materials laid out. And the older ones can learn knitting, or if they already know how, they can begin to make a scarf."

"That's simple?" Neither idea sounds simple to me.

"Very," Leonardo says.

"I can see it now. Eleanor and Leo rocking in rocking chairs, knitting away," Jen says. She laughs and nudges Lam. She made sure she sat down next to him—or more like on top of him. I'm sitting across from Lam, who's not saying much. He's staring down at his food, not eating a thing. I plan to grab his bowl of oatmeal after I finish mine. I've piled a whole mess of brown sugar, cinnamon, two-percent milk, and peanut butter on mine. I had left the peanut butter in the back of Lam's Jeep about a week ago, and I found it there this morning when I went to fetch my camp T-shirt that I'd also left back there. Everybody has to wear the WeightAway counselor shirt when they're on duty. Mine comes halfway down my thighs because it's a large so it will fit over my belly. I'm wearing it underneath my pumpkin dress so all you see are the short sleeves that come to my elbows. The MIL gave me bitch-eyes when I walked into the dining hall, but she didn't say anything, just kept following me with her squint till I got all the way to the kitchen door and disappeared from view. I was sweating like a horse under that gaze, but I just held my head high and kept on walking.

I stir my oatmeal and ignore Jen. I've decided to pretend she doesn't even exist. If she talks to me, I'll ignore her. If she talks to someone else, I'll interrupt her as if I'm not even hearing her. I hate people who are always trying to stir up trouble, and Jen is one of those kinds of people. She works down at the lake with Lam. This worries me because it's so obvious she likes him, but it's also obvious that Lam doesn't like her—I think.

I ignore her comment about me and Leo in rocking chairs knitting together, and so does everybody else, but that just makes her try harder.

"You better watch out, Lammy, or Leo's going to steal your wife away from you." She leans on Lam even more and talks into his ear, and I know her breath is tickling him. She's trying to turn him on. I see the way she rubs herself up against him.

Jen laughs. "By the looks of her, it shouldn't be too hard. Looks like she'll go with anyone who offers."

Lammy squirms away from Jen. He looks across the table at me and sees my eyes are filled with tears—so much for me ignoring the bitch. Lam stands up and climbs over the seat. Then, without saying anything, he grabs his bowl, comes around to stand behind me, kisses me on the head, and sets his bowl down next to mine. "I'm not hungry. You have this. For our baby."

I look up at Lam, and he leans way over and kisses me again. On the lips. "I'm the luckiest guy in the world," he says, looking right at Jen. "And you're not fit to sit at the same table as my wife." He touches me on the shoulder. I don't want the others to see how grateful I am, so I stare down at my food and jam some cereal into my mouth.

"I've gotta get ready for the testing. See you at lunch. Love you." He squeezes my shoulder and I whisper back, "Love you," because I can't say it any louder. I'm too choked up. Now I remember why I fell in love with Lam. When it's us against the world, he always makes sure we win.

*   *   *

I hate crafts. I *really* hate crafts. I try to learn how to knit, and Leonardo encourages me by saying that I should learn so I can knit a baby blanket or booties for the baby, but I can't do it. I've got ten fingers, and they're all pinkies as far as using them for any kind of craft goes. I'm useless teaching knitting or helping the kids with it, and they know it. Then the sailboats need glue, and the glue stinks so bad it makes my head hurt. I know it can't be good for the baby. Most of the morning I sit on the steps outside the crafts hut rubbing my head. And this is the easy stuff.

Mid-morning I see Banner walk up from the lake with a

group of girls following her and whispering to each other. Banner doesn't see me because she's got her head down and her hair hanging in her face.

"Hi, there, Banner!" I call out. "That was a blast last night, huh?" I say this partly because I want to make sure she enjoyed herself, and partly to see if she plans to accuse me of molesting her. I don't know how I think I'm going to figure that out, but maybe her expression, if she looks at me, will give me some information.

Banner does look up. First she glances at the girls behind her, then she smiles at me and waves. "That was really fun," she says. "I'm glad you'll be teaching dance this summer. Maybe it will be fun for a change."

"Yeah, right," I say, and wave her away. I see the girls snickering behind her and notice that Banner must have sat down on a freshly painted bench somewhere because the back of her beige shorts has a forest green butt-print on it. I think to call her back, rescue her, but I don't, because half my mind is caught up with what she said: "I'm glad you're teaching dance." Maybe it was only some whiny little girl who said it, but I have to admit, it feels nice to kind of be wanted—or at least appreciated.

After lunch I ditch the crafts hut and just kind of hang out wherever—my cabin, the latrine, the woods—wherever I won't get caught. In the woods I hear kids singing the camp song that begins with the line, "I left my fat on a tired ol' log, a tired ol' log, a tired ol' log," and I laugh and think about the camp T-shirt with the eggplants with tape measures squeezing their waists. I figure this has to be the corniest place I've ever been. It really is the pits. I wonder if I can ditch working in the crafts hut and the dance hut all summer without getting caught, or, if not both, at least ditch the crafts. Dance has got to be better than knitting and gluing blocks of wood together. That is, as long as I don't have to wear a leotard.

Since I managed to skip out on doing crafts all afternoon, I'm in a decent mood when I get back to the cabin just before dinner. Lam is already there slouched down on the couch, and I go and snuggle up against him and study his face.

He looks tired. He's got bags under his eyes that look like they could hold a month's worth of laundry. He's pale, too, especially his lips. I remember my mother fainting once when I cut my leg really badly. She took one look at all the blood and her lips went white and she passed out.

"Are you okay?" I ask. "You look ill."

Lam shakes his head. "I had way too much to drink last night."

"Yeah, I know. The cabin and this couch still kind of smell like beer and vomit."

"I didn't smoke anything—or do anything—in case you're wondering." He shoves his bangs out of his face and looks at me. "I thought of you sitting here all by yourself because of the baby, and I didn't think it was fair, which I know is stupid because I did leave you here and run off and I did drink my ass off, but maybe that was the last time."

I climb onto Lam's lap and hook my hands around his neck. "That's what you say now 'cause you feel so sick. We'll see how you feel a week from now when you've forgotten the pain. Believe me, I know what it's like—remember?"

Lam nods. His hands are around my waist, or around where my waist used to be. "Yeah, but you just stopped everything cold turkey. I really admire that."

I shrug, but I'm pleased that he's proud of me. "I had to. For the baby. Once I realized the baby wasn't going anywhere—you know, like a miscarriage—I figured I'd better clean up my act. Besides, I got so sick it was hard to do anything for a while. That helped."

Lam nods, but I can tell he isn't really listening anymore. He has this faraway look in his eyes, and I wonder if he's thinking about some girl he might have fooled around with last night. When he said he didn't do anything, did he just mean drugs or did he mean girls, too? I'm afraid to ask. "You okay?" is all I can say.

"Yeah—no—I mean, I was just thinking." Lam shifts himself, uncrossing his legs on the coffee table, and I move off of him in case I'm too heavy.

"You were fine," he says, but I don't climb back on. I kneel on the couch, facing him with my butt resting on my heels. I wait for him to tell me how he messed up with some girl on our wedding night.

"It's just, well . . . I was thinking that maybe we ought to consider keeping the baby." He blinks at me with his watery blue eyes. "It's ours, isn't it?"

"Well, yeah! But a baby? Are you sure?" I feel excited all of a sudden, because Lam's never really said he wanted the baby. He never said he didn't, either. He's just left it all up to me. So, I'm excited . . . but scared, too.

"A baby is forever," I say, trying to think it through with him. "They grow up and all, but it gets even harder the older they get—and more expensive. But then again, we grow up, too, and we won't always be like this." I lift my chin and take in the cabin. "We'll get real jobs and make lots more money." I roll off my knees and turn around so I'm sitting next to Lam. I prop my feet on the table and take his hand in mine. "Wow, Lam. Are you sure?"

"No." He laughs. "No, I'm not sure. I guess—I guess I just want to consider it—really consider it. I don't want to just automatically hand the baby over."

"No! No, me, either," I say. I take Lam's hand and place it on my belly and smile, and for a second I feel good—happy and safe and comforted—but then in a flash I feel anxious, and I don't know why, exactly. "What happened at that party?" I ask, figuring that the uneasy feeling has something to do with the party.

Lam shrugs, and I hold my breath, waiting for the bomb. If he tells me he had sex with someone else, there's no way I'm going to even consider keeping the baby.

"I don't know," he says. "All the guys were there, you know, except you, and we were just sitting around drinking, but I wasn't drunk yet, and I looked over at John Runyun and Bill

Hoover, and that group, and they just looked so, I don't know, so together. I thought how they're all doing something with their lives. They've got plans, college and jobs and all that, and then I looked at us, and none of us had any plans, really. And look at you and me." He squeezes my hand and bounces it on his thigh. "We just kind of fell into this. We just kind of fall into everything. We don't know what we're doing—do we? Every year I work at this camp. I work for my parents. I want to get away, have my own life. I'm tired of this. Man, I'm so tired of it. Like you said, I could get paid real money if I worked somewhere else. I'm tired of being under my parents' constant watch. I'm eighteen. I'm grown-up. We need a plan, Elly. We don't have a plan, that's our problem. We need goals, a future—a future away from here."

"Yeah, goals," I say. "I like the sound of that, but I don't know what I want to do with my life. I've never had any vision of my future, the way my sister has. She's always known she wanted to be a businesswoman of some kind, and to get married and have kids. And her wedding? She'd been planning that thing since the day she was born." I draw my hand away from Lam and bite on my fingernail. "I don't know what I want. I want to be happy, I guess, but how do you go about being happy? You can't plan happiness, can you?"

"No, but you can go after a dream. Going after dreams seems to make people happy. We just have to figure out what our dreams are."

"But can we go after a dream and keep this baby? Can we do both?"

Lam puts his arm around my shoulder, and he smells like the lake. "I don't know. Maybe not. I was just kind of thinking of what it would be like to take our kids hunting, you know, give them their first rifle, help them nail their first buck. And I can teach them to swim. They can watch me swim and dive and stuff."

"Yeah," I say, and I nod, but inside I find myself thinking, *But I'm only sixteen.* A family? Me? Us? I'm not even sure I want to be married. I'm not sure I want my kids to learn how to hunt. How many moose heads do I really want staring down at me from some wall? Shouldn't they be learning more important things? And if so, what are the important things? Am I smart enough to know? Could I ever become a good parent? I'm not sure. I'm not sure of anything. I'm only sixteen.

CHAPTER SEVEN

I'M RELIEVED when we get really busy over the next week or so and Lam and I don't have any real time to talk more about our future. The future has always scared me. I can't see into the future the way other people do. Other people will say things like, "The party is going to be so great," or "I know you're going to learn a lot from that class," and I want to ask, "How do you know?" Do they really know? Am I the only one in the world who doesn't know? What if I die before I get to that class? Then how educational will it be? Am I the only person who thinks like this? I think I started drinking and getting into drugs just to have something to do to keep my mind off the future. Will I graduate from high school? Will the baby be all right? Will Lam and I stay married? I'm afraid to ask, and I'm afraid to step into the future to find out the answers. I want to throw my hands in front of my eyes and just peek at the future from between my fingers. The present has always seemed so much more than I can handle, and anything else has always been too much.

There are all these books and TV shows that talk about being in the present, and how staying in the present will keep us happy, but I don't think so. I stay in the present because I'm afraid. I hate my past, or at least I hate myself in my past, because I've always been kind of a pain in the butt, and thinking about myself makes me unhappy, and I'm afraid of the future, so yeah, I stay present, but it's out of fear, and that fear never goes away. I don't know what's coming along in my life, but if my past is any clue, it won't be pretty—that's about as much of the future as I can predict. So what fun is that?

* * *

Leo hauls my ass over to the crafts hut every day, and he watches me to make sure I don't ditch it like I did the first day. "I need you here to help."

"But I don't know what the hell I'm doin'," I say. "I'm worse at crafts than the kids, and the glue stinks."

"Look," Leo says. "They don't need you to know how to do stuff. They just need your attention. You think you can do that? Think you can pay a little attention to someone besides yourself?" His scrubbed little face turns pink with anger.

"Yeah, sure, Dad. Whatever you say, Dad," I say, and even though I'm annoyed with Leo, I've got nothing better to do, so I stay. All week long I stay and watch Leo and talk to the kids out on the porch. I don't get any better at the crafts, but as nasty as Leo was to me, I discover that I kinda like him, and this totally surprises me. He's much more patient with me than I deserve, and he's funny with the campers, and I can tell they all love him. He doesn't take things too seriously, and he's good at what he does—the crafts stuff. I notice he's got really nice hands—nice work hands, or maybe artist's hands. He's going to be a ceramics major in college, of all things. Who knew you could major in clay? Best of all, Leo's open to suggestions, like when I said, "Did you know you eat with your mouth open? It's disgusting. Why don't you try keeping it closed?"

"Ay-uh, okay," he says, just like that, and he does it!

Or once I said, "No offense, Leo, but you dress like a dork. Can't you see how different you look from everybody else? You're an artist; you should notice stuff like that. I mean, come on, you look like the all-American tourist."

Leo didn't get all bent out of shape about what I said. He just laughed. "Ay-uh, that's the idea," he said. "We're all only tourists in this world."

"Is that supposed to be deep?" I asked. "Because if it is, it went right over my head."

"I'm merely stating a truth," he said. "We're all tourists, no need taking ourselves too seriously. Some of these campers act as if their world is coming to an end if they don't lose weight fast enough or if they've got a zit on their face or their craft doesn't come out perfectly. I'm just keepin' it light; that's all."

The only thing Leo really needs me as an assistant for, besides talking to the kids, is to keep track of the time so he can send the campers off to their next class on time, or so he doesn't miss lunch or dinner. They do ring the bell for meals, but he never hears it, because he's so involved with the kids. If any one of them does something great, some good deed, or a great job on their craft or something, they get to sign the back of his camp shirt. The first time I saw this, I couldn't believe how excited the kid got. He picked a colored sharpie out of Leo's back pocket and wrote his name with a flourish, and then paraded himself around announcing that he was the very first one to get to sign Leo's shirt. Big whoop! I didn't get it, but all the kids love it. It's what happens at Camp WeightAway. It's the camp tradition.

Leo always wears one of his Hawaiian shirts over the camp shirt, and kids love to try to sneak up on Leo and lift the shirt to see how many names he has back there. Leo pretends they've pulled a fast one on him.

Another thing that surprises me, besides liking Leo, is that I kinda like the kids.

Ashley Wilson, the girl who's so mean to Banner, is a real pill, and so are a few other girls, and there are some boys I'd like to bind and gag and abandon in a ditch somewhere, but most of the kids I enjoy . . . and they seem to enjoy me.

I spend most of my time on the porch outside the crafts hut talking with the kids who are knitting outside. They tell me about how they feel about coming to a weight-loss camp. Generally they love the camp, but they feel embarrassed that they have to be here. "I'd die if my friends found out where I am," one girl says, and another says, "There's kids a lot fatter than me in school, but you don't see them here."

Several of the kids, I find out, have been coming to Camp WeightAway for years, and they lose the weight in the summer and gain it all back in the winter. "Food is my best friend when I'm at home," a boy named Alfie says. "If I didn't have food for comfort, I wouldn't have anything," he adds, and everybody agrees.

They're supposed to talk about these weight issues during the morning "Health and Well-Being" sessions in the main cabin, but they prefer just talking outside on the porch while they're knitting, and where it's informal. Oh, and there are boys in these knitting classes, too. Just because they like to knit doesn't mean they're gay—another surprise.

I love to watch some of the older boys who think they're too cool or too tough to knit hanging around the crafts hut pretending they're just talking to the guys, or flirting with the girls, but really they're watching the knitting with this kind of hungry longing in their eyes that cracks me up, because I can see it. I can step back and see right through these kids. For all my life I've been just another one of those kids, and I could see through nothing, but now all of a sudden, maybe because of this baby, or because I have to act like an authority of some kind, I'm allowed to take that step back and just observe, and it's a hoot; it really is. And somehow, because of this ability I've got of being able to read these kids, I like them. I feel like I understand them a little, and that's a blast. It makes me think that maybe, if we do keep the baby, I wouldn't be such a crappy mother after all.

I'm supposed to help Haley the second week of camp, but after breakfast, Monday of that second week, the MIL and FIL ask to see me.

I talk to them at their dining hall table after the campers have left.

"We have a problem," the FIL begins.

"Well, I didn't do it," I say automatically. I run through my mind all the things I've done lately, and I try to figure out what I may have done that has got the two ILs looking so miserable. Except for leaving the cabin in the middle of the night without my bathrobe on a few hundred times, and swearing on occasion, I've been pretty decent.

The MIL waves her hand and gives me this irritated look. "Haley isn't feeling well. Her stomach is upset, and we have no one to teach the dance class except you. Do you feel up to teaching the class on your own?"

"Well, I didn't poison her or anything, if that's what you're thinking. I didn't do anything." This is so wild because I sort of imagined a scenario like this, where for some reason I get to teach the dance class but I don't teach ballet; I teach the kids all of my wacky fun stuff, but now it's for real, and I'm scared. I'm scared that I'll get blamed for making Haley sick, and even more scared that I'll actually have to teach the class. Daydreaming about teaching the class is one thing, but actually teaching it is another.

"No, of course not," the MIL says. "We wouldn't ask for your help, except there isn't anyone else. We're short a couple of counselors this summer as it is, and we can't afford to lose any of our waterfront counselors, so it's you or nobody."

Gee, thanks for all the love.

The FIL puts his hand on mine. "We need you for this, Eleanor."

Well, that's a new one. They need me. I love it. It's straight out of some movie. The hated girl comes to the rescue in the end and saves the day, and everybody loves her and she lives happily ever after. Yeah, I could live with that.

"Sure. Sure, I'll teach the class. Don't worry about it."

Both of the ILs look relieved, and the MIL actually thanks me and almost, just almost, smiles at me.

So my knees are a-knockin' when I get to the dance hut. The room is large and square, and there are those bar things attached to the walls, where you're supposed to hang on and do *pliés,* and one wall is covered by a huge mirror. The first thing I notice in the mirror, besides my big belly and a zit on my chin, is that I've got Ashley Wilson and Banner Sorensen in my dance class, and then I see all the other kids, all those wide eyes staring at me, and all those legs in pink tights and ballet slippers. I can't teach ballet! My knees get to knocking even more. I turn away and think to run out of the room, but I can't really run too well anymore, since I'm so pregnant, and I've got nowhere to run. No, I've got to be strong and remember I'm older than they are. I turn around again and take a deep breath. I try to smile, and I think of how hard it is for the MIL to smile at me. So then I really smile. I try to look friendly. I tell them about Haley being sick, and the campers groan.

"Yeah, so while I'm teaching the class, we're, uh, going to do things a little differently. But first, before we get started . . ." I pause and stare at Ashley Wilson. "If there is any name-calling or if anyone is mean to anybody else in this class, inside or outside of it, you will not be allowed to dance. You'll have to sit on the floor and watch for the period if you're mean once, but twice and you're out, and you can't get back in."

Ashley Wilson sees me glaring at her, and instead of hanging her head in shame, she lifts it higher and raises her hand.

"Yeah?" I say.

"All the classes are voluntary, so we get to choose if we're in a class or not, just so long as we have four physical classes and two rest classes, so I don't think you can kick us out."

The girl doesn't look a thing like me, with her red hair and dark, deep-set, beady little eyes, but she sounds like me. I know if a teacher had read me the riot act, I would have rebelled—I did rebel. Still, I walk right up to her and stick my belly in her chest. "Girl, just try me, okay? Just try me. I want this to be a fun class. If you aren't fun, out you go."

Another girl raises her hand. She's short and not really fat, so I don't know why she's in this camp, but some parents expect perfection, and she has bowed legs. Maybe they think if she loses what little weight she has, they won't be so bowed or something—who knows? "Do we get to vote people out of the class?" she asks.

I laugh. "No. I'm the only one who gets to vote you out of my class. So anyway, are you ready to dance?"

Some kids nod and some kids say a meek yes. "I don't hear you!" I shout. "Are you ready to dance?"

They all yell, "Yes!"

"I can't hear you!"

"Yes!" they scream.

I look over the CD selection Haley has left out on the table, and I put on some music by Dread-Locked. The music starts, and I shout, "Okay, let's dance!"

I start dancing to the music, and the girls just stand there watching me. I wave to them. "Come on, dance!" I shout.

The girls look at one another, but they don't move, not even Banner. I stop the music. "What's wrong? Why aren't you dancing?"

"Aren't you going to teach us some steps or anything?" Ashley asks. She looks pissed.

"Why? Are you afraid to just dance? Everybody can dance. You just move to the music."

"Is that all this is going to be? You play music and we dance to it?" Ashley Wilson sounds even more pissed.

"No," I say. "No, it isn't. There's going to be other stuff, but you've—you've got to warm up, don't you? Every *real* dancer knows that," I say, implying that she's not a real dancer. "So come on, swing those hips and kick those legs, girl, and let's dance."

I put the music back on, and again the girls just look at one another, their faces red with embarrassment.

Feeling desperate, I grab Banner's hand and tell her to grab the girl's hand next to her. Then one by one they all join hands and we form a circle, and I shout, "Let's skip into the center." We skip into the center—only my skip is more like a walk 'cause I don't want to bounce the baby. "And back out again. Four steps to the right. Four steps to the left. Now, everybody twirl!" I shout, remembering how much Banner loved to twirl. I watch them, and I can see they're getting into it. Their eyes sparkle as they wait for me to tell them what to do next.

I grab Banner's hands and shout, "Grab a partner. Bump bottoms with your partner!" The girls laugh. "Bump hips with your partner!"

While the girls are bumping hips, I notice out of the corner of my eye the MIL slipping into the room. She stands just inside the door, folds her arms across her chest, and just watches. I feel my throat start to close up and my knees get to knocking again. What is she going to do to me? Now she knows I'm not teaching ballet. What a nightmare. What do I say next?

The girls have stopped, and they're all staring at me, waiting for instructions. I start to speak, but nothing comes out. My mouth is dry. I clear my throat and try again.

"Uh, pretend you're the wind and—uh—blow all over the room!" I shout. Off they fly, around the room, watching one another to see if they're doing "wind" right.

"Pretend that you're snow falling gently, softly, shhh, shhh." The first song is over and the girls move like snow in the silence, on tiptoes, their arms in the air or held out to the side. One girl leaps, and then they all start leaping.

The next song begins, and I call out, "You're horses now, leaping, prancing horses!"

They love this, and I glance over to see if the MIL has noticed, but she's already left. I imagine the reaming I'm going to get after class and shudder. I turn back to the girls. Everyone is still leaping, everyone except for Banner, who is standing off to the side with her shoulders slumped and her hair in her face. *At least the MIL isn't here to see this.* I go over to her. "Come on, Banner—you're horses."

"I can't," she moans. "Not here. They'll laugh at me. My legs will jiggle, and they'll laugh at me."

"But everybody's legs jiggle. It's okay. I won't let them laugh. So come on. Let's see some horses, or maybe the girls will start laughing at you because you're just standing here like a stick."

That gets a rise out of her—but only a small, halfhearted one. She does a few tiny little leaps, barely-off-the-ground leaps, but at least I got her into the center of the room with the others, and nobody's laughing at her.

The music changes to this slow, dragging tune. "Now

you're crawling through mud," I call out, and everyone but Banner gets down on their bellies and pretends to be crawling through the mud. Banner just kind of squats, afraid to actually get on the floor on her belly like the others, so instead she looks like she's taking a dump in the middle of the floor, and really I can't blame them when the other girls laugh.

"Hey, look at Banner!" one of the girls shouts. "She's got the trots!"

I clap my hands and scowl. "All right, that's enough," I say to stop the laughter, but really, I'm proud of myself because although I'm laughing so hard inside, I manage to look stern enough that when I clap my hands, the girls actually stop laughing.

By the end of the class, the girls are flushed and happy, and I'm exhausted. I watch them file out of the cabin, and then Ashley Wilson stops in front of me and stares at me with her beady little eyes for a few seconds. I stare back. No way is some snot-nosed fifth-grader going to outstare me.

She tilts her head. "That wasn't real dancing," she says. "I take dance at home. I know how to *really* dance. That was just pretend dance."

"Oh, yeah? Well, then, you don't have to come back until Haley does, now, do you? If the only dance you know how to do is *plié* and *arabesque,* then go ahead and do them. No one's forcing you to be here."

Ashley Wilson shrugs. "Well, I'll think about it. It might be interesting to see what different stuff you'll do next time."

She smiles this evil-child kind of smile and pushes open the door. She lets it slam behind her.

Different stuff? I gave them all I had. That was absolutely all I could think of. I don't know what I'm going to do next time, but at least for one day, for this one class, it looks like a hit. I was a hit—with the girls.

CHAPTER EIGHT

I WAITED with my shoulders hiked up to my ears all day for someone to come tell me that the MIL wanted to see me, but nobody said anything about it. Did she approve of my class? Was she waiting until after dinner to speak to me? I didn't know. So I just waited.

Lam wasn't at dinner, and neither was Jen. Lam said they had to stay down at the lake for the junior lifesaving course they were teaching—together. I didn't like the way Jen was always trying to get Lam to notice her and the way she still put me down every chance she got, which was whenever Lam wasn't around to hear her, but I was too busy myself and too tired to worry that much about them.

By bedtime I still haven't heard anything from the MIL. At last I relax. I'm tired and I fall asleep before Lam returns from Junior Lifesaving.

I'm getting to know a lot of kids through the crafts hut, and they're always coming up to me between activities and before and after dinner, too. Some even follow me to the bathroom. The only place I can really get away from them is in my own cabin, or when I have my day off, which I spend in the library, because since I've been pregnant and quit all the drugs and drinking, hanging out with Matt and the guys the way Lam does on his day off isn't fun anymore. All they want to talk about is hunting and girls, and all I want to talk about is what it's like to be pregnant. Other counselors get the same day off that I do, but they're all old-timers here, and even though they invite me to join them, I can tell they don't want me dragging along. So all I do is drive Rambo around town for a while, just to feel my freedom, and then I sit in the library and read about being pregnant and what it's like to raise a kid.

The third place I can get away from the campers is in the counselors' break hut, where we take breaks from our activities. Ziggy and I have the same break time.

I told Ziggy that as long as he never sang to me, we could be friends, and it turns out I really like him, and he seems to like me, too. It just goes to show, my first impressions of people are always wrong.

There's a juice machine and a snack machine in the hut, and a couch and a coffee table and some chairs. Ziggy buys me a snack, because he knows I don't get paid one red cent in this backwoods place. The ILs like to keep me powerless. They figure their ratty old cabin with the ratty old sofa and lumpy bed is payment enough for my pathetic assistant counselor services. Maybe they're right. Anyway, I like Ziggy. I like how he knows so much about music, and it's cool that he's in his second year at the Berklee College of Music, and that he plans to write the music, or "scores," as he calls them, for movies when he graduates.

"Why would you teach music at a fat camp?" I asked him once. "I mean, wouldn't a music camp or something be better? Or maybe even just forming a band and performing in the summers or—or something else—anything else?"

"I like it here," he said. "I like the time away from all the intensity at Berklee. I like how remote this place is, and besides, I used to be a camper here. I just want to give back. The Lothrops have always been good to me."

That was a shock. The Lothrops, nice? Well, maybe Mr. Lothrop. Oh, okay, the MIL is great with the campers, too. I guess she just saves all her hate and venom for me, the girl who she thinks destroyed her son. And Ziggy used to go here? Big shock.

"You mean you used to be fat?" I looked at his wiry self in his baggy jeans and his skinny arms poking out of his too-big WeightAway T-shirt, and I couldn't picture it.

He nodded. "Yeah, a real doughnut. But I learned how to eat right and exercise, and it's at WeightAway that I got into music. They talk here a lot about finding your bliss and focusing on that instead of food. There was a great music teacher here— really cool guy. Here's where I got my start."

I thought about finding my bliss. Is Lam my bliss? The thought depressed me for some reason. *Maybe this baby I'm carrying will be my bliss. Is it okay to have people as your bliss?* Somehow I didn't think so. I think I'm supposed to have some kind of skill, or talent, or gift, but if I have one, I haven't found it yet.

I also like Ziggy because he's nice about the baby; he never asks questions, he just listens to me talk. A lot of the other counselors, especially the girls, and even the kids, are always either making snide remarks or asking me stuff like is it a boy or a girl, or aren't you kind of young to have a baby, or are you going to keep it or give it up for adoption? First of all, I don't know if it's a boy or a girl. To tell the truth, I haven't gone to a doctor since the first visit, which my mom took me to, because like I said, I hate doctors. Every time I had an appointment, I'd cut out, just like it was a class at school. I just couldn't face all their poking around. I've got my prenatal vitamin pills, I'm off all the bad stuff, I've read lots of books on being pregnant, so I figure I'm good. In the olden days they didn't have all this ultrasound and crap, and those babies turned out fine; why shouldn't mine? The MIL's always checking up on me about it, too, so I lie and tell her I have doctor's appointments scheduled on my days off. Anyway, I don't need to know which sex it is. Am I going to give it to Sarah? I don't know. I don't know what I'm going to do. I talk this over with Ziggy.

"I lie awake at night, staring up at the rafters at the 'Carrie was here' message written in glow-in-the-dark marker while

Lam snores next to me, trying to figure out what we should do with the baby," I tell him. "One night I think maybe we can handle it." I look at Ziggy and shrug. "That's when I've had a good day with the kids here. But then the next night I'm thinking, give it away. Get rid of it, and fast, because I'll stink as a mother. I don't want to be tied down—stuff like that. That's when I've had a bad day with the kids—or sometimes with Lam."

Ziggy listens and nods, resting his hand on my knee. He's always touching people, so I don't think anything of it. "I have a cousin who got pregnant young—well, at eighteen—but she didn't marry the guy, and she kept the baby. She's really struggling. She works three jobs and never sees the kid. The daycare people are pretty much raising her, but what can she do, you know?"

"Daycare. I forgot about daycare. I don't want my kid in daycare. But I don't want to spend all my days changing diapers and feeding and taking care of the baby, either—I don't think."

"You should move to Boston," Ziggy says, which sounds like a comment out of the blue, but then he explains. "There's just so much to do—so much culture. You could take your baby to the Museum of Fine Arts or the Museum of Science and go to outdoor concerts with it and poetry readings and walk with it along the Charles River."

"Yeah," I say. "Yeah, that would be great. I'd like that, for sure."

"I once thought I got a girl pregnant, but it was a false alarm," he says.

"Really? No kidding?"

"No kidding. So for a couple of weeks I was imagining doing all those things with her and the baby. When I found out she wasn't pregnant, I was glad but sad, too. Boston's a cool place to raise a kid. I'd love to show you Boston."

"Sounds great," I say. Then we sit there not talking for a minute or so while Ziggy slurps his grape Fanta and I eat my peanut butter–cheese crackers. Then Ziggy reaches for my hand and squeezes it. "You'll figure your life out," he says. He smiles at me. We're sitting really close and looking right at each other and I think, *He's cute*, and this zinging feeling goes from our touch right to my stomach, and the baby kicks. I spring to my feet, which, my being almost eight months pregnant, is hard to do, but I do it. I'm nervous. I've got that scared-of-the-future thing hammering in my head all of a sudden. I back away from Ziggy.

He jumps up. "You okay? Is it the baby? What's wrong?" He puts his arm around my shoulders, and there's that zinging thing again, and I make for the exit and knock into a couple of other counselors entering the hut. "Oh, sorry," I say, but I don't stop to see if they're okay. I run—sort of—up the hill to my cabin, and I get inside and slam the door behind me and fall against it. My heart is thumping in my chest, keeping time with the baby's kicking. I feel ill. I don't want to think about what just happened. Nothing happened. That's right; nothing happened, I tell myself. I'm emotional. I didn't kiss him or anything. But maybe I felt like it? Did I? Is that what I felt? I don't want to know. I push away from the door and cross the cabin to my bed and climb in. I check my watch. I have fifteen more minutes till dinnertime. I won't go. Lam won't be there, since he's teaching the lifesaving course, but Ziggy will be. No, I'll just lie still. I stare up at the rafters. There's the "Carrie was here" message and the "I lost fifteen pounds!" message, and the "If you're reading this, you're in my bunk" message. I read all the different messages left by campers from years past. They take my mind off of things, and I start to calm down. I hear the dinner bell, but I ignore it. I read more messages, and then before I know it I'm thinking of Ziggy and wondering what it would be like to kiss him. I mean, it would be okay. I'm not *really* married. Not really. We were pushed into this, so the marriage isn't real. So if I wanted to kiss Ziggy, if we became boyfriend and girlfriend, that would be okay, wouldn't it? Lam's been my only boyfriend. My whole world since I came back from Kenya has been about Lam. That can't be right. I should have more than one boyfriend before I settle down, shouldn't I? Would I be a bad person if I kissed him? I think of my parents, and I see their disappointed faces looking down on me from the rafters. They're shaking their heads. They're in Kenya saving the children, and I'm thinking about doing the nasty with Ziggy. Wait, no I'm not, just a kiss, just a simple kiss; that's all. Would kissing him hurt anything really? Kissing's not cheating. Sex is cheating. We just won't have sex.

There's a knock on the door, and I sit up. I call "Come in" and feel my face grow hot with embarrassment, as if Ziggy were with me in the bed.

The door opens and it's Ziggy, and my whole body flushes. He steps just inside the cabin and stops. "I was sent to find out if you're okay. Are you sick? Do I need to get the nurse or any-thing? Do you need me to find Lam?"

I shake my head. "No, I'm fine. I just felt tired, just really tired. So—so I came in here to lie down."

His worried expression relaxes. "Then can I bring you a plate of food? It's brown rice and bean burritos, a meal you ac-tually like."

He remembers I like the brown rice and burritos. I wonder if Lam knows that. Does he know what my favorite foods are? Do I know his? Do I even know his favorite color? No. What does it matter? I love Lam. He loves me. I just miss him. We hardly see each other anymore. Ziggy is just a substitute; that's all. Forget about all that kissing-Ziggy nonsense. I get off the bed and stretch. "No need. I'll go up to the dining hall. I wouldn't want to deprive the MIL of my presence, would I?"

Ziggy laughs. He's the only one who knows I call my mother-in-law the MIL. "MIL, like a millstone around my neck," I told him once, and he had laughed.

I wave him away. "You go on and I'll be right there. I've just gotta do something first."

"Are you sure?" Ziggy takes a few steps closer, and I worry he's going to touch me again.

"Yes! Yes, I'm sure. Go on." I wave him away again, and he turns and leaves.

When he's gone, I let out my breath. I shake my head. I've got to be more careful. What was I thinking? I love Lam and he loves me and we're married and we're going to have a baby and maybe keep the baby and everything's going to be great, just really great, just really, really great.

CHAPTER NINE

SINCE THE LIFESAVING course runs past the dinner hour, Lam gets his dinner later and so he gets to our cabin late, too. Two or three nights a week he has night duty, where he takes a two-hour shift of guarding the camp to make sure the boys stay on their side of the lake and the girls stay on theirs. I thought it was supposed to be only once a week, but Lam says since he's been in the doghouse with his parents because of us getting married and being pregnant and all, that he's doing extra duty to make it up to them.

All the male counselors except Lam sleep on the other side of the lake with the boys, but since Lam is married he's in the cabin with me on the girls' side. The girls love him, and one time they made him an honorary girl and put makeup on him and dressed him up like a girl, stuffing oranges in a bra and all, and he loved it. I watched the sweet way he let these campers fix his hair and makeup and the way he pranced for them once he was all done up, swinging a purse on his arm and everything, and I thought that he would make such a great father. He's patient. He would be patient with our children. I'm not patient, and I'm not patient tonight while I wait for him to finish his dinner and come home to the cabin. I need to be with him. I need to talk to him. I want to tell him what happened with Ziggy—or what didn't happen, but what might have happened. I kind of wish I could call my sister and ask her advice, and this shocks me, because since when did I ever want her advice? Maybe I shouldn't tell Lam anything, but then I think he should know. We should be honest. If our marriage is going to be worth anything, then we should be honest. Anyway, I didn't do anything with Ziggy. I just thought about it. I just lusted in my heart. Isn't that what it's called? That's allowed, isn't it?

Like I said, I have no patience, so I'm about to jump out of my skin by the time Lam gets to the cabin. As usual, he looks tired.

Most nights he comes in, shakes his head, and says, "Man, I'm tired." Then before he can even pull off his shorts, he falls into bed and goes right to sleep.

He won't let me tell his parents how tired he is, but I'm kind of worried. He's lost weight and he has these dark bags under his eyes all the time. He hates waking up in the morning, and it takes lots of pushing and pulling from me to get him going.

Tonight I cut him off before he gives me his "I'm too tired to speak" speech. "Lam, we have to talk," I say.

He lets out this long sigh. "Now? I'm just so tired. What about? Can't we talk in the morning?"

"No, because you're even more tired in the morning. I really think you should tell your parents how you're feeling, you know? You shouldn't be this tired all the time."

Lam waves my comments away and shuffles over to the bed. He falls onto it face first and rolls over. "So what do you want to talk about? The baby? I'm thinking we should give it to my parents. I think that's the right thing to do." He puts his hands behind his head and closes his eyes as though saying, "End of discussion," when that's not even the discussion I'm wanting to have—but since he brought it up . . .

"With your parents? What, have they been pressuring you? Last time we talked, you wanted to keep it. Remember? You were talking about growing up and being responsible and crap. What's changed?"

Lam opens his eyes. I go over and climb onto the bed. He's smack in the middle of it, so I climb over him and squeeze myself up against the wall. He doesn't even move his elbow, which pokes out from the side of his head and covers half my pillow. While I'm doing this, he's talking. "What's changed is I've come to my senses. I want to make something of my life. Get out of this hellhole and see the world. How can I do that if I've got to start out having to take care of a baby and all?"

A baby and all? What does he mean by "and all"? Am I the "and all"?

"So what are you saying?"

He stares up at the rafters. "I'm saying that maybe I want a little more in my life than just being a father and a husband."

"Yeah, well, who's stopping you? Go get more. We're going to need you to be more just to survive, so who's stopping you? Don't you think I want more, too? Do you think I want to spend the rest of my life in a fat camp with my in-laws scowling over my shoulder all the day long? I don't think so!"

I feel so mad, and I don't know why. I guess it pisses me off the way he talks like he's got himself all figured out all of a sudden, and the way it sounds like his plans don't include me. I know, I know, just a couple of hours ago I was daydreaming about Ziggy and my plans sure didn't include Lam, but it hurts the way he's talking, and that's why I decide not to tell him about what happened in the counselors' hut. There's nothing to tell, anyway, really, and I don't want to hurt him. I sit up and think about this a second.

Lam notices and touches my arm. "You okay? Is it the baby?"

No, it's not the baby; it's me, I want to say, but I don't say anything. It's just that it occurs to me that deciding not to hurt Lam feels so grown up. I feel so grown up all of a sudden. First, because I realized that the reason I was hot for Ziggy this afternoon was really because I was missing Lam; and second, because I realized that if I told Lam about my thoughts, it would hurt him; and third, because I decided not to hurt him, even though he had just hurt me. I smile to myself and look down at my belly. I rub it to comfort the baby. Tonight's a good night, so I feel like I want the baby. I want to take care of it and be a good mother to it, and I want Lam to love me and to make something of his life for the three of us.

"Eleanor?" Lam rubs my arm, and I lie back down and snuggle up to him, me and the baby.

"Lam, it's going to be all right, isn't it? You love me, don't you? And I love you. I'm going to be the best mother for this baby, and the best wife, and you know I have this idea about a teen pregnancy magazine—about creating one, with interviews and articles and, I don't know, real stuff, honest stuff, the stuff they don't tell teenagers. I'm not going to make it all pretty with pretty people and perfect kids and everything working out just perfectly, because that's not how it is, is it?"

Lam shifts away from me a bit so he can get a look at my face. "When did you decide all this?" he asks. He looks surprised and maybe, I don't know, jealous that he didn't come up with the idea.

"A couple of weeks ago—on our wedding night, I think."

"So, what, like you're going to have ugly people on the cover and tell all these horrible stories about what could go wrong and shit? Who's going to want to look at that?"

I punch him in the chest, and he grunts and brings his

knees up. "You're just jealous. Everybody's going to want to look at it, that's who. Everybody who's tired of reading all that phony-baloney stuff they've got in all the other parenting magazines."

"Oh, yeah? And what did you get in Language Arts this year on your report card?"

"Lam, shut up. Why are you shooting down my idea? Is it maybe because you're just all talk about making something of your life? Is it because you don't have a clue what you want to do, and I do? Huh? Is that it? Because if that's it, then you're just being mean, and even if it isn't, you're still being mean." I get up and crawl to the end of the bed and climb off. "I think it's a great idea, and so does Ziggy, so there. And, I'm thinking we should move to Boston as soon as we can afford it, because Boston is a great place to raise a kid."

Lam props himself on his elbows. "Well, screw you! I know exactly what I want to do," he says, then pauses and adds, "Ziggy? What's Ziggy got to do with it?"

"Oh, nothing," I say in this singsong voice. I go over to the windows and stare out at the dusky night and the campers parading past. There's a line of them heading up to the main cabin for their weekly weigh-in. Most campers weigh in in the morning, but the older campers check their weight at night because it keeps them eating light at mealtimes. If you lose even an ounce you get points for your cabin, and the cabin with the most points each week gets a special trip out of the camp. If you've gained

weight, your cabin loses points and everybody hates you for ruining their chances.

"What do you mean by, 'Oh, nothing'?" Lam asks. He
comes over to the windows and stands with his arms folded
across his chest like a genie granting a wish. Maybe he can blink
his eyes and make himself disappear, because I can feel where
this argument is heading.

"What the hell does Ziggy have to do with it? And why do
you suddenly want to move to Boston? Isn't that where Ziggy
lives? What's all this with Ziggy?"

I turn on Lam. "Nothing! Nothing at all. Only he's around
to talk to, and you never are, are you? And he listens and thinks
my ideas are good ones, and he thinks I'm smart."

"Who says you're not smart? I've told you a thousand times
that I think you're smart. Everybody thinks your smart. You've
always got your face in some book. You're a real bookworm. I
mean, who else in the world has read that big fat book you read
on ants? You're just lazy about school."

"Lazy? I've never been lazy a day in my life! Just because I
skipped school a lot does not make me lazy. If you recall, I was
skipping to meet you. I did everything for you. I'm the one who
snuck out of the house all the time to meet *you* in *your* basement.
I'm the one who stole the car twice so I could be with you and
we could go up to the cabins and be alone. I'm the one who
broke into—"

"All right! All right! You're not lazy. Wrong choice of

words. Forget it, anyway. Let's just forget it, okay? Go ahead and do your dumb magazine. What do I care? I've got my own plans."

"Dumb? Dumb? Just wait and see, and anyway, what's your great idea, Mr. Genius?"

Lam backs away. "Oh, I've got one, all right. I'm just not ready to talk about it, because all my ideas aren't fully formed. I don't just blurt out anything that pops into my head the way you do, and then act like it's a great idea."

I turn away from the window and watch Lam crawl back into the bed. "You know what? Just shut up, okay?" I say. "Don't say another word, because I swear, if you do, we're finished. And anyway, I hate the way we are now. Before we were married, we couldn't get enough of each other and we had all kinds of fun ideas, like running away to Hawaii, or hiking our way around Europe, but now—well . . . Lam?" I take a couple of steps toward the bed. Lam's eyes are closed, and he's breathing deeply. "Lam? Are you awake?"

CHAPTER TEN

HALEY WAS FINE again for a day or two, and I was off the hook. I just assisted the ballet class, which meant I went around poking the girls here and there when their butts stuck out too far or they weren't standing up straight. I also spent a lot of time standing by the CD player putting on whatever music Haley wanted. But then Haley got sick again, and it's been three days in a row that I'm teaching her class, and the kids are getting bored with my classes. They're tired of doing the same dumb dances in every class. I'm so embarrassed that I just want to melt into the floor. There are fewer girls every day. I've got some new kids, too, but still there aren't as many as the first class I taught, and I don't know what to do, because I feel like I'm making a total fool out of myself. Ashley Wilson keeps coming, and I think she just wants to look smug and see what stupid thing I'll do next.

So, we're all in a circle the way we usually are in the beginning of my classes, and I'm about to call, "Skip to the center," the way I always do, but then I see Ashley's disgusted expression and feel like picking on her, so instead I call out, "Ashley Wilson to the center," and she says, "What?" She looks trapped, and all her smugness just falls away.

"Do something into the center and out again, and we'll all imitate you."

"Oh," she says, and thinks a second. "Okay, I've got something." Now she's smug again. She does this leap-turn thing and lands on one foot with her other leg in back of her and pointing in the air. I don't know what she just did, but I'm pregnant, so luckily I don't have to copy her. The other girls try to do the leap-turn thing, and some do it and some don't, but they just laugh at themselves, except for Banner, who looks like she's about to cry, but what else is new?

"Let's do that again," I call out, and the girls try another leap-turn-arabesquey, as I decide to call it. "Do the leap-turn-arabesquey!" I shout, and Ashley says in this snotty voice, "It's called a *tour jeté*."

"I know," I say, "but in English it's called a leap-turn-arabesquey. Come on, everybody, do the leap-turn-arabesquey!" I shout again, and the girls spread out all over the room trying their best to copy Ashley. Then Ashley Wilson does some other fancy step, some kind of spin around on one leg, and the girls try that out. Then, before Ashley's head gets too big, I ask someone else to take a turn. "It doesn't have to be a real step. Make one up. Let's see how *creative* you can be. Everybody try to come up with a new step, and then we'll all take turns learning them," I say.

Everybody except Banner is trying to do some variation of the *tour jeté*.

I go over to where she's standing with her head down and her eyes peering out from her wall of hair. "Hey, come on, Banner," I say. "Why aren't you trying anything?"

"You know why. I'll look stupid, and they'll make fun of me."

"But everybody looks stupid. Really, you've just *got* to get over yourself." I lean over. "Check out Ashley Ryan. What's she trying to do? She looks like a duck trying to take off into the air. Look at her arms."

Banner giggles and wipes her eyes at the same time, like there were tears there, even though they look dry. I think she's so used to crying, she just automatically wipes her eyes, just in case.

"Go on," I say. "Give it a try. See how goofy you can make it."

She gets this upset look on her face again. "Goofy? It has to be goofy?" Her voice trembles, and I want to kick her. I do. I really do.

"No," I say, exasperated. "No, it can be anything you want. Come on, Banner, just walk across the room or something, anything. Just move."

Okay, now here she goes. She's crying and wiping her eyes. "I'm sorry I'm upsetting you," she says.

"Banner, you're not upsetting me except that you're upset, so that makes me upset, so stop being upset and I won't be upset, okay?"

She nods and wipes her eyes some more. I decide to ignore her and just get back to the class, even though ignoring her makes me feel like a total failure. I know Leo would do something to make her feel wonderful, but I'm not Leo, and I don't know what else to do.

"Okay, everybody," I shout. "Who wants to go first? Who has something for us to imitate?"

Girls raise their hands, and I pick SuSun Kew. She does her step, but it's more than a step, it's a bunch of steps that we all have to learn. The girls seem to like this a lot, and that gives me another idea. If I get stuck teaching this class on my own another day, I'm going to have them make up whole dances, in groups, and then they can perform them for each other. I don't tell them my idea right away, though. I let each girl take a turn teaching something. Some of them are really goofy, and we all laugh and have fun with these steps. I check out Banner to see if she's laughing, and she's at least sort of smiling, but she keeps in the back of the room behind all the other girls.

When we get through all the different steps and minidances, the class is almost over, and I'm just about to announce my idea for next time, when Ashley Wilson says in her snotty voice, "But Banner didn't take a turn. It's Banner's turn."

What a big mouth!

Everyone looks at Banner, and one girl shouts out, "Come on, Banner, you snifflepuss," and then they all start chanting, "Banner—Banner—Banner!" and she looks so frightened I think she's going to faint. I'm trying to decide which excuse to use for her—she has cramps, or we've run out of time—when Banner comes to the center, pauses, then lets her front foot slide forward, more and more, and she's getting lower and lower, and her legs are getting farther and farther apart from each other, and then she's in a split. She's doing a full-out split! All the other girls start trying the splits, and most of them get about halfway. Ashley Wilson gets the closest, but there's a bend in her back leg. I can't help it. I have to point this out. "Your back leg is still bent, Ashley Wilson. Banner's back leg is straight."

"Well, so what?" she says. "I'm closer than anybody else."

"Yeah, but close is only good in horseshoes and heart attacks."

"Huh?" she says.

That's an expression I learned from Robby, my sister's husband, and after I say it I want to go wash my mouth out with soap. If there's anybody I don't want to be like, it's that old stuffed turkey.

Then Banner, still on the floor in the split the whole time the girls are trying, turns her body forward, so instead of one leg being behind her and one leg in front, her legs are sticking out on either side of her, and it's awesome.

"Wow, I didn't know you could do that," Robin Ettlinger

says, and all the girls just stand around and look. They don't even bother to try to imitate her.

Banner wears this shy smile and wipes at her dry eyes.

The class time is over and I haven't even told them my idea, but I let Banner have her moment. My idea will keep.

CHAPTER ELEVEN

Okay, I KNOW I'm not the best teacher in the world, and it was so wrong of me to pick on Ashley Wilson the way I did, but everything came out all right, and Banner topped all of them, so I feel in some way proud of myself. I guess it's because I'm actually getting to teach something, even though I don't know what the hell I'm doing most of the time. I'm still doing it, and the girls are listening to me. It's wicked cool. I like that they seem to like me. I want them to like me. I imagine myself someday being like Leo. The kids drape themselves all over him, and they hang on every word he says, and he's so casual about it, like it's natural that they should want to be with him and listen to him. I wonder how it is that he never gets any-body acting snotty in his classes. Is it because he's a boy? I don't get it. I think how if I were one of the kids at this camp, I'd be making fun of the way he dresses, and the stupid, sign-the-back-of-his-shirt thing, but then I think maybe I wouldn't, and I wonder why I wouldn't. I decide it's because I respect Leo. I don't know why, exactly, but I do. I decide to watch him closely to see if I can figure out what it is, because if I have this baby and if we do decide to keep it, I'm going to want it to respect me, and I know I can't be picking on the kid just because he or she is snotty, the way I did with Ashley Wilson, even if it did turn out all right.

My mom and dad would say that God put me in this camp to teach me how to become a good parent, because they're real religious like that. I don't know if God put me here or not, but I think maybe it's good I'm here, because I'm learning stuff that might be useful with my baby someday, and knowing this gives me a better attitude about being here.

In the crafts hut some kids are making dulcimers. Yeah, real live musical instruments! So now we have knitting and ship-building and dulcimer making going on all at the same time, and I'm frazzled, but Leo's his usual cool, calm self. He and Ziggy do a demonstration on two already-made dulcimers to show everybody what they sound like. Leo's pretty good with the dulcimer, but Ziggy's fantastic. The only thing is, he's looking at me the whole time he's playing, and it makes me wonder if he likes me, too. I mean, I don't *like* him, like him—but maybe he likes me? I try to look away, but then I catch myself looking right at him again, and I blush. Shit! I look away again and wish he'd stop playing and go away already. Finally, after lots of applause, he leaves, but I know he'll be back to demonstrate for the next class, and I decide that's definitely when I'm going to have to go to the bathroom.

*   *   *

The dulcimers sound a little like guitars and a little like auto-harps or zithers—kind of like all three instruments mashed together. There are only four strings, and three of the strings are tuned in the same key. I don't get it, but the dulcimers do sound kind of cool, and they're pretty easy to play. I think they're a lot easier to play than to make. Yep, I'm making my-self one. I don't have to make the whole thing from scratch. The dulcimers come in a kit, but still there's some sawing and sand-ing and gluing and stringing to do. So far I've cut out the front and back pieces of wood, and I did a really crappy job of it. Now I'm trying to sand the edges, but as jagged as mine are, I'm going to need to sand this thing for a month to get all the edges smooth. It's embarrassing, because some of the ten-year-olds do a better job than I do. Still, I'm proud of myself for doing a craft, even if it does end up looking more like a wooden banana with quills than an instrument.

Toward the end of the third week of camp, I get a pro-motion. It turns out Haley has appendicitis. The ambulance came, and everything in camp stopped while they loaded her into the truck and rode off again. Then an hour later a camper comes by the crafts hut to tell me that the ILs want to see me in the main cabin. The FIL does most of the talking while the MIL sits beside him in a director's chair, looking sour. He says Haley's most likely going to be away a couple of weeks and that they're still very short-handed and that if I feel up to it and if my doctor says it's okay, they'd like me to take over Haley's cabin duties as well as the dance class for the next few weeks. "Leo tells us you do a good job with the campers at the crafts hut. He believes you can handle the cabin on your own, and, well, we have no other choice; we have no one else," the FIL says again. He looks worried, and I don't know if it's because he's worried about me taking over a cabin, or he's just worried in general about Haley and being short on counselors this summer, or what.

Then the MIL shakes her head and says, "I don't know what it is about dancers at this camp, but they're always getting sick or injured, or they're just plain nuts. Honestly, this is the last year we offer dance."

"So, it's okay that I'm teaching, uh, interpretive dance instead of ballet?" I ask. I had looked through some dance books at the library, and "interpretive dance" is the closest kind of dance that I could compare my class to, so that's what I've decided to call it. I don't know what I wanted the MIL to say. Maybe, "Oh, yes, it's so much better than ballet. You're the greatest teacher we've ever had." She's come to my class a couple of times now, and both times my mind has just gone numb while she was watching me, but still, I want to hear something positive from her.

"What choice do we have, really?" she says. "At least it's active, and the girls seem happy enough."

Coming from the MIL, that's high praise.

Anyway, I'm so pleased that they asked me to take over for Haley that I lie and tell them my doctor says I'm fine for any kind of activity. I feel fine—clumsy and ugly, but fine—so I figure it's safe until I don't feel fine.

So we set it all up, and now I'll be living in the cabin with the girls and I'll be a full-time counselor and dance instructor—hah! What a laugh. I got cabin seven, the eleven- and twelve-year-olds' cabin, which means it's Banner's cabin, which also means it's Ashley Wilson's cabin. As if I don't get enough of the two of them already. I think I hate Ashley Wilson, and I wonder what I'll do if my kid turns out to be just like her. Can you hate your own kid? If Sarah and Robby raise it, will it turn out to be all stiff and uppity and judgmental like they are?

Ashley Wilson's really good at turning all the other cabin-mates into mini she-devils. They treat me the same way I used to treat substitute teachers in school, meaning they completely ignore me.

"All right, everybody, fifteen minutes till lights out. You should all be in your pajamas," I say on my first night as a full counselor. I have my new list of "Cabin Counselor Rules" the ILs gave me, and rule number 7,845 is that all campers should be in pajamas and on their beds by nine thirty and lights out by nine forty-five. Well, only a few of my campers are in pajamas, and they all ignore my lights-out warning.

"Don't worry about me; I sleep in the nude," Ashley Wilson says to me in this aren't-I-clever voice when I yell once more for them to put on their pajamas. Then she runs up to Banner, who's heading for her bunk, and yanks down her pajama bottoms so her butt's showing. "Banny-fanny!" Ashley Wilson sings.

All the girls in the cabin laugh, except Banner, of course, who's pulling up her pants and looking at me with this helpless expression, waiting for me to fix what just happened.

"That's not funny! How would you like it if I did that to you?" I say, marching over and getting in Ashley Wilson's face. Her friends, who had been gathered around her, back away.

"Okay by me," Ashley Wilson says. "Anyway, Banny-fanny hasn't lost any weight. She's *gained* weight, and our whole cabin has to pay for it, so it serves her right," she yells in my face. Then she turns around, bends over, and moons me.

Some kids laugh at this, and some kids yell, "Woo-hoo!"

"Well, now, *that's* butt-ugly," I say, and the whole cabin laughs at that, and the war is on!

I can see Ashley Wilson is seething and probably plotting something evil in her pointed little head as she pulls up her pants and trots off to join her buddies in the back of the cabin, but I can't worry about that now, I've got to get some discipline around here.

I clap my hands to get everybody's attention. The girls ignore me. I shout, "In bed now, or you'll all miss breakfast in the morning."

That gets about half the campers into bed—the ones who

actually heard me—but Ashley Wilson has flitted over to where the sinks are, and she and her evil cronies have started a wet-towel fight. I turn off all the lights, yanking on the strings hanging from the ceiling as I march to the back of the cabin. It's dark by the time I get back there. I grab the towel out of Ashley Wilson's chubby little hands and yell, "Get in the bed! Now!"

The girls giggle and scurry off to their bunks—everyone but Ashley Wilson. "I don't have to listen to you," she says. "You're not a real counselor. You're just a counselor-in-training—so I don't have to listen. You're just a pregnant-nobody loser."

Behind me I can hear some of the girls climbing back off their bunks. I'm furious. I know it's a war between me and Ashley Wilson, and I figure I had better win.

"Well, nobody has to listen to you, either," I say. "And nobody *should*, especially not the rest of this cabin. They're all smarter than you are, and prettier, and none of them have your beady little pig eyes. They're all nice girls, unlike you."

I hear the girls gasp, and I know I've gone too far—way too far. And even though I know it's a total act when Ashley Wilson bursts into tears, I know I shouldn't have said what I said. She just totally pissed me off.

"You pig whore. You aren't really twenty years old—you're just a teenager who got knocked up, so there! Everybody knows you're lying," Ashley shouts through her tears, which gets more gasps from the other girls. "I'm going to tell on you, and you're going to get into so much trouble. My dad will have you fired for what you said to me." Then, like the true drama queen that she is, she cries harder and rushes out of the cabin to go tell.

By now I can see pretty well in the dark, and I pad back to the front of the cabin to my little bed by the entrance door. The girls are all whispering, but I don't say anything. They could light the place on fire, and I wouldn't say anything. I know I'm a terrible counselor, and I'm going to make a terrible mother, and this is my final decision—I am giving my baby to my sister.

Twenty minutes later, Gren comes to get me. She tells me I'm wanted up at the Lothrops' cabin and that she'll watch my girls for me.

I head up to the ILs' cabin, and on my way I see Jen strutting herself toward my place, where Lam is supposedly fast asleep. I call out to her, "Hey, Jen, don't wake him up. Leave him alone, why don't you? He doesn't want to see you."

Jen stops walking and stands so still it's as if she figures if she stands completely frozen, I won't notice she's there.

"Uh, hello. I see you," I say.

Then Jen comes back to life. "Yeah, okay," she says. "I was just going to ask Lam if he could get down to the lake on time tomorrow morning, because we have a written test to give for the lifesaving kids."

"Uh-huh, sure," I say. "Like I really believe that one." I take a few more steps toward her, and Jen moves away from the cabin a little.

"You can believe what you want. What do I care? Anyway,

maybe you ought to be asking Lam where he is every morning, because he's not at the lake, and we're all getting tired of covering for him." She says this and walks off, leaving me to stare after her wiggling little butt.

Oh, boy, the night has already been such a great success, I just can't wait to get up to the ILs' cabin to see what nice surprises they have in store for me.

*   *   *

I open the ILs' cabin door, and before I can take a step inside, they start in on me. They're both sitting in front of coffee mugs at the round oak table they've got in their kitchen/dining room/ living room. The camp cat, a tabby named Rufus, sits in the middle of the table like a centerpiece. The FIL looks upset but not furious. There's a softness that's always there in his eyes, and it's there tonight. The MIL is furious, as usual, and her eyes are pure steel.

"Did you call Ashley Wilson a fat ugly pig?" the MIL asks.

I step inside and pull the cabin door closed behind me. No need to let the whole camp hear this. "Well, not exactly, but that might be what Ashley Wilson heard," I say. Then I add, "Look, I know I went too far. But that girl's a little devil and she pushed the wrong buttons on me. I was just trying to get control of the cabin and she was calling another camper and me names, so I called her a few back." I try to remember if she called me a pig whore before or after I told her she was ugly and stupid. What does it matter? I know I'm in the shithouse either way.

"You're expected to act like an adult, not sink to their level," the MIL says, spitting her words out every time she hits the let-ter *t*. "You're expec*t-spit*-ed *t-spit*-o ac*t-spit* like an adul*t-spit*."

Even Rufus looks mad, the way he's squinting and blinking at me while I'm getting yelled at.

"I was wrong. I know, I know. Come on, it's my first night, and they were ignoring me, and Ashley Wilson was the ring-leader, and she just started acting out for some reason and—well, I have no excuse. I stink as a counselor. I know. You shouldn't have given me this job."

"And how do you think you'll be as a parent? How can you think you can parent a child when you can't even handle this?" the MIL says, and the FIL shushes her.

"All right, now. I think that's enough. We're getting off the track," he says.

"No, I don't think we are. You know she's not ready. She's too young. That baby is going to need a lot better care than she can give it." She turns her angry glare back on me. "You know you're not going to be able to keep that baby, and I'm—"

"Hey!" I shout out, interrupting her. Then I'm embar-rassed, and I quiet down. "Whatever Lam and I decide to do with this baby," I say, "it won't be to give it to you. You've had it in for me the minute we met 'cause you hate that I'm stealing your precious one-and-only son away from you. You're not even willing to give me a chance. You charged me with breaking and entering last year, probably thinking that would get rid of me, but here I am. And I had to serve time in juvie for that, when you *knew* Lam had told me to come over. He'd just forgotten to leave the basement door open for me and he fell asleep"—more like passed out, but I don't say this—"and so I broke in."

"And you broke the law. When you break the law, you pay for it; it's that simple," she says.

"Okay, well, I paid for it already, but every time we meet, it seems like you're still making me pay for it."

"I've just been trying to make it really clear that you're not ready to parent a child, and the fact that every time we meet you've gotten yourself into a fresh heap of trouble proves my point."

"Maybe it does, but it doesn't make me want to give this baby away to you, that's for sure. Anyway, if you hate me so much, why do you even want this baby?"

The MIL looks as if I had just slapped her in the face. She goes really white, and I remember what Lam once told me about how much his parents had wanted to have another child, and how their first child, a girl, was born with some kind of brain damage and lived less than a year. "They've never gotten over her death. And they've always hovered over me like I'm the Hope Diamond," Lam had said. "Maybe if they had another kid, they'd cut me some slack."

I look at the MIL, and I can see the pain in her face. She shrinks before my eyes, this big country woman. Suddenly she's meek and small, and when she speaks, her voice is tiny and soft.

She doesn't look at me but at the cat. "I want this child to have a chance. The first years of a child's life are so important. I know Lam isn't ready. He won't be there for you, Eleanor."

"Then why did you even want us to get married?"

She looks at me, and her eyes flash. "Because *you* insisted on keeping the baby, and your parents were leaving the country! I wanted you to marry so that I could keep an eye on things— make sure the baby gets a good start in life. At least I know with us, the baby'll have that good start."

"Yeah? Well, you can try being nicer to me. That might be a good start."

The MIL glares at me, and she's grown back to her full size. "It's not about being nice. This isn't a tea party we're holding here. We're trying to run a camp. It's about you following the rules and getting some discipline. How can you expect to discipline a child and gain their respect if you have none yourself?" She pounds the table with each word of the last sentence.

"Okay, okay, both of you." The FIL holds up his hands like he's surrendering. "You two could go at it all night, I'm sure, but we need to get our sleep, and I bet Eleanor does, too." He reaches over and pats the MIL's arm, and the woman slips her hands into her lap. The MIL keeps quiet, but she doesn't stop glaring at me. Neither does Rufus.

"Eleanor, it's not all your fault," the FIL says. "You're inexperienced as a counselor, that's all. We know that."

I didn't expect that. I want to run over and hug the dude, but I don't, of course.

"We pretty much threw you to the lions, but we were in a bind and we hoped you could handle it. I know a lot of the campers like you and even respect you. As I've said, we've had good reports from Leo, and even Ziggy and Gren, and some of the campers. You've been doing a good job on the whole."

I feel embarrassed by the unexpected compliment, and I lower my head and rub my belly for something to do.

"The problem is, we try very hard to help these children with their weight problems, and often the weight is just the tip of the iceberg. They have low self-esteem and problems at home and in school that they're trying to deal with, and they use food to cope. We can't call them names like pig or cow. We can't call them *any* names."

I look at the FIL. "Yeah, I know. It won't ever happen again."

"You'd better believe it," the MIL says, bugging her eyes out at me. "We expect you to apologize to Ashley Wilson in front of the rest of the girls. Maybe, just maybe, she won't go crying to her parents about this. But name-calling amounts to verbal abuse, and we can't have it—*ever*. Do you understand?"

The lecture sounded so much better coming from the FIL. I nod my head and say nothing. I figure saying nothing is best when I'm dealing with the MIL. I need to just let all her hot wind blow right over me.

CHAPTER TWELVE

THE ILs finally dismiss me and tell me to go back to the cabin. When I get there, Ashley Wilson is waiting for me on my bed.

"Where's Gren?" I ask. "Is she in the back?"

"Gone," Ashley Wilson says, not looking up at me. "I was supposed to wait here for you."

"Yeah, well, I'm sorry about what I said tonight. I didn't mean it." I raise my voice. "You girls all hear that? I didn't mean what I said to Ashley Wilson. I just lost my temper. It was all my fault, and I'm sorry, and Ashley Wilson is a smart and pretty girl."

"You left out nice," someone calls back, and some of the others giggle.

"She's strong willed," I say. "And that's a good thing. A strong will can get you far in life, as long as you make good decisions, too." I add this because I'm thinking of myself. My dad says I'm strong willed but I'm always making the wrong decisions about stuff, so it cancels out any good. My strong will makes me hold on to all the wrong things. I think of Lam, and the baby, and I wonder if they're just two more things I'm holding on to merely because I'm too stubborn and strong willed to let go.

"We should all have strong wills like Ashley Wilson and not be such followers. Be your own person; that's what I say."

I look at Ashley and feel my baby kick. It knows I'm afraid to say what I'm about to say because I'm afraid Ashley won't do it, but I take a deep breath and say it, anyway. "Now, would you please apologize to Banner."

Ashley Wilson stares blankly at me a few seconds, and I feel this rush of adrenaline as I try to think what to do next, but then she calls out, "Yeah. Sorry, Banny," and I just leave it. I figure it's the best I'll get out of her tonight.

"Will you read us a story?" a girl, maybe Banner, asks out of the blue.

"What? You're all supposed to be asleep." I walk into the main part of the cabin with Ashley. "It's late. Maybe tomorrow night."

"Please," Ashley Wilson says, and she looks at me with this sweet expression that I'm not sure I trust.

"Well—okay," I say. "But maybe I'll just *tell* you a story so I don't have to turn on a light." I'm hoping if I please Ashley Wilson a little, she won't go crying to her parents about what happened. I'm also hoping that this isn't the start of some camp-long emotional blackmail scheme on her part.

I tell Ashley to get into her bed, and she actually does it. Then I drag a chair into the center of the cabin and tell the story of how Lam and I met.

"Any of you ever heard of base jumping?" I begin. Nobody has. "Well, base jumping is when you jump off of a super-high building, or a cliff, or a really high bridge or something, with kind of like a parachute on. It's really, really dangerous, so don't any of you ever try it."

"Did you try it?" one of the girls asks, and I think it's the other Ashley in the cabin.

"Yeah, but only because I was too stupid to know how dangerous it was, and because I've always gotta try something at least once."

"How many times did you try base jumping?" someone asks.

"Oh, I don't know, a few, I guess, but I stopped the night I saw a jumper break his back. What a bloody mess he was. Now he's crippled for life. So don't any of you try it, unless you've got a death wish.

"So okay, there's this big kind of festival in West Virginia, where once a year you can legally jump off this huge bridge, and I decided I just had to go there and give it a try. Only I didn't have a driver's license because I was only fourteen, and I knew my parents wouldn't let me just take off for West Virginia to go base jumping, so I advertised on Craigslist for a ride. And just so you know, if your parents won't let you do something, they're right; you shouldn't do it. I learned that the hard way."

Actually, I'm still trying to learn that one, because I hate that my parents are always right about everything and that I'm always making the wrong choices, but I don't tell them this.

"If you've got to sneak around, then you know it's wrong, and wrong is wrong is wrong, and it will only hurt you and everyone around you," I add, because I know the ILs would like that I said this, and also because it's what my parents are always telling me.

"Yes, Mother," Ashley Wilson whines, and the other girls laugh.

"Yeah, well, anyway," I continue, "Lam answered my ad, only he said he didn't have a car. He said he could drive me, but I had to provide the car. Kind of kooky, I know, but it was the only offer I got, so I accepted."

"You mean you rode to West Virginia with a complete stranger? That's crazy! You're not supposed to do that. You could get raped!" Stephanie Berry says, and everyone agrees, including me, even though at the time it had never occurred to me.

"So where did you find a car?" Banner asks.

"My parents' garage, where else?"

This gets a laugh.

"This is another thing you should never, ever do. It isn't cool, okay? Never take something that doesn't belong to you."

"Yes, Mother," all the girls say at the same time. Then they all laugh.

"Yeah, well, it's not so funny when you end up in juvie for stealing a car, okay?"

"You were in juvie?" I don't know who asks me that.

"Yeah, and believe me, that's one place you don't want to ever end up. It will scare the hair off your head. There are some girls in there that would just as soon kill you as look at you. You take a carton of milk they wanted, and they'll try to knife you for it, and don't think they don't all know how to make weapons out of anything there, 'cause they do—shoelaces, shoes, a shirt, a plastic fork or spoon, whatever." I shake my head. "But that's another story. Back to stealing my parents' car. You see, it was an old 1949 Volvo. My parents never drove it. My dad just liked to work on it now and then. When we lived in Kenya, he had to leave it here in the States and he could never work on it, but when we moved back—"

"You lived in Africa? How long? Did you see any giraffes? Did you go on safari?" The questions come from all over. I was thinking I would tell them a story and they'd be so bored they'd all fall asleep, but the more I talk, the more excited they get. It makes me feel like I've led an interesting life.

It seems like it takes me hours to tell them how Lam and I stole my parents' car and drove down to West Virginia, and how the car kept breaking down, so by the time we got to the bridge, the festival was over, but we jumped, anyway—a day late—and got put in jail for the night and fined a thousand dollars each, and my parents had thought I had been kidnapped or something, until they found the missing car, and how Lam and I had so much fun on that trip, and how we both base-jumped together, holding hands, and how we just instantly hit it off, and how by the time we returned home to the police and our parents waiting for us, we were madly, deeply in love.

"Did your parents really have you put in juvie for stealing their car? Their own child?" Ashley Wilson asks when I finish the story.

"Yeah, but not that first time. The first time I took their car they just grounded me, but the second time I took it to go— well, never mind where I took it. The second time I took it, they called the police and said I stole it, and I got put in juvie, and it was the smartest thing they ever did."

"Why?" Everyone wants to know.

"Because when you break the law, you should pay the price. Breaking rules hurts a lot of people, not just yourself."

Okay, so I'm only just learning this bit of advice, and basically I stole this line from the ILs' lecture to me earlier, but still, better late than never.

"You should pay the price, otherwise . . . otherwise you'll just keep breaking the rules until you get into even worse trouble, the kind of trouble you can't ever get out of," I add—this only just occurring to me.

"Like getting pregnant when you're only a teenager,"

Ashley Wilson says, only she's not snarky when she says it; she sounds kind of sorry for me.

"Yeah, exactly," I say. I rub my belly, and my baby kicks me, as if to say, "Yeah, thanks a lot, Mom."

CHAPTER THIRTEEN

My BEDTIME stories are very popular with the girls in my cabin, and I don't have any problems with them getting ready for bed anymore. Even Ashley Wilson is less of a pill, so that's going well, and surprisingly so is my dance class. It's always the same group of girls who come, so there are only about fifteen of them, but we have fun. Right now I've got them making up dances about how they feel about being overweight, and even though the songs they've chosen are sad and their stories are sad, they seem to be having lots of fun making up the dances and performing them for each other. Several of the girls have asked me if they can perform their dances for the whole camp. That gave me the idea of having a talent show, and I've even asked the ILs about it. They said they'd discuss it and let me know. So that's good, and my dulcimer is coming along so-so.

But Lam and I aren't speaking. I'm not sure why, except that I'm never around and neither is he, and when we do meet, kind of by accident, he's just like, "Hi, how's it going? How's the baby?" And I'm like, "Yeah, going fine. Baby's fine. Getting close to delivery time, though." When I say this last bit, Lam just nods and stares down at his feet. Then after a few seconds he says bye, and we just go on our way, and I'm left kind of worrying about us and the baby. I've done nothing to prepare myself for this delivery. I don't want to think about it. I'm praying for some kind of miracle where maybe I just pass out and the baby comes out of me, and then I just get up and walk away and everything's fine, no pain, no mess, and off I go. I have those few things my mom got me before she left—the car seat and crib—but I don't have diapers or baby bottles, and since all of my friends are guys, they aren't about to throw me a shower or anything. Still, I figure, just in case Lam and I do decide to keep this baby, I should have something prepared, but the longer I put off thinking about it, the more I think giving it up is for the best. It all just wasn't meant to be.

* * *

Lunchtime at camp is also the time when they hand out the mail, and every camper and counselor loves to get mail. The only mail I ever get is from my sister, Sarah, and it's not really mail, or at least not really a letter. She sends me articles, like the one about how it costs a million dollars to raise a child to the age of eighteen these days, or she sends these stories about struggling single mothers, and the importance of the first three years of a child's life, and how those early years mark a kid forever. I know what she's trying to do, and it's working. I'm scared. I don't want to read the articles, but they're hard to resist. I end up reading them out loud to my baby, and I ask it what it thinks. "You think Lam and I can raise you? Are you worth a million dollars? I bet you are. Do you think Lam still loves me? Do you? Do you love me, little baby?" The baby is smart. It lies very still and says nothing.

Anyway, when the FIL calls my name to pick up a letter, I figure it's another struggling-mother story from Sarah. I pause a second and consider not even getting the letter. I mean, all right, already, I know how impossible it is to raise a kid. I get it. Do I have to keep reading about it? This time, though, it's from my parents! I'm so excited I can't even open the envelope. I wait until my afternoon break, when I'm alone with Ziggy in the break hut, to read the letter.

"You want me to leave?" Ziggy asks when he sees me hesitate with the envelope.

I shake my head. "No," I say. "You open it, will you? I'm just—I don't know, maybe it's just another lecture about the baby or something. Maybe it's just them writing to tell me how ashamed of me they are."

Ziggy eyes me a second, and I shuffle over to the couch and ease myself down.

"Okay," I say. "Go ahead and open it."

Ziggy tears open the letter like it's a Christmas present. He unfolds the paper and reads:

"Dear Elly,

Well, we made it! Not much has changed here in three years. Only the children's faces, but not even all of them. Remember little Catha? She's still here, and she asks about you. She's eight years old now, if you can believe it.

Your dad and I have been so busy getting adjusted to the old routine again, and to tell you the truth, it's worn your dad out. I wish he'd take a break every now and then, but you know your father.

We're living in a new home—simple but adequate. You'd hate it. I think you were right not to come with us this time. You made the right decision, Elly-belly.

So how are you? How's the baby? I do hope you've made up your mind to let Sarah and Robby care for the child. You know they'd be wonderful parents, and then you could finish school, go on to college, and start a career. You'll be seventeen in a few months, and a senior in high school. I know that feels old, but it's way too young to have a baby. Yes, I know we've discussed all of this before, but I hope now that we've all calmed down, my argument makes a little more sense.

How is Lamont? And his parents? I hope you've been keeping out of trouble. I hope . . ."

I hold up my hand. "Stop."

Ziggy lifts his eyes from the letter and looks at me. "What's wrong?"

I wipe at the tear running down my cheek. "Blah, blah, blech," I say. "It's the same old thing. 'I do hope you've made up your mind to let Sarah and Robby care for the child'—blah!" She sounds so formal, so—so impersonal. Who is this woman? I'd rather her yell at me instead of this bullshit stuff.

Ziggy comes and sits down beside me. He puts his arm around me, and I lean on his shoulder, and there's no zinging feeling, because I refuse to allow myself to feel that way about Ziggy anymore. I'm married—I think.

"The thing is," I say, "I *am* going to give the baby up. I've decided. I haven't told Lam this, but with the way things are between us lately, what else can I do?" I lift my head off Ziggy's shoulder. "It was stupid of our parents to make us get married. It's killed all the romance, which is probably exactly what they wanted to happen. I mean, we were so hot for each other, and now, overnight, we've both just gone cold. I don't know what happened."

Ziggy removes his arm from my shoulder and shrugs. "Maybe you just liked the thrill of doing something your parents didn't like. Now that you don't have to sneak around or screw in the back seat of a car or anything, it's not so exciting."

"Okay, first of all, we never screwed in the back seat of any car. I'm not cheap like that, despite what everybody, including my parents, think." I pause because I can't think of a second of all, and then I think about Lam again. "I guess maybe you're right," I say. "It's not thrilling anymore. Lam isn't thrilling. He's tired and boring these days, and since I'm not on drugs or drinking or anything, I can't pretend I'm still so in love with him." I draw in my breath and cover my mouth.

Ziggy leans toward me. "What? What's wrong?"

"I can't believe I just said that. Why did I say that?"

"Say what?"

"That I was pretending to love him. I did love him. I do love him—don't I?"

Ziggy shrugs. "Don't ask me."

"Maybe I just don't know what real love is. But my feelings weren't just because of the drugs, were they? We had fun. We had so much fun, base jumping and riding up to Sunday River to go snowboarding, and hot chocolate after his hunting trips, and hanging out in his parents' basement just listening to music and getting stoned. We could always talk about anything, but now it's always about the baby and the future and wondering if he loves me."

While I'm talking, Ziggy stares down at his high school ring and twists it around and around on his finger. He looks so deep in thought, and I wonder what he's thinking about, but I'm uncomfortable asking him, so I don't. I just stop talking for a second, and he looks up.

"What?" he asks.

"I guess I need to talk to Lam about all this, not you. I'm boring you."

"Hey." Ziggy squeezes my hand. "You're never boring me, but yeah, you should talk to Lam. You're about to pop that baby out any day now by the looks of things."

I grab the letter, which Ziggy left on the coffee table, and stash it in the pocket of my dress. I tell myself that when I get back to my cabin, I'll toss it out, but I don't do that. I shove it inside my pillowcase and decide to forget about it, only deep in my stomach, behind the baby somewhere, is this burning hole full of all kinds of unhappy feelings that need unscrambling, but I'm too messed up to deal with them right now. I wish I could see my parents and explain myself in a way that would make them understand me, but they always act like they've already got me all figured out, and I don't know how they could. I don't have me figured out yet, so how could they? And anyway, the parts about me I do know, they've got all wrong. I mean well. They don't get that, but I do. I don't mean to screw up my life, and their life, and everybody else's.

* * *

It's my night off, and even though I ought to go into town and get some supplies in case the baby comes—like, I don't know, some diapers, and maybe some extra Kotex or something for me—I don't. I stay home and wait for Lam. I wait and wait, but he never comes. I fall asleep. When I wake up, he's there getting ready for swimming, and I realize I've missed breakfast, and I didn't report back to my cabin like I'm supposed to on nights when I have off.

I climb out of the bed. "I'm so late. Your parents will kill me."

"Chillax, Elly. What can they do? Fire you?"

He sounds stoned.

"And where were you last night?" I ask while I'm still struggling to get across the mattress. I feel like a turtle flipped over on its back.

"Here. I played Ping-Pong awhile after dinner, then I came back here and you were asleep. I didn't expect you to be here."

"Yeah, well, it must have been like five in the morning or something, because you forget I gotta pee every five seconds, and every time I got up to pee, you weren't here."

"Yeah, I was. I heard you get up, but I was too tired to say anything. I was on the couch." Lam points to the couch, and I see a rumpled blanket and his pillow lying there. "Like I said, I didn't want to wake you."

Finally I make it out of the bed. I go over to where he's stashing his towel in his duffle, and I grab his arm. "Lam. Are we okay?"

He shrugs. "I don't know." He doesn't look at me. His blond bangs hang down in his eyes, and he doesn't brush them away. He pulls out a pair of flippers from his bag and examines them for cracks.

"What's happened to us?"

He shrugs again. "I don't know. Maybe it's this camp. It's the schedule. We've got completely different schedules. I think my parents must have planned it that way."

"Yeah, and if they meant it to break us up, which I think they did, well, they're winning."

Lam looks at me when I say that. "Oh, yeah?"

This time I shrug. "Well, aren't they?"

He scowls, and he looks real young all of a sudden, like he's four years old. "It's not their fault," he says finally. "We can't just blame them."

"What—"

Before I can ask him what he means by that, there's a knock on the door, and it's Gren. She blushes when she sees us, like she's seeing us naked and doing the nasty or something. That girl is the blushingest, shyest person, or non-person, I've ever met.

"Oh, sorry." She closes the door.

I go open it again, and there she is just standing on the stoop, looking at her feet. "Did you want something, Gren?"

"Oh, uh, the Lothrops want to see Lam, and you're supposed to be at the crafts hut, and I was sent to find out if you're okay."

"Yeah, yeah, I'm okay. Thanks, Gren." I turn back to Lam. "We'll talk later, right?"

"Right," he says.

CHAPTER FOURTEEN

E VERY FRIDAY night the camp does something special.
Most camps have cookouts with s'mores and marshmallows and
wieners and potato chips and all, but at this place, the something special doesn't usually include food unless it's fruit. One
time it was Christmas in July, and we watched Christmas movies and had secret Santas, where we gave handmade or nature-
made presents, and another time we had a camp-wide swim meet
and water-ballet show, but this Friday of the fourth week of
camp, it's skit night, and all the campers are going to put on skits
about camp life, featuring imitations of their counselors.

We meet in the main cabin, where there's a real stage and
everybody sits on the floor, except me and the ILs and Lam's
grandma, who's in her wheelchair. I'm surprised to see her
here, and I wonder how she gets up the mountain with her chair

and all. She catches me looking at her, and she squints at me the way Rufus does. I wonder what the ILs have been telling her about me.

I see kids hanging all over the counselors, sitting in their laps and leaning on them like the counselors are their most favorite people in the world, and I want this for me. I want kids in my lap, too, but I don't have a lap, and I'm sitting up high in a metal folding chair. A few of the campers do come sit by me and talk to me, but it's not the same. Besides, sitting high up on a chair feels dorky, like I'm an adult, like I'm one of the ILs.

The first skit starts, and the kids are really funny. They've got Leo down pat. A boy named Bob Hart, who's a natural class clown, anyway, plays Leo. He's got on the whole tourist getup, and he's darting around pretending like he's taking pictures of the campers, and kids are coming up behind him and sneaking peeks at his back, and one kid gets his head stuck under Leo's camp shirt and he's flailing about, but Leo doesn't even notice. He just keeps taking pictures. Everybody laughs, and I check to see how Leo's taking it, and he's laughing, too. Then there's Jen, and they've got her always blowing her lifeguard whistle. "Walk! Walk!" she shouts.

They even have the guts to imitate the ILs. The boy imitating the FIL is wearing the FIL's "Life is good" apron and pretending he's demonstrating how to make bread, because the ILs teach "how to cook healthy" classes here. It's a riot, because every few seconds the girl imitating the MIL interrupts the demo to translate what the FIL has just said into something far more complicated. I look over to see how the ILs are taking it, and they're both laughing. I have to admit it, they really care about these kids and this camp. It makes me wonder if maybe the MIL used to be fat. She's big boned, and I can see her as maybe once having a weight problem. It makes me, for just a teensy second, feel compassion for her. The FIL looks just like Lam, except he's kind of balding and old, so I figure he's always been thin.

So here I am laughing my head off and the baby is kicking, so I figure it's laughing its head off, too, and then along comes Ashley Wilson, and she's got a pillow stuffed under her Camp WeightAway shirt and she's waddling across the stage. A kid comes up to her and says, "Gee, looks like you're going to have a baby. How old are you, anyway?" Then Ashley Wilson says, "I'm twenty years old, see, and I'm married, see, so get your face out of my business, see." The kid slinks off, and everybody in the audience laughs. Then Ashley Wilson picks up the dulcimer I'm still working on in crafts, and it really is my dulcimer, so it looks pretty bad, and as soon as she picks it up, everybody laughs again, and my feelings get hurt, but I see the kids sitting around me watching me, so I laugh, too. I wonder if they all just think I'm a total asshole or what? Then Ashley Wilson sits in a chair, which takes a good minute, since she's imitating pregnant me, and a guy in swim trunks and flippers with a camp lifeguard hat on, obviously meant to be Lam, comes creeping across the stage behind my back. I'm trying to sand my dulcimer and talk to a camper at the same time and messing up royally, which gets a laugh, and so does the way the boy is creeping along behind me. He's like a cartoon, with his arms bent at the elbows, and his hands like claws, and he's trying to cross on tiptoe in those flippers. When he reaches the other side of the stage, there's a girl waiting for him. The girl's face is made up so her cheeks are bright red, and when Lam reaches her, he takes her hand, and she giggles. They both look at me and leave the stage. Everybody's laughing except me, and the ILs, and the old bat in the wheelchair. I guess Lam and Gren wouldn't be laughing, either, except when I look around, neither one of them is here. I see the MIL start to stand up, but before she can do anything, another skit has begun and it's all funny again, so she sits down, and the moment passes, but I'm just sitting there too stunned to laugh. What did I just see? And what did it mean? Is Lam creeping behind my back with that blah Gren girl? Gren? He's cheating on me with Gren? He's cheating on me? And we're about to have a baby? And we're married? Gren?

The rest of the skits take forever and a day to get through. All I want to do is get out of there and go wring Lam's neck, but I have to endure the rest of the "fun" and stand around afterward eating carrot sticks with the campers, pretending that it was all so funny.

I notice the kids in my cabin, my kids, the ones I thought liked me and my stories, are staying way the hell away from me, and when one of them catches my eye, she looks all sheepish and guilty and turns away again. Yeah, they should feel guilty. How mean can you get? And who was the ringleader of this little joke on me—hmm, I wonder? I give Ashley Wilson bitch-eyes from across the room, and at least she has the decency to look, well, I don't know what, but at least not triumphant.

My face hurts from pasting on my smile for so long. I walk around with my carrot sticks, complimenting kids on their skits and avoiding the girls from my cabin. Finally, the night is over, but before I can escape and go find Lam, Leo comes up to me and says the ILs need to see me in their cabin, pronto!

"Me? Doesn't she mean Lam? Am I going to get blamed for this, too?" I say to Leo. "It's not my fault that the kids all know I'm lying when I say I'm twenty. What a dumb-ass idea that was in the first place. Who were we kidding? And it's not my fault if Lam is cheating on me. Is he cheating on me? Did you know?"

"No. I never pay any attention to gossip."

"So everyone was gossiping about me? Great! Just great!"

"Elly, the Lothrops said pronto. You'd better go talk to them."

"Yeah, yeah." I hate that I have to go talk to the ILs. Whatever is going on should be between me and Lam, not me and them. Man, what a farce!

Leo gives me a hug. "I'm on your side, El. Let me know if you want me to do anything, okay?" He stares into my eyes. "I mean it—anything, talk to Lam, punch his lights out, whatever. Okay?"

I laugh and hug him back. "Yeah, thanks, Leo. You're the best."

On my way to the cabin I see the FIL heading down toward the parking lot with that old lady's wheelchair. I suppose he carried the old bat down first and she's waiting in a car somewhere. The FIL sees me and calls out. "Go on to the cabin. I've got to carry this chair down. I'll be back in a minute."

I do as he says and step inside to find I'm the only one there, besides Rufus, who's sleeping curled up in the empty fruit bowl, so I have to wait. I look around, and there are all these pictures of Lam on the wall—Lam with his rifle and a dead deer, Lam on his bike, Lam in the lake, Lam rowing a boat, Lam holding up his lifeguard patches, Lam in the lifeguard chair, Lam surrounded by younger campers, Lam's school picture at five, six, seven, and so on—Lam, Lam, Lam, precious, only-child Lam. It's a whole wall of Lam. No way can this interview go well for me. I consider just chucking it and going on to my cabin. I thought they wanted to see me pronto, so where is everybody? Where's the MIL? And why should I have to put up with the MIL accusing me of I-don't-know-what? Before I can get up the guts to really take off, in she walks, *clomp, clomp, clomp,* in her leather hiking boots and green shorts and plaid flannel shirt.

"Have a seat," the MIL says without even a hello. She indicates one of the kitchen table chairs, so I pull it out and sit. Big mistake, 'cause she stays standing.

"So," she says, leaning her fists on the table. "What was that all about?"

[141]

"Where's Lam? And—and Gren?" I ask instead of answering her. I mean, if I'm going to be tossed in the soup, then I'm going to make sure they get tossed in with me.

"I asked you a question," she says, and I think to say, "And I asked you one," but I figure that's not a good idea.

I just look down at my belly. It's awful quiet inside me and I figure the poor baby, so close to coming out, has gone into hiding until this ordeal is over. I clasp my hands over it protectively.

"And haven't I told you before not to wear that silly dress? You look like a pumpkin. Don't you *know* you're being made fun of?"

I lift my head and I can't help it, tears fill my eyes. "Well, I do now," I say. Then I really cry. The tears just roll down my face and my nose is runny, so I feel like a slobbering mess, but who cares? "I thought my cabin liked me. They acted like they liked me. Everybody acted like they liked me." I take the sleeve of my camp shirt and wipe my face on it.

"This isn't about whether or not they like you. You're not here to win a popularity contest," she says, but more softly this time, like she might actually care that my feelings are hurt.

She grabs a couple of napkins out of the napkin holder and pushes them toward me. "Use this, not your shirt."

"Nothing else fits," I say, thinking about my dress. It's true. In the last few weeks I feel like my body has doubled in size. This ugly dress, because it's the newest, is the only one that still fits. I shake my head. I can't believe this is me. I love clothes. I love shoes. I love shopping. I wouldn't be caught dead in what I have on if I were my normal self. I'm wearing a pair of ancient cheerleading oxfords that I found in the lost-and-found box here. *Ugly!* They have to be like fifty years old, no kidding, but they fit my swollen feet exactly.

"Well, your next day off, go into town and find something else."

I don't have any money to "find something else," but I figure now is not the time to remind her that she doesn't pay me one red cent. And maybe she's forgotten, but I'm less than four weeks away from my due date. Like hell I'm going to buy some ugly dress just to last me three and a half more weeks. And who cares now, anyway? I'm already the camp laughingstock.

I'm saved from having to say anything by Lam's and the FIL's entrance. The FIL has Lam by the back of his neck. Looks like I'm not the only one who wants to wring it.

"Found him in the boathouse with Gren. I told her we'd talk to her in the morning."

Lam's eyes dart in my direction, then shift to the floor.

I push back in my chair and struggle to my feet.

"Would you care to explain what you think you were doing?" the MIL asks Lam.

Lam lifts his head, and he's got the same steely look in his eyes that I've seen in his mother's. "I think I was gettin' stoned and screwin' Gren, that's what I think I was doing."

The FIL shakes Lam's shoulders and his head bobbles back and forth. "Don't you sass your mother. Do you think this is funny? Do you think you're being cute? What's gotten into you? You're married, son. And you've put us in a very awkward position. Your grandmother was here tonight. She saw the skit, and don't think she's too old to know what it was all about. You and Gren should both be fired for this, but we can't fire you, and so we can't fire Gren. Don't you realize we've got young children here?"

"Doesn't that mean anything to the three of you?" the MIL says, glaring at me.

I force myself to remember what the MIL had just said—something about children.

"Hey," I say. "Don't try to pin this on me. I'm not the one who cheated, and before you can blame me for not being able to keep my man satisfied, which I'm sure is what you're about to do, because everything is always *my* fault, let me tell you, you're the one who's kept us apart all summer. You're the one making Lam work extra hours at night on camp guard duty . . ."

"Elly . . ." Lam interrupts, but I ignore him.

"And you're the one who assigned the junior lifesaving classes during dinner."

"Elly . . ." Lam tries again.

"And you're the one who assigned me the job of counselor to cabin seven, so you're the one who's been keeping us apart. We don't even get the same day off each week!"

I look at Lam, and he's hanging his head and shaking it. The ILs are both glaring at Lam now.

"What?" I say.

"Lifesaving classes are first thing in the morning," the MIL says, still with her eyes on Lam. "Not during dinner. And we have *not* assigned any extra guard duty."

"Lam?" I say.

He looks at me and shrugs. "Okay. Okay. Come on. I just needed some space. I got scared. I don't know. Hell."

"But you had dinner after the lifesaving classes. And Jen was helping you, wasn't she? Or were you sleeping with her, too?" Before he can answer, I turn to the MIL. "Why didn't you notice he and Jen and Gren were missing from dinner if he wasn't teaching lifesaving?"

"Jen was eating out front with the campers," the FIL says, "and we didn't notice that Lam and Gren were missing because we assumed they were eating in the back with you."

"Lam?" I say again.

He glares at me. "What? What do you want me to say? It's nothing serious. I just—well, you're pregnant and you won't—you know, so I just wanted to have some fun. I just wanted to—to—You guys are always on my case." He looks from one parent to the other. "And I'm stuck doing this crap job for peanuts, as if you don't think I can get a real job in the real world. Maybe I don't want to grow up to be a fifty-year-old lifeguard, ever think of that? How are Elly and I supposed to live on what you pay me? You don't even pay her, as if the cabin and the crappy furniture are supposed to be her payment, so it's like we're each working for half the pay. I want my own life. I want—I want to be my own man. I want to be free. So just leave me alone, already."

"But you're not free, and you're not a child anymore, Lam," the MIL says. "You're eighteen. You have responsibilities. You've created a child with this girl, and Lord help you, neither one of you are ready to care for it, but until you both decide what you plan to do with the baby, and with your lives, you're to take the responsibility of your marriage and this child seriously. As for working here at this camp, we were hoping you'd someday take over. You know that. We want you to have it and to run it."

Lam takes a deep breath and lets it out. I can hear the irritation in his sigh.

"Yeah, yeah, okay, okay. I know." He glances at me. "Sorry, Elly. I'm a shit husband, and a shit son. What else is new?"

I step away from the table and go stand in front of Lam. "You know what, just saying 'I'm sorry, and I'm a shit,' and thinking that that's all you have to do to let yourself off the hook is such crap."

Okay, I know, I do this, too. Lam and I are a lot alike, but seeing everything from this new perspective, I see how lame it is to just excuse yourself by dumping on yourself.

"You think if you just knock yourself down and get us all to dump on you, then you're in the clear," I say. "Well, forget it!

You're not. Either we decide we're married or not. If not, then I'm getting the hell outta here and getting on the next flight to California."

"You can't fly at this late date. You're due in three weeks," the MIL says.

"Yeah? Well, I'm glad someone remembers that!"

I don't even know what I'm saying. I want to pummel Lam. I want to take his head off his neck and use it as a kickball.

There's this lull in the discussion, and we're all just standing there looking at one another, and nobody's saying anything for a really long time. It starts to get really uncomfortable, so I say, "Lam and I have lots to talk over. It's up to us to decide if we want to be married or not, and yeah, you're right, we're not ready for a kid with the way things are between us right now, but that train's already left the station, so we have to just deal. Just us. Me and Lam, not me and Lam and you two, and my parents, and Sarah and Robby. I'm going back to cabin seven now. Lam, I'll talk to you tomorrow morning during breakfast. I'll come over to our cabin. Will you be there?"

Lam spreads his palms to the ceiling. "Where else?"

I can think of a couple of where elses, but I just leave, and thankfully, nobody calls me back.

CHAPTER FIFTEEN

I DREAD GOING back to the cabin. Now that I know the girls all hate me and that they've been making fun of me all this time, I feel totally embarrassed. I don't want to go, and I especially don't want to see that Ashley Wilson. Doesn't she just think she's so great, now? I've been done in by an eleven-year-old.

It's really quiet when I get up to the cabin, and I wonder if they're even in there. Usually I can hear the girls laughing and talking a mile away. Then I think that maybe they're inside planning to jump out and yell, "Surprise!" or "Ha! Ha!" or something. I hate this camp. I really, really do. And if by some miracle I ever stay married to Lam, I'm sure as hell not going to run this place with him. I've decided I hate kids. All of them. They're mean, and sneaky, and cruel, and a royal pain in the ass.

I open the door of the cabin, and it's dark inside. I can see lumps in each of the beds, so I know the girls are all in here. "I know you're here," I say. "Do you think you're hiding or something? I can see you all."

"We're trying to be good," comes a voice right beside me.

I look down at my bed, and Ashley Wilson is sitting on it. *On my bed!* She's got nerve.

"Well, you must feel really proud of yourself," I say. "You looked just like me. And stupid me, am I the only one in the whole camp who didn't know what Lam was doing behind my back? You really got me good; that's for sure."

"We didn't know how else to tell you," this meek voice that sounds like Banner's says.

"So you put it in a skit where everyone can see it?"

"Like you said, you were like the only one who didn't know," Ashley Wilson says.

"Yeah," all the other girls chime in.

"We hated that he was sneaking around on you. It's not right. You're married and pregnant and everything," Ashley Ryan says.

The girls are all climbing out of their beds and coming into the alcove, where I'm standing. They gather around me, and I feel a little crowded in. The baby kicks and moves around inside me. I can feel it, the stirring of life. I put my hand on my belly.

Banner takes my other hand. "We all really like you. We think you're one of the best counselors in the whole camp. You're honest, and we always know where we stand with you. It's nice."

"Oh. Well . . ." I feel the tears starting up again. They like me. They like me. I'm surprised and touched, and I think that I really need to start being a better counselor to them, especially if they think I'm so great.

"We're sorry if we hurt you," Ashley Wilson says. She gives me a hug. Then all the other girls hug me, too.

I love kids. I love this camp.

CHAPTER SIXTEEN

O KAY, THEIR LOVE and pity was nice for about five seconds, but I totally feel like a fool when I get to the crafts hut the next morning and find that some of the campers, feeling sorry for me, sanded the pieces of my dulcimer. They must all feel I'm the dumbest, stupidest person in the world. Everyone was so nice to me at breakfast, too, especially the ILs. Yep, the ILs—nice to me. The MIL actually called me dear! It's enough to make you sick. I had wanted to skip breakfast to talk to Lam and get feelings straightened out between us and figure out what we're going to do, but the new rule, Lam informed me this morning, is that he and I have to eat in the dining hall *with* the ILs.

Lam sat across from me with his head down the whole time and said nothing to anybody. He barely ate, and when breakfast was over, he scraped back his chair and bolted before I could catch him and plan when we could meet.

I'm disappointed in the new eating rule because it means I can't sit in the kitchen with Leo and Ziggy, and I know I'm going to miss that. Both of them are good friends to me. Also, I was looking forward to telling them about what happened in the ILs' cabin last night and asking Ziggy if he had known about Lam and Gren. I figure he had to. Then I remember the nervous way he was twisting his class ring and not looking at me the last time we talked about Lam and the baby. Yeah, he knew. I'm kind of pissed that he didn't tell me, but I know I wouldn't have told me, either, and I probably would have been snickering behind my back, too.

When break comes, I go down to the counselors' break hut, and Ziggy is already there playing his guitar.

I step inside the hut. "Bastard," I say.

He nods. "Not my business to tell you. You might have thought I was trying to make a move for you or something. You would have accused me of making up lies about Lam as a way to have you to myself."

"Why would I think that? That's crazy."

I pick up the change that I know Ziggy set out for me so that I can buy a snack. I choose a granola bar. I face the machine and drop the coins in.

"Because I actually thought about doing that—telling on him, so that you'd maybe ditch him and, I don't know . . ."

I press the tab, and the bar drops into the mouth of the machine. I dig it out and pause before turning around. I'm trying to decide if he meant what I think he meant.

"You mean you like me? You *like* me, like me?"

Ziggy keeps strumming the guitar, but he's staring right at me—right through me. "Is that so strange?"

"Uh, yeah. You're in college. You're going to be this big Hollywood musician-writer person. You're probably going to be famous someday. And I'm, I'm . . ." I shrug.

I don't know what I am, but as much as I fantasized about Ziggy and me, it wasn't for real, was it? It couldn't be for real, because we come from two different places—two different soul places. I would ruin his life. I know that. I'm a walking time bomb. It's okay with Lam, because so is he. We're trouble times two. When I think of this, I feel a little better about Lam. I feel like maybe it's okay he cheated on me, because he probably only cheated first, and given enough time, I probably would have cheated on him with Ziggy, or with somebody else. That's what I like about Lam. He's comfortable. He's trouble, but that's comforting somehow. Does that make sense? I'm used to trouble. I wouldn't know what to do with someone who has his shit together the way Ziggy does. Maybe I'd be bored. Yeah, bored, and I'd always be afraid of messing up. I'd be afraid of messing *him* up. I would hate to do that. He's like the perfect person. Lam and me, we fit. We're two messed-up people.

"Don't you know how wonderful you are?" Ziggy says. "You're different from all the girls I know. You're funny, and nicer than you ever let on, and you're smart in this different sort of way. You're so natural and confident."

"Me? Confident?"

"You're strong. You're a fighter. You come from the school of hard knocks, and I feel like such a weenie next to you sometimes." He stops playing and rests his arm in the curve of the guitar. "I'm older than you are, but sometimes I feel like you're older. You're, you're a powerful person, Elly. You make things happen."

"Me? Powerful? Look, Ziggy, I don't come from the school of hard knocks. My parents are well-educated teachers, and they're missionaries. I come from the planet of disaster, a disaster of my own making. I'm always making the wrong decisions. I'm always acting before I think. For once, I'm trying to think first, and what I think is if we ever got together, I'd ruin you in five seconds flat. Not on purpose. I think you're *really* hot and all, and it would be fun to kind of—you know, but that's all, and that's not good enough for either of us. I'm married now. I've got a baby on the way."

"Hey, would you sit down? I'm getting a crick in my neck," Ziggy says, so I sit, even though my back has been bugging me and it kind of feels better to just lean against the snack machine.

"I think I could handle your kind of trouble. Anyway, I think you underestimate us." He sets his guitar on the floor by the coffee table and inches closer.

I've unwrapped my bar and I take a bite. Half the bar comes off in my mouth. I bite into the half in my mouth and half again falls into my lap. I lift my arms. "See what I mean? Disaster." I scoop up the piece of bar and the crumbs and look at Ziggy. "What do you mean I underestimate us? I don't get that."

"I think we'd make a cool couple. I think you're going to go far, Elly. You just need to be challenged, that's all. And don't you know opposites attract? We'd be good for each other."

"Well, whatever. I'm married, so unless Lam divorces me, wherever I go, I'll be going with him."

"So you really love him, then?"

Ziggy's face kind of just droops, and his gray eyes get dark and smoky-looking—sad.

The baby kicks, and my heart skips a beat. "I don't know. I'm too mad at him to know how I feel right now. Maybe I just always loved the idea of us. I love who we used to be before we got married. It felt like we could conquer the world together and that there was a world to be conquered. We were fun. Life was fun. I guess I feel with you, that maybe the world has already been conquered, and that there would be nothing left for me to do—know what I mean?"

"That I'm boring?" He inches even closer, and because I take up the other half of the couch, I've got nowhere to go, so I kind of lean away from him, which is wicked uncomfortable.

"No. No, Ziggy, just—I don't know. Really, I don't. I don't know what I'm saying. I'm just blurting out whatever pops into my head, and that's never a good thing."

As I finish saying this, and before I even get all of it out of my mouth, Ziggy is on me. He kisses me on the lips, and there it is, that *zing* feeling that makes my toes curl and the baby do somersaults. It scares me. I don't want to like him more than Lam. I love Lam. I'm married to Lam. I want to keep on kissing Ziggy, and yet at the same time I want to push him away. I see out of the corner of my eye Ziggy's hand heading for my boobs and I push him off of me. "No, Ziggy. I can't. I'm married." I say this because it's the only defense I can think of. I don't really know how I feel, but getting groped in the counselors' break hut I know is wrong. I don't do it in the back of cars, and I don't do it in the middle of a kids' camp, either. I don't have time to say any of this, though, because while we're staring at each other, trying to figure out what really just happened, Lam shows up at the door.

"Knock, knock," he says.

I have my back to the door, so Ziggy sees him first, and he looks alarmed.

I turn around, and I see that Lam has a pot of geraniums in his hands—my favorite flowers.

I struggle to my feet. "Lam! What are you doing here? Do your parents know? Aren't you supposed to be teaching swimming?"

Lam enters the hut and hands me the pot of flowers while at the same time he kisses my cheek. "Yes, and yes," he says, in answer to my questions. "I just wanted to give you these and maybe talk to you. I've only got about fifteen minutes, so if you don't mind, Zig, I'd—"

Ziggy jumps up and bangs his head on the overhead lantern. He grabs at his guitar, fumbles, and almost drops it. "Sure, sure," he says, clutching the instrument to his chest. "I'll get out of your way. Later, Elly." Then he scoots out the door so fast you'd think Lam were threatening to beat him up, which he would have done if he knew what had just happened in here.

"What the hell is that all about?"

I shrug. "So, Lam, what was it you wanted to say to me? We only have a few minutes, you said."

He twists around and stares at me a second, then, coming to, he takes the plant from my hand and helps me to sit on the couch. He sits beside me and takes my hand and gazes into my eyes.

"I'm really, really sorry, Elly. I've just—I've been acting like a crud. I know it."

"Yeah, Lam. You totally made a fool of me. Everybody knew, except me. Now everybody's going around feeling sorry for me. It's terrible. And Gren, of all people. And you cheater! You cheated on me! We've only been married a little over a month, and you cheated on me. What does that say about our marriage?" I withdraw my hand from his, and Lam sits back on the couch.

"That it's a sham. Let's face it, El, we never would have married if you hadn't—if we hadn't had to."

"So, so, that's it? So it's over? Are we supposed to get a divorce now because you cheated and our marriage is a sham?"

I feel dizzy all of a sudden, and it feels like the baby is using my belly as a punching bag. "We're about to have a baby, Lam!"

Lam stares down at his thumb a moment, then sticks the edge of it between his teeth and chews at a loose piece of skin. His nails are bitten down to the quick. Something about his hands, those nails, makes me feel sorry for him. I don't know why. I don't want to feel sorry for him. I want to hate him, and fight with him, but I feel tired, and I just want to get past the fight and make up. I want us to either agree to a divorce or agree to stay together.

"Well?" I say, still waiting for some kind of answer. "Do you love Gren?"

Lam sneers. "You know I don't. She was just—available, if you know what I mean. Come on, Elly, give me some credit."

"Why?"

Lam frowns. "Yeah, why. So, I guess you want a divorce. I guess we're going to give the baby to my parents—or your sister."

"I guess," I say, and my heart stops. "That would make everybody happy—your parents, my parents, my sister."

Lam gets this glint in his eye. "Well, screw them. I'm not trying to make them happy. Screw them. We should just stay married and show 'em."

My heart starts up again. "Yeah, screw them. We could show 'em good. We could act like a real married couple, all lovey-dovey and responsible, and really show 'em. What do they know, anyway?"

"Yeah," Lam says. He starts working at the skin on his other thumb. "You know, I think I really love you, Elly. I haven't wanted to be married. I don't feel ready, but . . ."

"I love you, too, Lam. I love you, anyway, you crud. You're such a crud." I stand up, and he stands up, and he takes me in his arms and his skin's all cool from being in the lake. It feels so good. He feels so good. My first love. My only love. My husband. "I love you, Lam," I say.

"I love you, too, Elly."

CHAPTER SEVENTEEN

LAM AND I plan to start all over again. I decide to push what happened with Ziggy in the break hut to the back of my mind and really concentrate on being a loving wife.

Lam and I agree to make an effort to be together whenever we can, so now during my break, I head down to the lake, teetering on the rocks and roots along the way, and watch Lam teach the campers swimming. He has the older kids, the ones who already know how to swim, and to tell the truth, he's not the best teacher, but they all love him 'cause he's cool. He struts around like some big important dude, swinging his whistle on a lanyard so it wraps and unwraps around his index finger. He's tall, and tan, and blond, and he's still kind of got a young boy's face instead of a man's, and the girls all seem to like that. Okay, and so do I. All the older girls flirt with him, and they don't care that I'm sitting right there watching them, but then again, they flirt with all the male counselors. Lam takes it all in stride like he knows he's good-looking and like the whole point of being down at the lake is to just strut back and forth for all the girls. He's always been like this, but now it kind of bothers me, after what happened with Gren.

On Tuesdays Lam has a bunch of boys to teach during my break time, and he's so totally different with them. He's gruff and makes them do laps endlessly, and he slouches in a deck chair the whole time, twirling his lanyard around his finger. I watch Jen and Gren teach their groups while I'm down there, and I have to admit Jen's a pretty good teacher. She's good because she's very serious, and I think she cares about the kids. It makes all the difference. It makes me wonder, do I care about my kids, the ones I work with, and the ones in my cabin? Or am I just here because I have to be? If I was told I didn't have to be here anymore, would I leave, even though the kids need someone to be in the cabin with them? The answer is, I don't know. I want to care. Maybe I do care, but I think that maybe I care even more about them liking me, and that gets in the way of me really seeing them. I make a note to myself to try to really see them, to pay attention more to who they are.

The ILs have changed everybody's schedule around for the second four weeks of camp, even though most of the kids here sign on for eight weeks, instead of two, or four, like at most camps. I figure their parents want to make sure they can see a difference in their kids' weight by the time they get them back. Already, most kids have lost at least eight pounds, with Josh Billingsgate losing the most at sixteen point four pounds, but he was pretty hefty to begin with, and in the camp rule book it says the more weight you have to lose, the faster it will come off.

Anyway, the ILs made sure Lam and I got the same day off this time so that we can spend quality time together. It's like the MIL finally gets it; if she really wants the baby, then she has to be nice to me, not jump all over me because she's mad I married her precious son, and if we decide to keep the baby, then it's better for the baby if Lam and I are actually happy together, so now she's so sweet to me it makes me want to barf. It feels so fake. Still, I guess it's better than getting blamed for everything that goes wrong at this camp.

So today, Lam, Ziggy, and I all have our day off at the same time, and I'm looking forward to the three of us having a good time. And yeah, okay, I know how much of a threat Ziggy could be to our marriage, but I'm not going to let anything happen. We can all just be friends. It can work, can't it?

The MIL surprised me this morning by handing me an envelope with fifty dollars in it. She said, "Go buy yourself a new dress today; my treat." That was pretty nice, but I don't want to buy a dress. I'm three and a half weeks away from my due date, and I feel like I ought to fix up our cabin better and get all the junk off the floor and put it in some drawers or something. I want to buy a chest with the money. I don't wear dresses normally; it's just that they're the only things comfortable right now. Everything else is too binding, including my underpants and the straps of my sandals. I can't wait to be rid of this baby inside me. It's really dragging me down. I want to sleep all the time now, but when I do lie down, I can't ever get comfortable.

I've been looking forward to my day off just so I could take it easy, maybe go into town for a bit, then get a bite to eat and take a long nap.

"So I was thinking," I say to Lam and Ziggy as we're heading down to the parking lot by the lake, "I want to go to this secondhand furniture store they've got in Rumford and see if I can pick up some kind of chest for my clothes. Then we can all go get pizza or something."

"Or you and me could go to the Adventure Center in Bethel, and then get some pizza," Lam says, taking my hand and helping me over the rocks, which I can barely see 'cause my stomach's in the way.

"No pizza," Ziggy says. "Remember, Elly, how dizzy you got when they served pizza here last week? You went chalk white like you were going to faint."

"Oh, yeah, and I felt all clammy. Yeah, that was bad, but maybe it was because it was fake cheese. It was that low-fat soy cheese crap."

Lam looks mad about something.

"What's wrong with you?" I ask.

Lam shrugs. "Nothing. I just thought we should have some time alone. No offense, Zig, but three's a crowd."

"But I've spent my days off at the library all alone every

week. I'm ready for some fun. Come on. Let's have some fun—the three of us," I say.

"I wouldn't mind looking at that secondhand furniture place. I need a new chair for my desk in my apartment at school," Ziggy says.

"Since when is looking at other people's garbage considered fun?" Lam says. His voice sounds snarly.

We're at the cars now, and Lam opens the door to the passenger side of his Jeep for me. Ziggy stands aside and looks like he doesn't know if he's supposed to get in, too, or not.

"Come on, Ziggy," I say, then to Lam I add, "We can do the Adventure Center, but Ziggy's coming."

"Fine," Lam says, "but when our whole marriage falls apart because we have no time together, don't blame me."

Ziggy steps back from the car. "Okay, look guys. I don't want to cause any friction. You two go on and have fun. I'll be fine on my own. Just tell me where that furniture store is. I think I'll have a look around." I give Ziggy directions while Lam taps his fingers on the soft top of his Jeep. And I always thought Lam was a patient person.

The whole way into Bethel, Lam and I argue over Ziggy. Lam says we're too close and that it's worse than him and Gren because there was nothing really between them, but Ziggy and I clearly have a relationship going on.

"Yeah, nothing but sex with you and Gren," I say. "How much more intimate can you get?"

"Lots," Lam says, and I realize, thinking of Ziggy and some of our conversations and how I'd much rather be shopping at a used furniture store with him than going to the center with Lam, that maybe he's right, so I shut up about it and try to change the subject. Lam won't have it.

"What gives him the right to know that pizza makes you sick? Why didn't I know that? Why didn't you tell me that?"

We're riding down a long, steep, twisty hill, and Lam keeps looking over at me, and he's staring too long instead of keeping his eyes on the road. It makes me edgy. "Hey!" I shout. "First of all, I didn't even remember about the pizza, because I didn't consider the crap we ate real pizza. Then, second of all, you weren't there because you were busy screwing Gren, so don't give me this hurt-little-boy act like I'm whispering secrets to Ziggy. Third, aren't we supposed to be having fun? Is this the fun part? Because I'm not smiling."

Lam calms down after that and pretty much keeps his eyes on the road, at least for a little while.

We do have fun together, and it almost feels like old times except I'm not high—just Lam is, and what I want to know is, did he always act so stupid when he was high and I just didn't notice, or is he just now acting stupid for some reason? He's driving like a maniac on purpose, speeding up and over Paradise Road like he thinks we're on a roller coaster. My baby doesn't like this one bit, but does Lam listen? No!

We spend a couple of hours at the arcade in the Adventure

Center, and Lam gets into the zone, kind of like he's hypnotized, then we rent a canoe, which is crazy, I know, because we can paddle one anytime for free back at the camp, but it's not private and romantic like it is paddling alone on the Androscoggin River. It's such a gas, too, because I need Lam and two men to help me in and out of the canoe, and my end sinks down almost as far as Lam's does. Speaking of gas, man, do I have it. I read about getting gas in the "having a baby" books, but I didn't really get how bad the gas could be when you're pregnant. Still, Lam thinks it's a riot, and so we have a good time. We stay up where the river is lazy and just paddle along and talk, and Lam tells me he's thinking about opening a cigar store some day.

"A cigar store? Lam, you don't even smoke cigars."

"Yeah, but I'm planning on starting up. Lots of cool guys smoke cigars."

"But they stink."

"So does pot, and that never bothered you," Lam says.

We're in a really still spot on the river and we're not even paddling, just letting the canoe drift along. The sun is high and there's a breeze, and it's a perfect day.

"Still, it's a dumb idea," I say.

Lam flicks his paddle so water splashes on me. "No, it's not."

I laugh and flick my paddle back at him and he gets wet. "Is, too."

Then he strikes back, and then I do, and then it's war, and before long, Lam is standing in the canoe so he can really dump the water on me, and I'm screaming and laughing at the same time because he's rocking the boat. I know he's going to fall overboard. I shift just slightly to get in a better position to soak him back, and the canoe flips, and we both fall in.

"Pregnant lady overboard!" Lam hollers, but there isn't a soul on the river to hear him.

We have a time flipping the canoe back over, even though it's one of the first lessons he teaches the campers, mainly because I'm not helping any. The water feels so good and cool on my body. I'm just floating on my back. It's the most comfortable I've felt all summer.

"Hey, why don't you just leave me here until after the baby comes? This feels really good. Now I know why some women have babies in the water."

"Forget about it. You're going to the hospital."

That's when I decide that I really ought to call that doctor I saw three or so months ago and let him know that I'm still pregnant and due in a few weeks. Hopefully he'll still deliver the baby even if I haven't been seeing him. Maybe I can lie and say I've been out of town. I don't know. I've been lying to everyone about seeing the doctor, and I feel guilty about it because everyone, including the MIL, has believed me.

Since we're soaked, after we return the canoe, we order stuff from McDonald's and eat it in the car, then when Lam goes into the gas station to buy a pack of Camels, I hook up my cell phone charger to his cigarette lighter, dig through my purse for the number of the doctor, and speak to someone called a nurse practitioner. I tell her that I'm still pregnant and stuff. I lie and say I've been in Kenya and that's why I haven't been to see the doctor, but I'm back now. She suggests I come in so they can make sure everything's okay, and I say how I only have this one day off this week, so wouldn't you know she tells me I should come right now.

Lam comes out with his Camels, and I figure he's going to be mad that we've got to go to the doctor's, but he isn't. He says he's proud of me for thinking of it. We head to the doctor's office, and I'm shaking, half because I'm scared and half because I'm still wet and they have the air conditioner on high. People are staring and making snarky faces at me and Lam because we're wet, and Lam and I are having fun with that. He holds my hand, and like old times, it's us against the world, and screw them.

The doctor doesn't do much except listen to the baby's heartbeat, check my pelvis and uterus, weigh me, take my blood pressure, and ask me a bunch of questions. He gets me good with, "When did you get back from Kenya?" because I tell him I only just got back, and he says with alarm in his voice, "You mean you flew eight months pregnant all the way from Kenya?"

"Oh, no," I say. "When I mean I just got back, I mean like a couple of months ago, only I haven't had time to connect with you."

I know my face is beet red, and suddenly I'm not freezing

anymore—I'm drenched in sweat, but he doesn't go on about it. He probably knows I'm lying my ass off.

Finally he says, "Well, everything looks to be a go, young lady. The baby is in the right position—everything's good. Of course you know your pelvis is very narrow. We'll have to do a C-section. You'll need to prepare yourself for that, but otherwise, it's all going to go just fine, so you can wipe that worried look off your face."

Worried? More like panicked. C-section? A C-section!

"They can't cut me open—no way," I whisper to Lam on the way out of the doctor's office.

"They'll give you some awesome drugs, and you'll be totally out," Lam says. "Don't worry. You won't know anything until they put the baby in your arms."

"Yeah, I'd better not."

On the way out we actually schedule the delivery date for the last week of camp, on Tuesday, my day off. Can you believe it? How crazy is that? Scheduling it like it's a hair appointment. Then the nurse talks to us about insurance and stuff. My parents had set that up because they still claim me as a dependent, even though I just got married, so everything is ready, and I guess I'm glad I called and showed up this time for the exam.

Lam and I are feeling all lovey-dovey after the doctor's visit, and after we get back to camp, we talk in the car about how this baby inside is made from the two of us. "How amazing is that?" I say.

"Scary amazing," he says, nodding to himself.

"Yeah, 'cause no offense, but I wouldn't want either of us for a kid," I say.

"Exactly." He keeps nodding. "But neither one of us looks like chopped liver, either. It might turn out to be pretty good-looking."

"I hope it has your eyes," I say.

"I hope it has your mouth. You have the perfect mouth." He leans over and kisses me.

So we're kissing and whatnot in the parking lot by the lake. Lam parked in the shade and it's dark and hidden from any nosy campers there, but after a few minutes I see Ziggy's car pull up right next to ours.

I push Lam off of me. "Ziggy's here," I say.

"So what?" Lam says. "Let him watch." Lam grabs me, and I push him away again.

"Lam, come on, stop. That's not nice."

Lam scoots away and crosses his arms and scowls. "Your crush on Ziggy's what's not nice. He's a wuss."

I slap Lam's arm and laugh, even though I don't mean to. "Shut up!"

Ziggy is at my window, and he motions for me to roll it down. I glance at Lam, then open my window. "Hey," I say. "Did you have a good day off?"

"Yeah, great. I found a chest of drawers for you. I think you'll like it."

"What? Ziggy, you shouldn't have." I blush and glance at

Lam again, and he's got this punk-like pout on his face. I don't know what to do, but then Ziggy opens my door and holds his hands out for me, so what can I do but take 'em and get out of the car?

Lam gets out on his side and slams the door and kicks it. He's pissed, and I think Ziggy wants him to be. I'm hoping the chest is really ugly, or too beat up, so Lam won't be so mad, but no, the chest is wicked cool.

Ziggy has the trunk of his car open and tied down with a piece of rope. The chest is sticking out about a third of the way, and as soon as I see it, I know I love it. It's old and it's painted a teal blue. I love teal.

Ziggy unties the rope and lifts the lid of his trunk, and I see a small bouquet of flowers painted in the center of each drawer, and each drawer has these old red glass knobs for drawer pulls. "Awesome!" I say, before I can catch myself. But really, it's too awesome. I'm so excited. It has to be the prettiest chest in the world.

"Wow! Ziggy, where did you find this? Thank you. It's so pretty. Lam, isn't it so beautiful?" I take Lam's arm in mine, hoping he'll see that even if it is pretty, I'm still on his side, but Lam just lets his arm hang limp. "Yeah, it's real girly," he says, and I know he's implying that Ziggy is real girly, and so does Ziggy.

"Anytime, anywhere," Ziggy says. He punches his fist into his other hand and glares at Lam.

Lam loves a good fight, and I'm pretty sure he'd crush

Ziggy. They're both about the same height, but Lam is used to fighting, and I doubt Ziggy is. I've seen Lam's hands do some major damage. I find myself wishing Leo were there, just in case they really start to fight. I don't know why. Maybe he'd throw himself into the middle of the fight and get his head knocked off, but somehow I think everything would calm down if Leo were here.

"Come on, guys," I say. "Don't spoil a good day. It's been such a great day, and now I'm really tired. I need a nap."

Ziggy keeps his eyes on Lam, but he says to me, "I'll take the chest up to your cabin."

"No, I'll take it up," Lam says.

"Like hell. I bought it, I'll take it up."

"Like hell. She's my wife. I'll take it up."

I always thought having two guys fighting over me would be so cool, but it's not. I ignore the both of them because I'm just too tired not to. I leave them arguing over the chest, imagining it forever remaining in the trunk of Ziggy's car because they can't agree on who should bring it up.

CHAPTER EIGHTEEN

I LEAVE LAM and Ziggy to duke it out and trudge up the hill, feeling tired and achy because I haven't been sleeping all that well, and, wouldn't you know it, coming down the hill to greet me is the MIL.

"Oh, great, what fresh hell is in store for me now?" I say under my breath, even though I'm smiling and trying to open my eyes wide and look perky so she doesn't know how tired I am. Even sweet the way she is now is annoying, and I'm way too tired to deal with her. The MIL is smiling and greeting the campers she passes on her way down to me, and her smile and greeting don't look fake at all until she reaches me.

"Eleanor, I'm so glad I caught you," she says, and I can practically see the sticky-sweet syrup oozing from her mouth. "How did the shopping go? I don't see any clothes bag in your hand."

I hate how fake it sounds. I'd rather have her old angry hag self back, if you want to know the truth. At least it's honest.

"Lam didn't want to go shopping today," I tell her. "He wanted to go to the Adventure Center, and then I had a doctor's appointment, so we didn't have time. I'm sorry."

The MIL crosses her arms and frowns. "So what did you do with the money? Spend it on a big fancy lunch, drugs, beer, what?"

Ah, there's the bitch-lady I know and love. I reach into my purse and scrounge around for the fifty dollars she had given me earlier. I pull it out, but before giving it to her I say, "I don't do drugs. I'm pregnant, and drugs are bad for the baby. But if I did do drugs, I still wouldn't steal someone else's money to pay for them." I hand her the bill, expecting her to say something like, "And yet you do steal cars and break into houses," but she is back to being her fake syrupy self.

"Well, now, you go ahead and keep it. I gave it to you." She hands it back to me, and I mumble a thank you and stash it in my purse. The money still feels like it comes with strings attached, so I don't really feel all that grateful.

"I didn't come here to get the money back or to see what you bought, anyway. I just thought you'd be pleased to know that we've decided to go ahead with your *wonderful* idea of putting on a talent show, only it won't just be the campers, but the whole camp, counselors and campers, and we'll have it on the last night of camp."

I look at the MIL, and she looks so pleased with herself for being able to bring me this good news. Originally, I had come up with the idea of a talent show because some of the made-up dances the girls in my class are doing are really great, and I thought it would be neat to showcase them and some of the other things that are going on here at the camp. The ILs are always talking about "finding your bliss" in their self-esteem pep talks they give each morning, and every day when I'm walking around the camp, I can hear kids singing or playing instruments, and they sound so wonderful. I know Ziggy puts on a little music show every couple of weeks, but what about all the cool stuff that Leo and the kids have made in the crafts hut? What about my dancers? I'd like to see them get some recognition, too, and if they all had a performance to work toward, I figured it might help bring a little more order and direction to my classes.

For the most part the class has been going okay, because the girls like getting into groups and making up different dances and performing them for each other. The only problem I've been having is with Banner. She's such a crybaby. Everything seems to upset her: being late for class ("Oh, I'm late—are you going to kick me out? Do you hate meee?") or not getting chosen to help me with the music ("Are you mad at me? How come you didn't pick meee?") or getting stuck with bathroom-sink-cleaning duty in the cabin ("Meee? Again? Did I do something wrong?") all said with that squeaky whine of hers. She acts like she's getting picked on, when everybody has to take a turn cleaning the sinks once a week. So, of course the girls don't like having her in their groups. I've had to step in and force a group to take her, and then she feels like crap, and so do the girls in the group. No wonder she gets picked on all the time. She all but walks around with a "Kick me" sign on her back, the way she mopes and moans and sulks.

Still, when I stand back and watch Banner dancing in my class, I realize there's something cool and powerful and vulnerable, all at the same time, in her movements. As heavy as she is, she's so light on her feet. Sometimes she looks like she's just floating. So lately I have been thinking if the whole camp could just see her perform, it would help people see Banner in a different way, and if they did, maybe she'd stop acting like such a victim all the time.

I smile now at the MIL as we stand together on the hill, and my smile is sincere. "That's fantastic," I say. "Thank you! The kids are going to be so excited."

She nods, looking very pleased with herself. "Now, anyone who wants to be in the show should be allowed to be in it. We don't want anyone to feel excluded, and hopefully you'll be able to find something to do for those campers who don't wish to be in the show but want to get involved in some way. Don't take this all on yourself. It's too close to your due date. Get a group to help you."

"Sure. Sure. I'll do my best," I say, but already in the back of my mind I'm wondering who I'm going to get to help, because I'm going to need a lot of it. I don't tell the MIL just yet about the C-section, but it's only a week away.

"Great, Eleanor. Mr. Lothrop and I are really pleased with you taking the initiative on this. I'm sure it will be a big success." She smiles, but it's more like a grimace, as if it pains her to have to compliment me.

"Thanks." I want to lie down. I want to sleep. "Well, I better get planning," I say, making a move to leave.

"Good, good," she says, and she continues down the hill, while I continue up it.

* * *

So now I'm thinking that I need help. I need a co-producer, and I think of Ziggy, because he's a natural when it comes to shows and performing. That's what he does at school. But since Lam is so jealous of him, and because the next time I see him after the standoff with Lam down at the cars I see he's got a big bruise on his cheekbone and Lam's got a bloody, maybe broken, nose, and the chest of drawers is still lying in the trunk of Ziggy's car, I've decided against going with Ziggy on this.

I think about it all through dinner and again while I'm telling the girls in my cabin a bedtime story about the time a hyena chased me halfway across Kenya. Then I hear these girls talking outside the cabin, and I'm sure it's the nasty ones who came to my class a few days ago, and I wonder if I dare ask them to help me with the show. These girls are fifteen, and they think they're hot shit, and I can tell they look down on me for being pregnant.

I'm only a little older than they are, and they know it. Nobody bought that I was twenty or even that I got pregnant *after* Lam and I got married. I always knew lying was a bad idea, and I can't even tell everyone it was the MIL's idea, because then parents would probably be pulling their kids out of this camp left and right. Just having me here at all is a risk for the ILs, I suppose, because I know if I had a kid I was sending to this camp, I wouldn't want them influenced by someone like me. That's why I'm okay with saying stuff like don't smoke, and don't drink, and don't have sex, the way the MIL told me to, just so I won't be the bad influence I know that I am.

These girls came into my class as a group—four of them, all kind of leaning into one another and whispering and laughing and glancing over at me. I called the class to order, and they just kept talking. I told everybody to form a circle, the way I usually start the class, and these girls formed a separate circle made up of just them. I told them to come join our circle, and they giggled and stayed where they were and whispered stuff to each other. They ignored everything I said. The class was impossible. My everyday girls were dancing around, and these other girls purposely bumped into them, then pretended it was an accident. They sang off-key to the songs I played, and every time I said something to the class, they repeated it as if they were an echo, only they used this whiny voice. Ha, ha, very funny.

Yeah, okay, if I weren't me teaching this class, I'd be them, and be just as obnoxious, but since I am teaching the class, they really pissed me off. I wanted to cuss them out up one side and down the other and maybe tear their hair out of their heads, but I couldn't do that without more trouble from the ILs. Man, were these girls pushing my buttons!

Finally I said, "You girls either act right or get out of this class."

They said, "'You girls either act right or get out of this class,'" in a chorus, and all whiny.

"I'd watch out if I were you. You think we counselors don't talk? You think your mommy and daddy don't tell us stuff, and you don't think we talk about you behind your backs?"

Well, that shut them up. I was totally making this up, but since it was working, I kept going.

"Yeah, that's right, I know a couple of you have talked to a counselor or two around here and told them things you don't want people to know, and guess what? We know all about your issues"—I figured we all have issues, so I took a stab that this might scare them—"and I have half a mind to tell the class right now exactly what I know, and believe me, you'll be sorry. So, unless you want me to blab all over the camp what I know about you"—I looked especially at this one girl who reminds me of what Ashley Wilson could turn out to be like when she gets older—"then I think maybe you ought to leave."

The girls stood there with their bitch-girl looks, squinting at me for a second or two, and then, just like that, they left, single file this time, and silent.

The rest of the class clapped, and I turned around and got

busy selecting the next piece of music so they couldn't see how scared I was. What kind of trouble would these girls get me into with the ILs? I wondered. But they didn't get me in trouble. Nothing else happened, so while I'm telling my campers about Kenya and the mad hyena and I hear their voices outside the cabin, I ask myself, why don't I give those girls something to do besides cause trouble? Maybe if I had had more to do, like a job, I wouldn't have gotten into so much trouble with Lam. I decide to ask them in the morning.

* * *

I go early to the girls' cabin. I bang on their door, and Gren, their counselor, calls out, "Come on in."

Gren, I find out, isn't half as shy as she acts, but whenever she sees me, she still blushes and gets all nervous, and I don't blame her. I heard she really got a reaming from the ILs, and anyway, I'm fierce when I'm angry, and I'm plenty angry at her. I'd like to twist her arms and legs off and toss her in the Androscoggin for messing with Lam. Call me whatever you want, but I won't cheat if someone is already taken. That's dirty pool, if you ask me.

I step inside the cabin and do the snark face at Gren, and she has the good sense to blush and look at her feet.

"I've come to talk to some of your campers." I look into the main part of the cabin and see the girls making their beds at the back. "There they are back there." I point them out. "What are their names?" I whisper this, because I don't want the girls to know that I don't know their names, or they'll figure out that no way could I have any gossip on them.

Gren sees where I'm pointing, and she looks happy to give me the information, as if that somehow will make us even. Yeah, right, uh-huh.

She points to the one who's the leader. "That's Elizabeth," she says, also whispering, "and the one next to her is Abby, and then the short one is Marissa, and the other one is Cath."

"Great, thanks," I say. I shuffle back toward the girls, and as I move through the cabin, the chatter and cleaning stops and the girls all watch me. Some say hi when I pass, because I've talked to them during crafts, but I don't know most of these girls. They keep more to themselves than the other campers.

"Hey, I need to talk to you guys," I say when I catch up to the unholy four.

The girls share two sets of bunks right next to each other. They all look up when they hear my voice, and they look kind of nervous. I feel suddenly like I'm the MIL, and it's not a good feeling. I try to smile, but it feels fake, so I stop and just say what I need to say.

"I'm putting on a talent show and I thought you four might like to help me."

"Help? Why? Why should we want to help you?" Elizabeth says. She's taller and thinner than the other three, except she has a wide butt, and she's got really long, thin hair that's kind of limp looking. She wears it close to her face, I think to make her face look thinner, and it does, I guess, but if you ask me she'd look better with her hair really short and spiky.

"Well, because I thought you'd like being in charge of the other campers, and I thought you might like to be more like a counselor instead of just a run-of-the-mill camper."

"Would we get paid?" Cath, the girl with the biggest boobs, says. Speaking of boobs, mine are huge now, and they hurt. Being pregnant sucks, but at least once I have the baby, my breasts should get back to normal. It makes me feel kind of sorry for this Cath girl. She'll have to starve herself for the next twenty years to get her boobs down to a size that doesn't poke you in the eyes when you look at her. She slouches, and I bet I know why.

"No. No payment," I say. "Just the fun of being in charge of putting on a show."

"What would we have to do?" Marissa asks, and they all look interested.

I tell them about my idea of everybody sharing their talent, singing or dancing or playing some instrument or acting out a short skit. "I also thought we could have an art show at the same time, displaying all the things people have knitted, or built, or drawn, or painted. We'd have those all around the perimeter of the main cabin." I tell them I need them to help me organize it and decide who goes when so that all the music and singing isn't clumped together at the beginning and all the dance at the end. "We want it to be a mix, or it'll be boring. You'll also have to tell people if their stuff is a snore. Like, we don't want slow, fall-asleep music. It needs to be lively and entertaining. Any-body can be in it, but they can't just do anything."

"If everybody can be in it, won't the show be kind of long? And what if they stink?" Elizabeth asks.

"Yeah, I was thinking of that, and I thought we may have to do the show in two nights, and if we think somebody stinks, we're going to have to help them to make their performance better somehow so it doesn't stink. Maybe just shorten it so it's a minute long or something, I don't know. We just don't want anybody's feelings getting hurt."

"But what if we want to be in it? Can we help organize and be in it at the same time?" Abby asks.

"Yeah, sure you can be in it."

So, surprise, surprise, I get the four mean girls involved in the talent show, and we become friends, and they become more a part of the whole camp, and then they're not such bitches, and I'm feeling very proud of myself.

"Okay, look," I say to Lam finally. "I'm going to put all my stuff in the chest, because this place is a dump, and it was nice of Ziggy to think of us, so I'm going to use it. You're just going to have to deal."

"He wasn't thinking of us. He's not so great. He was just trying to score points with you."

"Well, it worked," I say without thinking, which of course was the wrong thing to say, because now it's war.

After dinner, while I was in the main cabin with a bunch of kids auditioning for the talent show, Lam set out in his parents' pickup to go find me a bigger and better chest. It takes both him and Leo to haul it up from the parking lot, and he sets it down outside the cabin so all the campers can see what a big, fine chest it is. When I see it, all I can say is, "It's big all right."

"You got that right," Lam says. I look at Leo, who says nothing, and I can't tell by his expression what he thinks, but I'll tell you what, if there were an ugliest-chest-of-drawers contest, this would win it, hands down. It's made out of this fake wood stuff that's kind of charcoal gray, or dirty gray, and it's done like panels, the kind you put on a basement wall if you want to look cheap, and it has these fake, chunky brass handles that are as long as my foot, two on each drawer, and on the top someone has put on some black and white tacky paper, the kind you might line the chest of drawers with but never put on top. I open the top drawer and it makes this loud scraping sound. The inside smells like sour cream and onion potato chips.

Ziggy comes by to see what all the campers are looking at, and when he sees it he laughs. "Did you make that in Leo's crafts class, Lam? Must have used your feet."

"Ha, ha, very funny. This is a *man's* chest. Not some girly thing made out of cardboard," Lam says.

"Oh," Ziggy says, "so you got it for *you*. Oh, now I get it. Good choice." He raises his thumb and walks off, and so do I, not with Ziggy, but into the cabin.

The next day after dinner, Ziggy comes by the main cabin, where we're auditioning people, and he's brought his guitar. I see on the sign-up sheet we had posted in the dining hall that he's auditioning. The unholy four tell him that he's number six on the list, and he smiles and comes to sit by me. "How's it going?" he whispers.

"Fine, but I wish you and Lam would stop fighting. You know how it is, Ziggy."

"But it doesn't have to be. You're not happy with him. He's a loser. Come on, that chest of drawers? Please."

That chest is butt-ugly, but it makes me feel sorry for Lam that he would think I would like it, and that he's so proud of it. "Look at how much junk you can put in this one drawer," he said to me this morning. He had jammed all his clothes inside, and there was still plenty of room, so he went over to the pretty chest that Ziggy had gotten me and started pulling all my clothes out.

"What are you doing?" I said, still in bed and not wanting to get up yet.

"I'm putting your stuff with mine, where it belongs. You can put the baby's things in that little chest."

"If we keep the baby."

"Right. Well, my parents can have the chest—even better. Or we can throw it on the campfire the last day of camp."

I let Lam put my clothes in the drawers, and so now I smell like sour cream and onion potato chips. I'm making myself nauseous with the smell.

"Please don't tell me my husband's a loser," I say to Ziggy.

He puts his hand on mine. "Okay. I'm sorry. You're right. I just want to be your friend. Can we still be friends?"

"Yeah, friends, of course," I say, trying to ignore the lusty, zinging feel I get every time he touches me.

When it's Ziggy's turn to audition, he goes and stands in front of the stage. He tells us he's written a new song that he'd like to sing. He gets up on the stage and sits on the edge of it instead of on a chair, and he begins. His song is about love, and yeah, I know most songs are love songs, but he's looking at me, so I kind of get the feeling he wrote the song for me. I'm not the only one who thinks this, either. The unholy four are sitting around me, and I can hear them saying, "Aw," and "I wish somebody'd write me a song," and "Lucky," and "That's pretty."

I know I'm blushing, and I feel stupid for blushing, because maybe the song isn't for me at all and just something he wrote. Anyway, the tune is really pretty.

Ziggy's still singing when from the back of the room I hear Lam's voice. "What a bunch of sap!"

I turn around and see Lam coming toward me with something in his hands. "Lam, not now," I say.

He comes over to where I'm sitting and stops. "What a loser!" he says. "Why doesn't he find his own girl?"

The girls around me giggle and whisper to each other. I wonder how I manage to get myself into these situations.

I get onto my feet and frown at Lam. "Come on, Lam, leave it."

"I'm not the one writing love songs to someone already married."

"Yeah, well, neither one of you is scoring points with me, lately. I wish you two would stop already."

"I vote for Ziggy," Elizabeth says.

"I vote for Lam," Abby says.

They're whispering, but I can hear them.

Lam hands me something that looks like a book in wrapping paper. "Anyway, for you," he says, and his voice is loud so Ziggy and everyone else in the room can hear. "For us."

"Lam, what is this?" I open the gift because I can't help it, I'm curious.

It's a book called *The New Mom's Survival Guide: How to Reclaim Your Body, Your Health, Your Sanity, and Your Sex Life After Having a Baby*. It's by Jennifer Wider, M.D.

With sex in the title, I know why Lam picked this book out, but it was still sweet and much nicer than the chest of drawers he gave me.

I smile. "Thanks, Lam." I kiss him on the cheek, and I see Ziggy hop off the stage and leave the cabin by the side door. My heart sinks. I feel badly. I don't want Ziggy hurt, and I don't want Lam hurt. I don't know what to do. I never even said how much I liked the song.

* * *

Before the first crafts class the next morning, I talk to Leo about what's happening.

"Leo, I don't know what to do. You're always so sensible. What would you do? What would you do if you had two girls fighting over you?"

Leo's unloading these honking big chunks of clay from a tall plastic sack. Some of the campers are going to make hand-built mugs and bowls out of it. Leo demonstrated in the classes yesterday how you roll pieces of clay between your hands until you have these long, round strips that you then coil around in the shape of a mug or a bowl. You place one coiled strip on top of another, and then you wet your fingertips and use them to smooth the clay out so that instead of strips you have one smooth surface. It sounds easy, but I know somehow I'll make a mess of it. I'm still nowhere near finished with my dulcimer!

"Honestly, Eleanor, if I had two girls fighting over me, I'd sit back and watch the show."

"No, you wouldn't. I know it. I'm hurting their feelings. Last night Ziggy sang a song he wrote for the show, and I never got a chance to say how much I liked it and all, because Lam showed up with a present for me. So Ziggy got hurt and left. And you saw Lam the other night when you two brought up that ugly chest and Ziggy made fun of it. I know it hurt Lam's feelings."

Leo sets a big chunk of clay into my hands. "Feel that. Doesn't that feel good?"

I raise it up and down in my hands. "Hefty." I smooth the surface out with my fingers. "Yeah, it's cool," I say.

"If you're asking me," Leo says, "then I think you should just lay it on the line. Either you're married and you want to stay married, or you're not and you're interested in Ziggy. Tell them and put them out of their misery."

I dump the clay on the table. "Okay, first of all, I already told Ziggy just what you said. I told him I was married and I love Lam and that's that."

Leo hands me another hunk of clay. "Well, I think you're sending mixed messages."

"You do?"

"Yeah, I do."

I think he's right, because I'm kind of confused about how I feel. Being sober all the time makes me not like Lam so much. I love him still, but I don't like him all the time. I don't think he's the greatest thing to come into my life anymore. He can be a jerk and all that, but I know him, and I'm comfortable with him, and we're a lot alike, because I can be such a jerk, too, and so I forgive him when he's one.

I like Ziggy, too, though, and maybe I'm even starting to fall in love with him. I don't know. He's new, and he's talented, and he's different, and he's in college, and all of that is so interesting to me. We can talk really well together, too. I feel Ziggy listens to me in a way that Lam doesn't. Lam is all about himself. I think Ziggy cares about more than just himself, but like I've said, maybe he's just too together for me—maybe.

I try to explain this to Leo, and he surprises me. "You know, Elly, you act like you have to choose between these two guys," he says. "There's a whole world of guys to choose from. Maybe you really don't want either of them. Maybe you haven't yet met that one special person. Maybe that's why you're having so much trouble. You have a baby on the way. That's a big deal. Maybe you all should be thinking more about that, and not so much about who loves who more."

"Yeah, wow, Leo, you sure put me in my place," I say.

Leo takes a piece of wire and slices down the center of one of the chunks of clay like it's a hunk of cheese. "Ay-uh, I did, but you asked," he says.

Just before dinner Ashley Wilson comes to the crafts hut and tells me I need to get down to the lake.

"What for?" I ask.

"Ziggy and Lam are racing."

"Swimming? Lam will win, hands down. I don't need to see that."

"No. Canoe. Around the whole lake."

"Are you kidding me? It will take them at least three hours to do that." The lake isn't all that wide at our end, because we're located on the inlet. It's less than a quarter of a mile across to where the boys' camp is, but it gets wider just beyond the inlet, and the distance around the lake is ten miles at least.

"Well, that's what they're doing," Ashley Wilson says. "Are you coming?"

I look back at Leo.

"Go ahead," he says. He waves me off.

I make my way down to the lake, and there's a small crowd of counselors and campers gathered and the boys are hauling their canoes out from the boathouse. I thought they'd be on the water by now. I say this out loud, and the kid standing next to me says, "They've been fighting over the canoes."

Lam and Ziggy both slip their canoes into the water, and I see their angry faces and know I'm the real cause. I mean, this is just too stupid.

Jen is standing on the dock with the starter gun the camp uses for the kids' races. Once they both get settled, Jen raises the gun in the air. "On your mark—get set—"

Before she can say go, both boys are paddling. They're in the inlet, and they're paddling so hard they knock paddles.

"Get out of the way! Can't you steer?" Lam shouts.

"We're not driving cars," Ziggy says. "You guide a canoe, you don't steer."

"Thanks for the language lesson, buddy. Here's a little lesson for you." Lam takes his paddle and jabs Ziggy with it. It gets him in the ribs.

"Oh, so that's how you wanna play, is it?" Ziggy jabs back, and then Lam stands up and kids are cheering, and then Ziggy stands up and Lam tries to get a good swipe at Ziggy with his paddle but misses and falls in the lake, and Ziggy, seeing his chance, jumps in on top of him.

Now everybody is clapping and cheering, but it's not funny because they're really going at it, and it looks like they're trying to drown each other. First Ziggy is on top of Lam, then Lam's on top of Ziggy. Jen and Gren and Alfie and Rod—all the lifeguards—jump in to break it up. By the time the two of them are dragged to shore coughing and spitting, Ziggy's got a bloody nose and Lam's got a cut above his eye. I've seen enough, so I leave.

I know Leo's right and I need to say something and make it clear to Ziggy that I'm married and that's that, end of story, but something keeps me from saying it. I said it once, and to tell the truth I was sorry I did, because maybe I'm interested in Ziggy in that way—you know, in a romantic, long-term kind of way. Maybe I've grown out of my relationship with Lam. This is what I'm thinking as I head up the hill. I know Leo said that I'm acting like these are the only two guys in the world and that maybe I haven't met the right guy, and I need to be focusing on the baby, but I can't keep my mind from wondering this stuff. Like, how do I know if Ziggy's not the right guy unless I give

HALEY, THE COUNSELOR who had to get her appendix out, has returned to camp, and so I'm back in my own cabin with Lam. The cabin smells funny—not good funny. It smells like someone who hasn't bathed, but not quite like B.O., you know, oily skin and dirty hair, and soggy-sweaty feet. Since Lam has been living by himself the past three weeks and hasn't had a cabin he's in charge of, he hasn't had to do any cleaning, and it looks it. I get busy in my spare time, which isn't so spare because of the talent show, and I open all the windows and clean the place as best as I can. Ziggy has brought up the chest of drawers, but nothing has been put inside it, because Lam says, "I'll be damned if I'm going to use that," and so all our stuff is still on the floor. It's ridiculous. I don't want to hurt Lam's feelings, but it would be nice to put some of my clothes away.

him a chance? But then, am I a slut for thinking this? I'm married. I'm married! That's supposed to mean something. I shouldn't be thinking about anybody else but Lam and the baby. I decide I have to be the worst human being on the planet because I'm thinking of Ziggy and not Lam, and not the baby. But maybe Ziggy isn't as boring as I thought. Seeing him fighting out in the water—well, I can't help it, it was exciting, and I think . . . yeah, I think I was rooting for Ziggy, just a little bit.

"What is going on down there?"

I'm so into my thoughts that I don't even see the FIL coming down the hill. I stop in my tracks and wonder if I should tell the truth or lie. He'll find out, anyway. All the campers will be talking about it at dinner.

Speaking of dinner, the dinner bell rings and I'm saved from having to say anything, because the FIL continues marching down the hill while the campers begin streaming up it.

CHAPTER TWENTY

I'VE BEEN so busy with the audition and the classes and, in my spare time, thinking about Lam and Ziggy that most of the time I'm able to stash the whole scary C-section part of giving birth in the back of my mind. I'm not sleeping much, because everything about my body bugs me, my back, my swollen legs and feet, getting up and having to go to the bathroom a million times, just getting up, standing, sitting, lying. I am so ready for this baby to be out!

I catch Leo staring at me sometimes when I'm busy working on my dulcimer or working with one of the campers. Finally it bugs me so much I have to say something.

"Leo, you keep looking at me. What's up?"

"I'm just thinking how I don't think I've ever met anyone like you."

"Yeah, well, right back at you. I've never met anyone like you, either, Leonardo. But what do you mean?"

"Most girls who are sixteen would be pretty nervous or excited about having a baby, but you seem so together. So calm."

"Do I?" I smile at the thought. Am I together? How can I be? I'm still trying to figure out how I can avoid giving birth—like avoid the C-section. I still don't know who should get the baby. I don't even know how I really feel about having a baby. I should know. At first I didn't believe it—that I was pregnant, and then when I did believe it, I had this growing thing inside me and I was trying to get off drugs and caffeine and alcohol all at the same time. I felt like hell for two months, and then my parents were giving me such a hard time, and then I got married and came to work at the camp, and so I really haven't had much time to think about things. I try to explain this to Leo, and he just shakes his head.

"Amazing," he says.

* * *

Two days before *the day,* the FIL comes and gets me at the crafts hut, where I've just finished writing my secret message inside my dulcimer. This is Leonardo's idea. He tells everyone to write a poem, or a message to yourself, or words from a song on the bottom piece of the dulcimer before we glue all our pieces together. I write a message to my baby.

Dear child of mine,
Wherever you are, and wherever you go,

some part of you will always belong to me
and some part of me will always belong to you.
We are forever no matter what happens.
Your mother,
Eleanor Allan Crowe

The FIL tells me my sister is on the phone. I turn my dulcimer over to hide my message, and walk with the FIL back to his cabin.

He has his hand on my back like he's trying to help me walk. Ever since I told the ILs about the C-section, the FIL has been sweet and gentle with me and treating me like I'm sick or fragile or something. I kind of like it.

Once inside the cabin, I pick up the receiver. "Sarah?"

"Elly, hi. How are you? How's the baby? I've been keeping track. You're due in a few days right?"

"Yeah, a C-section in two days. I have an appointment." I say the words "C-section," and my heart pounds. "Narrow pelvis," I add.

"Oh, wow, sorry." She pauses and then, "So listen, I'm flying to Maine for the event. I want to be there for you."

"For me, or for the baby?" I ask.

"Well, both. I'm hoping you've reconsidered. Did you get the articles I sent you?"

"Yeah, I got 'em. If raising a kid is such a struggle and so expensive and all, why do you want to do it?"

"Come on, El. I'm in a different place than you are. I'm ten years older, and I'm married, and I've got a good job. I can give this baby what it needs."

I'm silent a second too long, and Sarah says, "Elly? You still there?"

"I'm here. I still have to talk to Lam about it, but maybe, Sarah. I'm not trying to be spiteful. I'm just not completely sure, but maybe. I'll—I'll let you know when you get here, okay? Before the C-section."

"Super! That's super, El. Okay. Oh, and Mom and Dad ought to be arriving in the States tomorrow."

"What? Arriving here? What do you mean?"

"Yeah, they wrote you, didn't they? Mom wrote me and said she wrote you, too, to tell you they were coming, that they'd be there for the birth. Didn't you get their letter?"

"Yeah, I got it, but I didn't read it all the way through. I thought it was just going to be a long lecture. I think they're still pretty ashamed of me."

"That's not the way it sounded to me. Mom said in her letter to me how she felt badly about the way she and Dad handled things with you. They shouldn't have forced you to get married."

"Wow, really?" I say. I'm stunned. I never expected them to feel sorry, and for some reason I feel guilty, like they shouldn't be feeling badly, especially since I've done nothing but give them grief all my life. And I'm the one who pushed them into pushing us to get married.

"But they believe in no sex before marriage and marriage before babies and all that," I say. "I can't believe they're sorry and they're coming home. Wow!"

If they were coming home, then Grandma Lottie had to be doing all right.

"Well, maybe all that religion works on paper, but the reality is different," Sarah says. "They're sorry, El. They were just so fed up with you. You have to admit you've been a real delinquent, especially the past three years."

"Uh-huh."

We're both silent for a bit, and I want to tell her that maybe I've changed, that maybe I'm not such a delinquent anymore. I'm off the drugs and alcohol, and I think I'll stay off them. I'm working really hard with the kids here, and I'm doing a pretty good job, too. I want to tell her that I think maybe I'd make a good parent someday, but I don't. I'm too full of so many feelings, worries about having a C-section, and now everybody coming home, and the talent show, and me and Lam, and besides that I gotta get off the phone and go pee.

"Oh, well, anyway, we'll all be there for you, El," Sarah says, breaking our silence. "We'll be there for you and the baby. I'll rent a car in Portland and go directly to the hospital, okay? So, see you in two. Good luck."

"Yeah, okay. Thanks. Bye." I hang up the phone and just stand there a second. That had to be the best conversation Sarah and I have had in years. I don't know if it's because I've changed so much or if she's just trying to be nice so I'll give her the baby.

I use the bathroom in the ILs' cabin, then hurry off to glue my dulcimer. After I finish, I plan to find Lam and decide what to do once and for all about the baby.

CHAPTER TWENTY-ONE

I'M ON MY WAY down to the lake to talk to Lam during the short break between the last class and dinner when Ziggy stops me. He comes out of the music hut carrying a music stand in one hand and a grape Fanta in the other. He pauses on the stoop and sets down the stand. "Hey, stranger," he says. "I sure miss seeing you at the break hut."

"Hey, Zig. Yeah, I miss seeing you, too," I say, "but planning the show takes up all my spare time. How's the nose?"

He touches the tip of it with his index finger. "It's okay. So, I guess you're going down to see Lam?"

I rest my hands on top of my belly and nod. "Yeah, we have some decisions to make. My sister's coming from California to pick up the baby, only I haven't discussed it with Lam. We need to come to a decision once and for all."

Ziggy hops off the stoop and walks up really close to me. "You know I'll take it. I mean, if you want to keep the baby, I'll help. Either way, if you want to come live with me in Boston after it's born, I'd take great care of you—both of you."

"But we hardly know each other," I say, because I'm still not sure my feelings for him are a good thing. "You don't know me. I'm a pain in the neck. You don't see—"

"How do you know what I see? Maybe I know you better than you think I do. Maybe there's such a thing as love at first sight, and maybe I want a baby. Maybe I want to be a father now."

I touch Ziggy's arm. "That's so sweet, Zig. Wow. I don't know what to say." I shrug and tilt my head. "But I'm still married."

Ziggy rolls his eyes. "I know you're married. You tell me that every time I see you, but, come on. Lam isn't serious about the marriage. It's a joke, a farce to him. He's young. I don't mean in age, I mean maturity-wise. He's still a little kid. You need a man. You need someone more serious. And I can support you, and the baby, too. That's important. You've got to think about that, Elly."

"I do. I will," I say. "I'll keep it in mind, really. I just don't know how I think about you. Maybe I'm falling in love with you, but I don't know. I've told you before I'd probably ruin your life in ten seconds flat, and maybe you're just too—too tame for me."

"Tame? Tame? I beat your husband up. How's that for tame? And anyway, what do you want? Why do girls always go for the dangerous ones? Ever think Lam might just ruin *your* life? Why are you so self-destructive? I'm a great catch!"

"Look, Zig," I say. "Maybe I am self-destructive; I don't know. My feelings are all mixed up, and I just can't handle this right now. I'm too confused. I've got to go give birth in two days. Is that insane or what? I really can't think about anything else. I just need to go talk to Lam."

"Okay, El. I understand. Just know that I'm here for you, okay? And I'll be with you at the hospital when the time comes, too, and Lam will be the one passed out on the hospital floor, if he shows up at all."

I sigh. "See ya, Ziggy." I leave Ziggy, and as I'm making my way down to Lam, I have a little conversation with my baby.

"I don't know what I want, baby cakes. If I were older and happily married, I'd be so excited about you—about your arrival. But I'm scared and not just because of the C-section. We've kind of grown attached to one another, you and I, haven't we? Maybe we already love each other." I whisper this because I'm so afraid to admit it. If I give this baby up, I don't want to make it harder on myself than it already is, but this baby has already been better company than most people I know. Does that even make sense? Probably not. I just know I feel this love, this protective love for what's growing inside of me.

I have my hands cupped around my belly, and my belly is

warm, and the baby is moving inside me, and my heart breaks for this unborn life because, really, what kind of mess am I bringing it into?

"I want you to have everything," I say, leaning forward, trying to see past my stomach to the rocks jutting out from the earth. "I want you to have the best and most loving parents, only the happiest of days, and I want you to never feel lonely, but how can I make that happen? I don't know what to do."

I stop talking out loud, because I notice a couple of campers on their way up from the lake watching me.

And what do you think, baby cakes, what do you think about Ziggy? I know he's a great catch and there's definitely an attraction. I don't know what's wrong with me. I should be happy that he's interested, and that he wants you, because I'm pretty sure Lam doesn't, even if he says he does. Ziggy's right. Lam's got a lot more growing up to do, but then so do I. You deserve better than all of us—even my stiff-necked sister and her pinched-faced husband, and maybe even better than the Lothrops, although they're great with all the campers. But look at the mess they made of Lam. Sarah wants you because she keeps miscarrying, and the MIL wants you to take the place of her dead baby, but is that what I want for you, to become a replacement baby, the baby that neither couple can have on their own?

The baby is still and it's so quiet all of a sudden I feel panicky, like I'm all alone and the whole rest of the world has blown up or something. I don't like it. I hurry the rest of the way down the hill. I reach the lake out of breath. I look around for Lam and catch Jen's eye. She's wrapping a rope around her arm from her elbow to the palm of her hand, around and around. I see her glance toward the boathouse then back at me. I see the last couple of campers have wrapped themselves in towels and are scurrying up the hill to get ready for dinner.

"Oh, hi, *Eleanor*," Jen calls in a way-too-loud voice. She keeps winding the rope. "Great to see you, *Eleanor*." I check the other lifeguards on the lake and none of them are Lam or Gren. Both seem to be missing. I shake my head and start off toward the boathouse, but just then out come Lam and Gren carrying a canoe between them like that's why they were in there. Yeah, right.

I walk over to them, and Lam does this whole act like he's so surprised to see me. He's got a bandage on his nose from the first fight with Ziggy and another one over his eye. The bandages only make him look cuter. "I came here to discuss the baby, because this might be our last time to make a decision. My sister is coming, and she expects an answer when she gets here, but judging by the two of you, I guess there's nothing to discuss. I guess my sister gets the baby."

"Yeah, well, my parents might have something to say about that. They're the baby's grandparents, and they have legal rights."

He and Gren are just standing there like dopes still holding on to the canoe, and it's like we're talking about the last piece of cake or something, not about a life. To Lam it's all the same—no big deal.

"Your parents have legal rights as grandparents, maybe, but not as parents. So—"

"It doesn't matter. This baby is both of ours, so I have a say in where it goes, too, and I think my parents should have it."

"Why, because they did such a fantastic job with you? What a dickhead. Were you two actually going at it in there, after everything that's happened? What assholes." I glare at Gren, and she blushes and stares at her stupid, ugly, stubby-toed feet. "Yeah, and you can cut the phony shy-girl act there, Gren. You suck. Both of you suck."

I turn to leave, and Lam drops the canoe and calls after me. "Elly, wait." I hear Gren howl, and I turn to see her pulling her foot out from under the canoe. Fake out on her. She got what she deserves.

"We weren't doing anything, I swear. We were only getting the canoe out because it needs fixing. All the good canoes are already out. Really. Look."

Lam points back at the canoe that Gren is still hopping around. "See that split near the tip?"

I look and I see the split, but really, who cares? "Whatever, Lam. Look, neither one of us is ready for this. I don't know what's going to happen to us, but we can't take care of this baby. We'd make such a mess of it, just like we've done with this so-called marriage. You're fun and all, but I guess fun isn't enough, is it? Not when we're talking about a family. Not when we're talking about forever."

I continue back up the hill, and Lam comes after me. "I love you, El," he says. "When camp is over and it's just me and you again, you'll see. I'll be different."

"So what are you saying, Lam? I mean, really, what are you saying?" I keep climbing, because if I stop I know it will be harder to get going again. I've reached the steepest part of the climb back up to the cabins.

Lam walks beside me. "I'm saying that I'm not ready to lose you, and my parents really want the baby, and I think they should get it because, okay, I'm screwed up, but that's mostly my fault. Yeah, they spoiled me to make up for losing their first kid, but I'm the one who's been the asshole. They got all that spoiling out of their system, so now they're ready, and anyway, they're here, in Maine, where we are, and they love kids, and they work with kids all summer long, and they've got experience."

"And they're old, Lam. They're in their fifties. My sister is only twenty-six and Robby's twenty-nine. They're the perfect age, and she's never had a kid, and anyway, I don't get the connection between you saying you love me and how you don't want to lose me, and saying your parents should get the baby— unless . . ." I stop, in spite of the hill. "Oh. Oh, I get it. As long as we stay married, you figure your parents still have a chance of getting the baby, and they're putting the screws to you, is that it? They've told you to give me a pot of geraniums and take me out and show me a good time and be good to me so they can get the baby. Your mother's being nice to me and letting me put on this talent show just so I'll agree to giving them the kid? Yeah, yeah, I see how it all fits. You don't care about us. They don't care about us. Wow! Wow, what a scam."

"No! It's not like that. Don't put the mess I've made of things onto them. They had nothing to do with it, I swear."

I'm walking again and so is Lam, and I feel like pushing him down the hill and watching him roll all the way into the lake. I hate him and his parents and this camp and blushing Gren and my whole stupid life. How did I ever get into this fix? I'm going to give birth the day after tomorrow. I'm going to have a C-section, and I've got all these people who want my baby, but I'm not sure anybody really wants me—not even me.

CHAPTER TWENTY-TWO

I N THE EARLY hours of the day of my C-section, at about one thirty, I get up for the third time to go pee. I slide into my sandals, ignore the bathrobe rule because my bathrobe doesn't even begin to fit around me anymore, grab my flashlight, and head out to the latrine, which is farther away now that I've returned to my old cabin. On my way back I notice some kind of movement out of the corner of my eye. I look to my left and see someone, and I think it's Lam. I quickly turn the flashlight on him and say, "Got ya, you bastard."

A startled Banner stands frozen with two loaves of bread, one in each hand, and squinting in the light.

I'm just as startled, and for a moment neither one of us says anything. Then Banner lets go of the loaves and they drop and roll in their plastic wrappers down the hill toward me. "Please don't tell on me," Banner whispers. "Please, please, please," she says. She's standing there in her Camp WeightAway shirt and the boxer shorts with kittens all over them that she wears as pajamas, and her little knees are pressed together as if she's desperate to go to the bathroom.

"Banner? What are you doing?" I say. I know, stupid, right? I can see what she's doing, but I just can't believe it. I walk up the hill toward her, and she crumples to the ground and starts whimpering with her hands over her face.

"Hey, Banner. It's okay. Everything is okay. What's going on?" By now I've caught up to where she is, and I struggle, and I mean struggle, to get myself down on the ground so I can put my arm around her and show her she's not in any trouble.

Banner really starts sobbing when I do that, but it's this funny sob because she's trying to be quiet and she's all torn up at the same time. Her whole body shakes with her sobs and she falls against me, and I grab hold of her and hug her even though her elbow is pressing into my thigh because of the awkward way we are both sitting. I'm super uncomfortable. "Come on," I say. "Help me up, and we'll go down to the counselors' break hut and talk."

When we get to the hut, we sit on the couch and Banner starts crying all over again, only louder now that we're inside and alone. I've set the loaves of bread on the coffee table.

I ask her about the bread and where she got it, and she tells me that she got it from the kitchen. She admits to me that she sneaks out every night and takes two loaves and eats them at night and during the day.

"I can't help it," she says. "I'm so hungry all the time. And I know the whole cabin hates me because I'm not losing any weight, and my parents are going to hate me even more than they already do because I'm so fat."

I think of the Hollywood-type parents of hers. I brush the hair out of Banner's face and look into her eyes. She's serious. She believes her parents are going to hate her because she's fat. "Banner, they won't hate you," I say. "You know they love you. They don't really care how much you weigh. I'm sure they just want you to be healthy."

"No, they don't. Why do you think I'm here? My parents put me here. They think I'm ugly—fat and ugly." Banner sits up and wipes her eyes. "My mom works for *Vogue* magazine, and my dad's a publicist. It's all about looks and image. That's what my mom says. She says, 'You can't get anywhere in this world without looks and image. You'll always be at a disadvantage if you're fat. People will hate you if you're fat.'"

"But that's not true. Only dumb, ignorant people would hate you for how much you weigh. Only unimportant people."

"Well, my parents are very important, and they hate me." Banner takes my hand and examines my wedding ring. It's just a silver band, nothing special, but she's looking at it like it's smothered in diamonds. "My father says no one would ever marry me if I'm fat."

"What? That's so stupid. My great-great-grandmother is huge, and she's been married four times! And never from divorce. They all died before her. She's ninety-nine years old, so there."

"I don't want to go home. Camp is almost over. I want to stay here. I can't go home. I can't. It's even worse there than it is here. I want to stay here. I want to live in one of the cabins all by myself. Then we can be neighbors."

"But you know you can't do that, right? Nobody's here in the winter."

"You'll be here," she says, and she strokes my arm. "I could live with you and take care of the baby."

"Look, Banner, I don't think I'm going to stick it out here after the baby's born. Anyway, your parents wouldn't let you stay here. There's no cook here in the winter—there's nobody here. And despite what you believe, your parents would miss you too much."

"Nobody would miss me. Nobody. My parents are divorced," Banner says, letting go of my hand and leaning her head on my shoulder. "They argue over who's going to have to take me for the weekend. I told them I wouldn't go to this camp unless they both took me. Big mistake; they totally ignored me and fought all the way here. Neither one of them wants me. They're too busy. The only time they talk to me is if they have something to say about my weight."

"Well, okay, that sucks. You've got everyone picking on you."

Banner nods, and fresh tears roll down her face.

"Hey, now. So what? Don't just curl up and let everybody kick you around. Fight back, Banner. You know? Screw 'em. You'll show them."

"I will?" She peers up at me with this trusting look in her eyes that breaks my heart.

"Sure you will. Anyone ever gives me a hard time or tells me I can't do something or whatever, I just say, screw 'em, and then I show 'em. I just show 'em good."

"Yeah, show 'em good." Banner nods and stares down at her lap.

I look at the bread on the table, and I ask Banner how she ever managed to sneak past me every night. "I'm a light sleeper, and I'm always getting up to pee."

"Yeah, I know. I wait until you're almost to the latrines, and I sneak out. Then I wait until your next trip and I sneak back in. Only tonight you were in *your* cabin, so I wasn't sure where you were, and then I thought I saw a bear or a moose, and I got scared and had to go a different way, so you caught me on the way back this time."

I laugh at this, and Banner kind of laughs, and then we get to talking about bread and we each have a slice, and then Banner has several more. I watch her eat, and she looks so hungry, but I don't think it's for bread.

After our talk, and after I promise not to tell on her, we decide it's time to go back. I watch her go into her cabin, then I return to mine. I climb into bed, careful not to wake Lam, and for a few minutes I lie there thinking about Banner. I'm glad that I could make her smile and that she knows I'm her friend. It feels good to help somebody like that, really good.

Soon I'm asleep again, and I dream about Banner's parents. They're ten feet tall and beautiful and all powdery and they say *dahling* all the time and they have diamond-studded cell phones. Banner's in the dream, too, dressed like Cinderella covered in soot, only she's wearing my orange maternity dress, and she follows behind her parents with a broom and sweeps up all the clouds of powder that falls from their faces.

In the morning I get up to go pee and I think, *Today's the day. This is the day I meet my baby and see Sarah and maybe my parents. This is the big day.* I feel so—so aware, so different somehow. I hear myself on the way to the latrines saying hi to the kids I pass, and I call out, "Tie your shoe, Janet," and I'm so paying attention to what I'm saying, as though I'm watching myself on television, or like this is an out-of-body experience. I like hearing myself say "Tie your shoe, Janet," because it's what I say every time I see her, and I think, *This is me. This is my life, with these campers, going to the bathroom, saying hi, hugging a camper good morning, telling Janet to tie her shoe. This is my life, and it's wicked cool.*

I notice everything I do and say, and everything feels so important, so wonderful and important. I feel so awake. I feel such a part of everything—of the whole world. I'm marveling at this as I make my way back to my cabin, and I think all these campers are beautiful and wonderful, and this day is just going to be perfect. I start to sing "Everything's Coming Up Roses," a song my mom and I used to like to sing together. I see a necklace hanging on our door latch. I'm still singing while I examine it. It's one of the ones some of the campers made in crafts out of clay. All it is is this piece of clay that you press your thumb into to make like an oval shape, and you pull it some at the top and form a little loop for the piece of rawhide to slip through and then you draw some kind of small design on the thumb print, or a symbol or a word, using a pin, and then you leave it to dry. It's the first craft I actually could do. I lift the necklace off the handle and notice the heart on the front. Lots of campers drew hearts. I turn it over and I see the initials *B. S.* I stop singing. It's Banner's necklace. She wants me to have it as a thank-you for last night. I slip it over my head and smile to myself and go back inside to get dressed. Lam is still sleeping, so I try to be quiet. I think about Banner and our conversation, and I feel the necklace hit my chest every time I lean forward and stand back up. Then something comes over me. I'm scared all of a sudden. I hear Banner's voice from last night saying, "Nobody will miss me," and I see the necklace hanging from my neck, and a chill runs up my back. I hurry into my sandals, go back outside, and make my way up to cabin seven.

I step inside, and all the kids are busy with their cleanup duty. They're making their beds and cleaning the sinks in the back of the cabin, tidying up the closets, sweeping the floor, collecting clothes and books and junk and putting them away. It's all the normal morning stuff, and this reassures me. Everything's okay. Everything's normal. I look around for Banner, but I don't see her. The counselor's in the back with the girls doing sink duty, so I just call out, "Banner?"

There's no answer. "Anybody seen Banner?" I ask. I wait and get no response. "Anybody seen Banner this morning?" I call out again.

"I heard her get up around four to go to the bathroom," her bunkmate says. "I'm not sure she ever came back."

I look at her bed, still unmade. It looks so empty. "Thanks," I say. "I'm worried about her. I'm going to go look for her."

The counselor, Haley, hears me and turns around. "Everything okay?"

"I don't know," I say. "I'm worried about Banner. She was really upset last night, and she's missing. I've got to go look for her. Tell the Lothrops, would you?"

"Yeah, sure. I knew somebody was missing," Haley says.

I hurry to the latrines, but she's not there. I check the kitchen, but she's not there, either. Then I decide to go to the counselors' hut, thinking maybe she went back to get the bread and just fell asleep. When I get there, the bread is still on the table, but she's not asleep on the couch.

Where could she be? Did she run away? Did she give me this necklace as a going-away present?

I step out of the hut and look about. Could she have taken off into the woods? I hear all the campers cleaning and talking in the cabins, and occasionally a counselor calls out some kind of order or reminder for the day. It's all happy noise, and it's comforting, and I try to get into my earlier mood. I look toward the lake. Someone's left a raft out. Probably Lam, or maybe Banner took it out and left it. I head down to the lake, remembering how much Banner likes to swim. Maybe she just went for a swim and now she's in the bathroom down there. Don't they say the simplest explanation for something is the most likely? I make my way down the steep path through the pines, and I notice that the air smells sweet. It's still cool like it is most mornings and evenings, but since I'm pregnant I like the coolness. I don't even need a sweater or a jacket the way I usually would if I weren't pregnant. I think for a second how the next time I climb down to the lake, my stomach will be flatter and I'll have had a baby. Me, a baby. I wrap my arms around my belly.

I come out into the clearing, and I stare out at the lake. The thing I thought was a raft now looks more like a shirt. Another chill runs up my spine, all the way to the top of my head. It's a Camp WeightAway shirt, and it looks all puffed out—bloated, almost as if . . .

I hurry now to the far end of the lake, near the boys' camp. "Banner!" I call to her, because now I'm sure that's who it is. "Banner! Please, no. Banner!" I hold my baby from underneath my protruding belly and I run. "Help, somebody!" I call out. "Somebody help me!" I keep running, and as I get closer I can see the hair, all that beautiful hair fanning out around her head.

"Eleanor?" I hear somebody call, and I look up. It's Leo. I

wave, then point at Banner. "It's Banner," I say. "Help! I think she's . . ." I can't say it, but I don't have to. In a flash Leo's in the water, swimming out to her, and other counselors and campers are coming out of their cabins to see what's going on. One of the counselors thinks to go ring the big bell, and suddenly people are streaming out from every direction.

Leo reaches Banner, and he rolls her over onto her back while someone from shore tosses him one of those orange rescue tubes. I'm standing on the edge of the lake watching and crying and feeling hysterical. I can't believe what I'm seeing. I keep saying no, and I can't shut up. "No! Banner, no! No! Please, no. Come on. You're all right. Please, you're all right." I'm slobbering all over myself with my tears and snot, and Leo's got his arm across Banner's chest and he's pulling her in while other counselors are diving in and swimming out to them. People on my side of the lake join me, and I hear the FIL's voice behind me and he's calling out orders, and then Banner's on the shore and we can hear sirens, and everybody crowds in while Leo, Ziggy, and Jen take turns doing CPR and mouth-to-mouth. It's obvious by the colorless tone of her skin and her open stare that she's dead, but they keep trying because otherwise we'd all just be standing around staring at a dead body, waiting for the ambulance.

The MIL is ordering the counselors to get their campers back into their cabins, and I realize I don't have campers I have to take back to a cabin. I don't have the excuse of leaving, but I can't take it. I can't stand looking at her. I don't know what to do. I want to leave, but I can't make myself move. I don't know where to go, back to my cabin to sit there by myself? No, I need to stay. Stay put. Stay still. Stop crying. I wipe my eyes. I've got to stay. I've got to see the ambulance come and hear the medics say it, that she's dead, because I can't believe it. It just doesn't make sense. She was smiling when I said good night to her. She wasn't that unhappy, was she? Everybody loved her dance, and she could do the splits. Why would she do this? I hugged her good night, and she was smiling. I had made her feel better. I had showed her I was her friend. How could she do this? I just can't believe it.

A police car arrives with the ambulance, and then it's hustle-bustle while they get out all their life-support stuff and a stretcher or whatever it's called, and rush over to Banner and check her out, but they shake their heads, and I know it's hopeless; Banner is dead. Campers are crying, and little ones are screaming and want their mommies, and counselors are yelling for the kids to go back to their cabins, but nobody is listening. It's all so crazy and surreal, and I just have to get away. I have to get out of this place. I look around for Lam and find him leaning against the camp flagpole, chewing on his thumb. I scramble up to him, calling to him as I climb, but he doesn't hear me until I'm almost in his face.

"Lam, I've gotta get out of here. It's almost time to go, anyway. Can you take me now? Please? I've got to go now!"

Lam sees that I'm a wreck. I can't stop crying and I'm shaking all over. He puts his arm around me and guides me back down the hill toward the parking lot. Everybody's so busy watching the medics that nobody notices us slipping behind the ambulance and getting into Lam's car.

"Get me out of here, Lam. Fast!"

Lam backs out slowly, but as soon as he's clear of the ambulance and the other cars, he floors it, and the tires spit out rocks and dirt and we tear out of there, down the narrow dirt road leading out of the camp and onto the paved streets—away, away from that terrible, horrible scene.

CHAPTER TWENTY-THREE

I CAN'T STOP crying. Lam drives all over town, up one back road and down another, and we say nothing to each other. I cry and he drives.

It's all my fault. I know it is. I review our talk in the break hut, and I remember how I told Banner to show 'em. I meant for her to get mad and get even, but I didn't say that, did I? No. I said show 'em. Well, she showed them all right—her way, not mine. I'm a murderer. I killed her. I cry harder, and Lam pats my leg and tells me it's okay.

I scream at him. "No, it's not okay. It's never going to be okay. She's dead. She's dead and I—I . . ." I can't even bring myself to say it. I lean forward into my hands and cry harder.

Lam pulls into the Bethel movie theater parking lot and stops the car. He reaches across me to the glove compartment, rifles through the junk he's got in there, and pulls out a joint. "Come on, you need to calm down," he says.

I rock side to side and keep crying, and I'm crying so hard I can barely breathe. Lam reaches into his pocket and pulls out a lighter and lights up. He takes a pull, then hands it to me.

I stop crying and take the joint. My chest is still heaving. My face hurts. I've got snot running down my nose. I wipe my nose on my shirtsleeve and stare at the joint. I try to calm myself.

"Go on, you need it," Lam says. "It can't hurt the baby now. It's coming out today, right?"

I don't know what to do. It's tempting. It's so tempting. I try to clear my head and think. Would it be okay? Would the baby be okay? The nurse practitioner said not to have anything to eat or drink after midnight the night before the C-section. Would this count as eating? Would I have to tell them that I smoked a joint? Would it make me throw up when they give me anesthesia? I bring the joint closer and remember the good old days when Lam and I used to get stoned. Wait. No. What am I thinking? It's crazy. I can't. I'm going to have a baby. I don't want to do this anymore. I don't want my life to be about getting stoned anymore.

There's a rap on Lam's window and I look over, and wouldn't you know it, it's the Bethel police.

"Shit!" I say, flicking the joint on the floor.

Lam swears, too, while the policeman motions for Lam to roll down his window.

Lam rolls it down and the policeman steps back. "Very aromatic in there. Can I see your license?"

Lam digs in his pocket, pulls out his wallet and gets his license, and hands it to him. The guy looks at it for two seconds. "Would you get out of the car, please?"

"It's not what you think."

"Get out of the car, please. Both of you."

This cannot be happening. The very first time I've held a joint in months, and I get caught. And we know better than to park in an empty parking lot. Police always come check that out. We're so stupid.

I climb out of the car and come around to where Lam and the policeman are standing. Lam is cradling the back of his head with his hands. I put my hands behind my head, too.

"Oh, brother, would you look at this?" the policeman says when he sees I'm pregnant.

"I didn't have any. I was holding it, but I didn't smoke it."

"You can tell your story over at the station. Get in the car." He gets behind us and herds us toward the car. Lam gets in, but I stop. I'm crying again. I turn to the policeman.

"I've been good to my baby. I've been so good and I'm scheduled to have a C-section this morning. I'm supposed to be at the hospital, and they said don't be late."

"Yeah? Then what are you doing here? This is not the hospital parking lot."

"A girl—A girl—I can't—and Banner's—Banner's . . ."
Now I'm really crying, because it's like my whole life is flashing

before my eyes. I see my parents' angry faces, and the juvenile detention center, and the judge, and me sniffing cocaine and dancing on a table, and the camp, and the MIL's angry face, and Kenya, and me with dysentery, and the orphans and their crying, and my crying, and the whole world crying.

Lam leans out of the car and speaks for me. "A girl at the camp where we're working just committed suicide. Elly was close to her. I just wanted to calm her down, but she didn't smoke it. She's clean. You can test her."

The officer nods. "Yeah, I heard there was something going on up there, but that's no excuse. You're both in possession." He looks at me. "What time are you due at the hospital?"

"Eight o'clock."

He checks his watch. "You've got twenty minutes. Get in the car."

I get inside and Lam slides over. The policeman slams the door, then goes over to Lam's car, fishes around for the joint I threw on the floor, takes the keys out of the ignition, closes up the car, and walks back over to his cruiser.

"Sorry, Elly," Lam says, and I think of how many gazillions of times Lam has had to say that to me. I get arrested while I'm in the middle of breaking into his parents' basement, and while I'm getting hauled away, Lam steps out all groggy and hung over and says, "Sorry, Elly." I get suspended from school for having a pocketknife in my backpack—Lam's pocketknife that I didn't even know he had put there—"Sorry, Elly." I get stopped by the police for erratic driving and fined $150 because Lam was picking on the way I was driving and kept trying to take the steering wheel out of my hands—"Sorry, Elly." I get pregnant because the condom Lam used was like five years old and it broke—"Sorry, Elly." Finally, I'm waking up and realizing for the first time that as long as I'm with Lam I'm going to keep ending up riding around in police cars and hearing his voice, his sickening voice, saying, "Sorry, Elly."

The policeman gets in his car, talks into his radio in some kind of code, but I hear him mention the hospital, and I hope that's where he's taking us. He starts up the car and we speed off—and I mean speed. The guy should be arrested.

I arrive at the Rumford hospital just in time. It's a long brick building that's always reminded me of an old high school—so it's like the hospital and high school, the two things in the world I hate the most, rolled into one. I wait for the policeman to come around to the door to let us out. He opens the door and we start to scoot out, but the officer shakes his head. "Just the girl. You're coming back to town with me."

I get out, then turn around and look at Lam. "Sorry, Lam."

CHAPTER TWENTY-FOUR

THE OFFICER walks me into the hospital lobby, this rotunda kind of place with big picture windows, and checks to make sure I really am scheduled for a C-section. Never have I been more glad that I was actually telling the truth. Before he leaves, he warns me, "You stay out of trouble. You've got a baby to think of now."

"Yes, sir," I say. "I know that."

I don't have my driver's license or the insurance card my parents left with me, and that slows everything down, but the admitting lady calls the camp, and the MIL agrees to bring it down. That's all she needs on top of what's going on at the camp. I don't have to wait for her to get here, though. They admit me to the hospital, and they lead me to this room where I get undressed and tie on a gown. A nurse helps me onto a bed and puts these monitors all around my belly to "check my vitals" as the nurse says, and to check the baby's heart rate and stuff, and then I wait a long while, and while I'm waiting, Sarah shows up. I start crying again, and she comes over to me, and she's so sweet.

"Hey, baby, what's wrong? It's okay. It's all going to be okay. I'm here." She gives me a hug. "Mom and Dad are on their way. They'll be here in about an hour."

"Good, 'cause—oh, Sarah, this is the worst day of my life. Really. I don't know how I'm going to make it through all this today. Banner's dead, and Lam's at the police station, and—and I'm going to have a C-section." I'm really wailing now, and Sarah keeps shushing me and patting my head, and I like the comfort of her patting me, but I know I don't deserve her comfort. Nobody can comfort Banner ever again. I thought I had comforted her, but I hadn't. She was just pretending. "'Show 'em.' I told her to show 'em, and she didn't understand."

"Shhh. It's okay. It's all right, baby. It's going to be fine. It's all right. Honey, you've got to calm down. This can't be good for the baby. I'm going to go see if they can give you something to calm you down."

I think of Lam trying to calm me, and the joint I almost smoked, and I cry even harder.

A few minutes later, Sarah comes back with a nurse who wants me to sign some forms, and she makes Sarah sign them, too. Then she hooks up an IV that she says will shoot fluids and medication into my veins during the surgery. I've never had an IV before, and I'm so grossed out, I cry about that, too.

Sarah sits close to me and pats my hand. Eventually, even without a sedative, I start to calm down some.

"I'm glad you're here, Sarah," I say. I grab a tissue off this little tray-thing they've got by my bed, and I blow my nose.

"Me, too. You look well, Elly. You look like you've gained enough weight and everything."

I nod. "Yeah, I read how teens who get pregnant don't always gain enough weight and that's bad for the baby, so I made sure I gained weight. The doctor says everything looks good."

Sarah nods, and we're silent for a while. I try not to think of Banner, or Lam, or the C-section.

"So," Sarah says, "have you made your decision about the baby? You said something about Lam being at the police station?"

I nod. "Yeah, he got arrested for smoking a joint."

Sarah shakes her head. "I've always said he was bad news, Elly."

"I know, but so am I. I'm bad news, too. I'm really, really bad news. I'm like the black widow of bad news."

I sniff, but I don't cry—well, just some slow tears rolling down my cheeks, nothing dramatic this time.

"So? About the baby?"

I look in Sarah's eyes. She's so hopeful, expectant. "I love this baby, you know," I say.

Sarah nods, and I see a bit of a frown forming at the edges of her mouth. She controls it, though, and pats my head. "I'm sure you do, El. I'm sure you want what's best for it."

"I do. I want what's best for it." Now more tears are spilling down my face, because I know what I'm about to say, and I can't stand to hear myself say it. Not after all these months together, me and baby cakes. "Okay, Sarah, I—I want you to have it. I've decided. But . . ."

Sarah's face lights up, and she leans over me and hugs me so hard, and then she's crying and laughing at the same time, and I can see how much this means to her. I didn't know. Until this moment I didn't know how she must have been feeling waiting in the background all these months, waiting to hear me say that she's going to be a mother.

Sarah cries and laughs and hugs me over and over, and she wipes my tears away and then hers and then mine again.

Finally she calms down enough for me to finish what I had started to say. "Listen, Sarah, Lam and his parents want the baby, too. I don't know what happens when two sides want the same baby."

Sarah slides back in her chair and wipes her face. She straightens her back and gets that stiff-necked look of hers that means she's put out about this. "Well, if we can't come to an agreement, then a court will decide, and that can take months. They could put the baby in foster care until a decision is made, and by then the baby has bonded with someone else, if it's bonded at all. I wanted—I want—I want the baby right away. You can see how that would be best?"

I nod. "Uh-huh, I see that, but I think Lam's parents want it, too."

"If it's a boy we'll name it Robert after Robby, and if it's a girl we'll name it Ethel, after Great-Great-Grandma." Sarah smiles down at her lap and smoothes out the skirt of her already smoothed-out suit.

"Ethel? Why would you want to do that to the baby? Great-Great-Grandma's super and all, but what will kids call her at school? Eth? Thul? Ethie? Yuck!"

"I think it's a sweet name."

I feel guilty that I never even thought about a name for the baby. I haven't even thought of it as a boy or a girl. Just baby cakes, just a generic baby.

Is that proof of how little I really want it, or of how sure I am that I won't be keeping it? I know I've been too afraid to get attached to it, even though I have, anyway. I think Lam has been afraid, too. Maybe that's been our problem. Maybe our marriage has been such a fiasco because we haven't been able to really celebrate being pregnant. We haven't bonded over the pregnancy at all. It's torn us apart. Maybe Lam even resents the baby.

I start to worry over this thought, but then Sarah says, "El, you know we're the best ones for the baby. We're young and we live in a beautiful home. The baby will want for nothing—you know that."

"Yeah, Sarah, I know. Despite the way we are with each other, I know you'd make a great mother."

"I've always gotten on your case, El, because I care about you and because I care about our family. I would see you tear into Mom and Dad all the time and whine and complain about living in Kenya and having to share your life with all the orphans, and you just never let up. For four years you never let up, and then we moved back home and you hooked up with Lam and you went insane. I was just looking after you, El."

"I know." I nod. "I know."

"I just wanted peace. I like peace. Your baby will grow up in a peaceful, loving household."

I don't want to hear any more about my baby and where it will grow up, but I don't know how to shut Sarah up. She's so excited. Then I hear Ziggy's voice out in the hallway, and I'm so grateful he's come.

"In here?" he asks. Then he pokes his head in and sees me and smiles. He comes into the room and right over to me. "Elly, are you all right? Where's Lam?"

Sarah stands up. "Who are you?" she asks.

"Ziggy Grumbauer, a good friend of Elly's. Who are you?"

"Her sister. I'm Sarah."

Sarah sounds so haughty that I'm embarrassed for her. Why does she have to do that? She sounds like such a snob, and she dresses like one, too, in her perfect little suits and matching pumps and flashy jewelry. I'd been loving how real she'd been acting for a change.

Ziggy sticks out his hand for Sarah to shake, and she hesitates, like she's afraid his beard and earring and long hair all have cooties. "Nice to meet you," Ziggy says, waiting for Sarah's hand.

"Yes, delighted," Sarah says, finally sticking her hand out. "Listen, El." She turns to me. "There's a snack machine in the other hall. I'm just going to go get a little something to eat while you talk to your friend. I'll be back." She checks her watch. "Mom and Dad should be here soon."

She leaves, and Ziggy calls after her, "Nice to meet you."

When Sarah is gone, I say, "She's really not so bad. If she'd just pull the stick out of her butt, I'm sure you'd like her."

"She's just careful and protective of you. I know the type. I have an older brother just like her."

Ziggy smiles at me and takes my hand.

I smile, but it's fake. I'm worried. I want to know about Banner. "So, what's going on at the camp? How could you leave? Don't they need you?"

Ziggy shakes his head and sits down in the chair Sarah had used. "Everybody's in the main cabin watching movies. There's a grief-counseling team there. They're interviewing kids who seem seriously upset. They talked to everybody as a group first, and now they're taking kids one by one. Some kids have gone home. It's really a disaster for the Lothrops. And for Banner's family, of course. Poor kid." He shakes his head and leans forward on his elbows.

Disaster. That sounds about right. If I've had anything to do with it, then it has to be a disaster, and I had plenty to do with Banner's death.

I look away and stare out the window. It looks like such a

pretty, sunny day, and that feels all wrong. It should be raining out. There should be a storm outside. A hailstorm.

"So where's Lam?"

I turn back to face Ziggy. "In jail probably, so go ahead and say it: I told you so."

"Jail? How . . ."

"Don't ask, okay? I'm lucky I'm not there with him."

Ziggy brushes the hair out of my face. "Just remember, I'll take the two of you. You and your baby. I've got a really nice apartment in the city. You'd love it."

Of course Sarah walks in with her coffee and Danish right as Ziggy's saying this.

"What's that? Elly? You're not changing your mind, are you? Please tell me you aren't. Who is this guy?" She looks Ziggy up and down and scowls. "Who are you?"

"Ziggy Grumbauer, remember? We've already met." He sticks his hand out again, and Sarah waves him away.

"Another one of your brilliant friends, El?"

"As a matter of fact, I scored a—"

"Stop!" I say, or really I sort of shout it. "Please stop. Please, I just need to be quiet."

Then the doctor and Mom and Dad come in at the same time, and I'm so happy to see my parents that I burst into tears again, and they rush over to hug me, and I think now that they're here maybe everything will be all right. They'll fix it. They'll make it all better.

My parents only get a short visit with me, though, before the doctor shoos everyone out so he can talk to me before the surgery.

They hug me and tell me how much they've missed me and how sorry they were about the way they left things here. "You just are the most stubborn person, sometimes, Eleanor," my dad says. "And to your own detriment."

"Yeah, I know, Dad. I know. I'm sorry. I'm sorry about the hell I've put you two through the past—well, all my life, I guess. I know you were really fed up with me when you left."

"You really placed us between a rock and hard place, El. We had to get to Kenya to be with Grandma Lottie. We couldn't cancel no matter how much we wanted to. If you had just been willing to come . . ."

My mom puts a hand on Dad's arm. "Let's not go there. It's all over."

"Well, you got there, didn't you?" I say. "And Grandma's still hanging on, so—"

Mom and Dad exchange this weird, uncomfortable look.

"What? What is it?"

"It was in the letter your mother sent you. Unfortunately, we didn't get there soon enough. Grandma died, honey," my dad says.

I'm stunned. I didn't expect that, but I should have. I tell them it's all my fault, too. I remember what I said about wanting to be in hell if she was going to be in heaven, and I cry my eyes out all over again.

My parents try to calm me down, and Mom reminds me that the universe doesn't revolve around me and that I'm not that powerful. This is comforting. More comforting than she knows, but I'm still bawling. She says I need to calm down, and she wants to know if they can give me anything to calm my nerves. Sarah, who's been standing over by the windows just glowing with the joy of knowing she's getting the baby, butts in and says she already tried that, but the nurse said that a sedative would sedate the baby, too, so they won't give me anything. "Too bad," Mom says, gazing down at me. "I had valium when I had you."

"So that's what's wrong with me," I say. "It started at birth."

They all laugh at my joke, but I don't think I'm kidding.

* * *

Once everybody's out of the room, the doctor explains to me in all the gory details what's about to happen.

"When we get into the operating room, we'll insert a Foley bladder catheter to drain your bladder."

"Drain it? Like in a sink?"

"What we're actually doing is deflating the bladder."

Now, that sounds gross, this empty rubbery bladder flapping around in the breeze—*flap, flap, flap.*

"But I haven't had anything to eat or drink since midnight, like you said. Do you really need to do that to my bladder?"

"Yes, we do, but not to worry. You'll be glad it's in place."

"I doubt it." I'd rather pee all over the bed than have a catheter.

"Then the anesthesiologist will administer a regional anesthesia so you'll be able to stay awake during the procedure."

"That's the spinal epidural. I've read all about that. That's supposed to be a killer. I don't think I need that. I don't want to stay awake. Knock me out. I don't want to know anything. Give me a whole-body anesthesia."

The doctor just pats my hand and tells me that it wouldn't be the safest way to go for the baby or for me. Then he gets all excited when he tells me about cutting my uterus open. It's all science to him. To me it's my body, and I've got blood and guts and stuff down there, and hearing about getting cut open makes me wanna puke. Then he asks me if I have any questions, but I don't. I just want the whole thing to be over with.

"Just realize once the baby's out we won't be putting it in your arms right away like you see in the movies. We'll cut the umbilical cord, and the nurse will take it directly to the warmer, where our neonatal resuscitative team will check your baby out and help get all the fluids out of its lungs. Okay?"

"Yeah, sure, okay." I nod.

The doctor gives my family a few more minutes to be with me, so in walk my parents and Sarah and Ziggy and the MIL. I'm so surprised to see the MIL, but then I see she has my purse and the duffle bag I packed last night, and I remember she had to bring my driver's license and I'm embarrassed. I thank her, but I hate that she had to come here, today of all days. Her eyes look bloodshot, like she's been crying, and she looks exhausted . . .

and she looks angry. They all look angry, especially her and Sarah, so I figure they've been out in the waiting room arguing over the baby. I close my eyes because it's more than I can take. They're like vultures. That's what it feels like.

They gather around and pat my arm, my hands, my head—anything they can reach.

I wonder if the MIL knows about Lam. I wonder if he's going to be here for the birthing. The father is supposed to be in the room with the mother. That's what the doctor said. He said after my abdomen had been sterilized and I was draped, Lam could come in and hold my hand during the birthing.

I don't know if I want Lam there or not, but I want somebody. I want Ziggy. I open my eyes and look at all of them staring down at me. They're all smiling, yet no one seems happy.

"Hey," I say, "I'm about to have a baby. How 'bout that?"

They nod and smile and coo at me.

I'm starting to feel really sleepy all of a sudden, and I remember that whenever I get really scared I always get sleepy. I think it's some kind of protective mechanism. I guess that's why I was especially tired yesterday, and why I was actually able to sleep some last night. I was filled with too much fear to stay awake. I always get sleepy studying for final exams, too. My mom calls it test anxiety. My dad calls it failure to thrive. I never do well on the finals.

I smile at Ziggy. "Ziggy, will you hold my hand in the operating room? I don't think Lam is going to be able to make it."

I see that Mom looks a little hurt when I ask Ziggy, and the MIL looks annoyed.

I squeeze Mom's hand. "I just can't handle any judgment right now," I say, and she nods and pats my shoulder.

"Me, either," she says, and I understand. She left for Africa when I needed her most, and she made me marry Lam. She made mistakes, too. Maybe she'll forgive me now for mine, or for at least one of mine. I think about Banner for a second, then brush the thought away. Not now. It's too much.

The MIL glances at Ziggy through the slits of her eyes. "Ziggy, what are you even doing here?" she asks.

"I'm here for Eleanor," he says. "I'm here to look after her and her baby, if she needs me to."

The MIL shakes her head in disgust. I'm sure she thinks I'm doing the nasty with him, but whatever. I'm too tired to defend myself.

"Lam's coming. I know all about this morning. He'll be here," she says. "Don't you worry; he'll be here."

Finally it's time to go to surgery, and everybody kisses me, including the MIL, as a last-minute suck-up, I'm guessing. She must really want this baby. I wave, and the nurse rolls me out of the room. I'm going to have my C-section. I'm going to have a baby.

CHAPTER TWENTY-FIVE

IT TAKES a while for everything to be ready with the steril-izing and then the epidural, which is a killer; I don't care what the doctor says. I've never felt so much pain. I don't think they did it right, and I tell them this and they laugh like I'm kidding. I'm not kidding. Nothing that's supposed to numb the pain should hurt so much going in.

It doesn't help any that the doctor and his assistant—a lady doctor—explain everything they're doing, and I mean *every-thing,* in great detail.

The operating room has these two giant round lights that shine down on me from the ceiling and all this machinery and a TV screen thing and wires and a table with scary-looking medi-cal tools on it. I close my eyes, and the doctor starts to tell me some horrible thing he's about to do to me.

"Okay, you know what?" I say, interrupting him. "I don't want to hear a blow-by-blow. I mean, does anybody? Really? Why don't you sing a song or something instead?"

The lady doctor surprises me because she asks me what I want her to sing, and I ask her if she knows "Everything's Coming Up Roses" from *Gypsy*, but she doesn't know it. She sings "Ob-La-Di, Ob-La-Da" by the Beatles instead. She's got a terrible voice, and when she's done I tell her not to quit her day job.

As soon as they adjust the drape so it's above my chest, they let Ziggy in, and now I'm sorry that my mom's not here, because she knows "Everything's Coming Up Roses," and I really want to hear that song.

I ask Ziggy if he knows it, and he does.

"Yeah, I know it, and I could sing it, but sorry, you don't want me to ever sing to you again," he says. "So my lips are sealed."

"Please? Just for this special occasion, and not like a lady opera singer, okay?"

The doctor can't help himself. He forgets that I told him not to tell me what he's doing, and so he says, "I'm going to begin the incision now."

"Oh, sing out, baby June!" I holler, quoting from *Gypsy*. I grab Ziggy's hand.

Ziggy's dressed in a gown and those funny blue paper shoe covers and he's wearing a mask over his mouth and nose, but he sings, and his voice is nice. It's got a wiggle in it—what do they call that? Vibrato? He sings almost every word with a wiggle, but it's okay. It sounds right, and I like when he sings, "Honey, everything's coming up roses for me and for you!"

The nurse and the assisting doctor clap when he finishes. I'm too busy trying not to feel all the tugging and pulling and yucky stuff going on down below to remember to clap, but I've got tears in my eyes. I miss my mom. I should have asked her to be with me. Anytime something went wrong or whenever I was afraid, she would sing me that song, and then when I got to know the words, I would sing it with her. We'd sing it from Maine to Massachusetts whenever we drove down to visit my grandma and grandpa, just for the hell of it. We never got tired of that song, but Sarah did. That made me like it even more.

Now it's quiet, except for the machinery and the doctor's voice and the gross noises coming from my body, so I ask for another song, but then the door to the operating room opens and a nurse comes in and whispers something, and the doctor nods. Then he looks at me. "Lam's here. Do you want him to switch places with your friend here? Only one can be in the operating room."

"Can we do that? Switch, I mean?"

"Whatever you want," he says.

I look up at Ziggy. He squeezes my hand. I think of Lam out there, fresh from the police station. I think of our life the past couple of years, and I remember what I realized in the cop car as we were rushing to the hospital. If I stay with Lam, it's always going to be rides in cop cars. There's always going to be another Gren. That's the kind of relationship we have—troubled. I decide it's time to grow up. I've got a guy here who loves me even nine months pregnant, even all cut open. I've got a guy I think I could really love—a grown-up kind of love, not a teenage crush/fantasy kind of love. I picture us living in Boston, going to concerts and museums and walking in the park—him, me, and the baby—with no drugs, no drinking, no base jumping and stealing cars. Then I remember about the baby. I'm giving it to Sarah.

I look at the doctor, who's waiting for my answer. "Let's just stick with Ziggy. I want Ziggy."

Ziggy kisses my forehead. "I love you, El," he says at the same time the doctor says, "You're the boss."

Things get tense after that. Cutting me open takes forever. What are they doing down there? I feel like they're pulling on me. Like the doctor's down there trying to pry me open with his elbows. I mean!

"I think—I think . . ." Ziggy says in this strange voice like he's suddenly drunk.

He's looking at something in the assisting doctor's hand. "I think I'm going to faint."

The nurse moves fast and guides Ziggy out of the room.

"Ziggy?" I call after him.

I'm wondering what he saw. I don't like the sounds I'm hearing or the constant tugging and pulling, and now I have no one to hold my hand.

I'm feeling this pressure like they're pushing on my stomach. The doctor says, "You're going to feel a little pressure now." Uh, yeah!

"What are you doing? Do you get a baby out the same way you pop a zit?"

The doctor chuckles. "Kind of."

Gross! I was only kidding.

A few minutes later and I hear, "Here—we—go. We've got us a real live baby. Here it—*she* comes!"

"A girl! It's a girl?" I squeal, and look around for someone to share the good news with, forgetting I'm on my own.

Then I see my baby, wow, my baby, born from me—a miracle. She's all covered in crud, and the umbilical cord is hanging out of her belly. I see arms and legs moving, and the doctor does something to suck out fluid from her mouth and nose, and the baby cries and I cry and I can't believe it—I have a baby, a baby girl, a baby girl named Emma Rose.

CHAPTER TWENTY-SIX

I KNOW, I know, I shouldn't have named her, but the name was right there. I had had it all along. It was hidden deep inside me. That's the way it is with me. I've got all kinds of thoughts and feelings and bits of information I know, that I don't realize I'm thinking, or feeling, or knowing, until all of a sudden there it is right in front of me, like it's been there all along and it was just waiting for me to notice. That's the way it is with the name Emma Rose.

They whisk the baby off so fast and I want to follow, see where she goes, but the doctor says that was the easy part. Now he has to get me put back together right so that there's no infection and no unusual bleeding.

While that's going on, in walks Lam, and I'm worried about what he's going to say. Is he going to yell at me right here in front of the doctors and all for choosing Ziggy over him?

Lam looks tired, and I smile at him to get him to smile back. "Hey, it's a girl," is all he says, his voice kind of flat.

"Sarah would love a little girl," I say. "She should go to Sarah, don't you think?"

He shrugs again. "My parents were hoping for a girl—to replace . . ."

"Yeah, I know, Lam, but no kid can replace another one. Not really. And your parents have you. They adore you. You should treat them better."

"I know. I know," Lam says. "Well, whatever you want is okay with me." His face is blank. He's already checked out. It's clear the story of us is over.

When the doctor finishes putting me back together, they wheel me into the recovery room, and before you know it I just totally conk out. They must have put something in my IV fluids, because wow! I'm out!

A while later the doctor is waking me up. He sits on my bed and takes my hand. The lights are off, and it's gloomy in the room. I notice the blinds are drawn. The doctor looks so serious.

"What? What is it? Is Emma Rose okay? Is she dead? What's happened? Why did I go to sleep? I shouldn't have gone to sleep. I should have stayed awake for my baby. It's my fault."

The doctor pats my hand. "She's alive, and she has all her fingers and all her toes. The surgery went fine. You're in great shape."

"But?" I know there's something. I know something's coming.

"Do you know what Down syndrome is?"

"Down syndrome? Yeah, I read about that. That's where the kids all look alike with big lips or tongues or something that makes their mouths hang open a lot, and they've got that bowl haircut and they're retarded, right?"

"Well, something like that, but . . ."

"But, she couldn't have that if that's what you're going to say. That's what old ladies have. They have Down syndrome babies because they're too old and they shouldn't be having babies. I read all about that in this book. I'm sixteen. So it can't be that."

I'm searching the doctor's eyes for some hint that he's kidding, but he's serious.

"You're right, it's rare for a teen to give birth to a Down syndrome baby, but it happens. Of course we'll do the blood test, but we're about ninety-nine point nine percent sure she has it. And as for retardation, every child is different. As she gets older, she'll need to be evaluated. She could be only mildly retarded. Of greater concern right now are her heart and lungs. Many children born with Down syndrome have congenital heart disease or even high blood pressure in the lungs. There are some serious issues that come with a child born with the syndrome." He pauses and sees that I'm crying. The tears leak out the corners of my eyes and spill onto my pillow. He hands me a tissue. "I'm sorry for the shock, Eleanor, but I want you to know that children with Down syndrome usually grow up to be a family's pride and joy. They're usually wonderful people who make you happy just knowing them."

"It's my fault. I took drugs. I smoked and drank those first couple of weeks. It's all my fault. I thought I'd just have a miscarriage like my sister and mother. Why didn't I just have a miscarriage?"

"It's not your fault. It's nobody's fault. Eleanor, if you took drugs and smoked and drank, your baby could have been born with a number of disorders, but Down syndrome isn't one of them. I explained that to your sister."

I look up. "She knows? She blames me, doesn't she? Does everybody know? Where are my parents? Do they know? Does Lam? And the MIL and Ziggy? Does everybody know? What do they think?"

The doctor is nodding while I'm speaking. "Yes, yes, they know, and I explained to them just what I said to you. It's not your family's fault because the Crowe women have a tendency toward miscarriages, and it's not the Lothrops' fault because they had a child born with brain damage. It is an entirely different circumstance. Okay?"

I nod.

The doctor had been sitting on the edge of my bed; now he stands. It's obvious he's ready to get out of here. "I think your parents are saying goodbye to your sister, but they'll be in as soon as they get back."

"Goodbye?"

"That's right. Your parents will come see you in the post-partum room soon, and a nurse will bring your baby to you then. I know you'll want to see her. She's precious."

As soon as the doctor leaves, a nurse comes in and wheels me into the postpartum room. The room is painted blue with a border of children's toys, building blocks, and trucks and such. It's a depressing room. For some reason it's just so depressing. I've been trying to digest the news about Emma Rose, but I can't. I can't quite believe it. The nurse tucks me in and messes with my pillows and tells me I'm going to need lots of rest. I ask when I'm going to see my baby, and she says, "Real soon," but she doesn't look at me when she says it. "Your mother wants to talk to you first—as soon as she's through speaking with the doctor."

I wonder what my mom has to say to the doctor, but the nurse leaves before I can ask, and then in walks Leo with a package in his hands. He looks hilarious because he's wearing a retro jacket and tie. It's a plaid jacket in tan and white and forest green and rust, and he's wearing tan pants and a really loud shirt in red and blue, and a green tie with tan somethings on it. I can't imagine anybody bringing dress clothes to camp. A suit jacket! And I never would have expected to see him here.

"Leo? What are you doing here? Where's Ziggy?"

Leo looks behind him as if he's expecting him to walk through the door, then he turns back to me. "They all left. Mrs. Lothrop and Lam and Ziggy all left."

"Did they say anything? Are they coming back?"

Leo comes over to the bed. "I would think so. I don't know." He smiles. "Hey, how are you?"

"Well, crappy. I feel crappy and I hurt, and I just—I think I just got the worst news." Tears start leaking again, and I try to sit up so I won't soak my pillows anymore, and Leo sets his package down and helps me. Up close I see that his tie has these Greek-like statues with missing arms and heads on it.

"I heard about the baby," he says. "I was there when the doctor came in and told everybody."

"Yeah, and?"

"And everybody was upset."

"And? What else?" I want to know what they said. I want to know that they're coming back and that this is okay.

"Well, I guess your sister and Mrs. Lothrop took it the hardest. Sarah was brokenhearted, really, and Mrs. Lothrop said something about how she couldn't live through that again, whatever that means."

I nod. "Yeah, I bet they were upset. They both want my baby—Emma Rose. That's what I named her."

"That's a pretty name."

"Yeah, I think so. The name was just there. It was like I just plucked it off a name tree—Emma Rose." I'm staring off in the distance picturing this pretty little girl, this pretty Emma Rose, but then I remember she has Down syndrome, and I return to Leo.

"So what did Sarah say? Did she say anything? Did she see the baby?"

"Elly, I don't know if I should be telling you this. Do you really want to know?"

"Yes, and be honest. Please be honest with me, Leo. Please?"

"It's just been such a hard day." He wipes his hand over his face as if he's trying to wipe out the memory of the day from his brain.

He does that, and I remember Banner. How could I have forgotten her so soon? I'm sure this Down syndrome is punishment for her death, and for all the other terrible things I've done in my life. How can I ever forgive myself? I've destroyed so many lives. That's who I am, the destroyer.

"Sarah blames me, doesn't she?" I say. I can't stop the tears from spilling. I dab at them with a tissue, and more just keep coming. I so hate myself.

"Yes, well, she did, because of your using drugs, but your mother and Mrs. Lothrop set her straight about that, and then Sarah blamed your mother."

"Mom?" I sniff and blow my nose. "Why?"

"She yelled at your mother. She said that all the Crowe women are defective. All the miscarriages, and now this."

"Sounds like she was really, really upset."

"Yeah, but Eleanor, I saw the baby. She's beautiful."

My heart skips a beat. "You did? She is?"

Leo pushes the package he brought toward me. "Here, this is for you. Something I made."

I pick up the package. It's wrapped in a grocery bag, and the

Hannaford grocery name is right on the front of the package. It feels like it's soft inside. "I bet I know what this is," I say.

I tear open the package, and I find a knitted baby blanket in white and pink and yellow and blue pastels, with matching baby booties and a bonnet.

"Leo, you shouldn't have. They're so beautiful." I rub the blanket against my cheek. "And it's so soft. You're the sweetest, really. And look at you. Where did you get that coat and tie?"

"I brought it with me. I have a wedding to go to as soon as camp is over."

"But why do you have it on now?"

Leo shrugs. "I guess I thought it was a special occasion, so I wanted to dress up."

I shake my head and smile, even though I'm still crying and feeling sorry for myself. "You really are the weirdest, Leo."

My mom comes in, and she asks Leo if she and I can be alone, and I feel bad because Leo got all dressed up and brought me a gift and came all the way down here from the camp.

"I'd better go, anyway," Leo says.

"But I wanted to know about what's going on at the camp. Leo, last night—I was with Banner. I mean, not when she—not when she drowned, but earlier. I need to talk to you about it, okay? Will you come back?"

Leo nods. "Tomorrow's my day off. I'll stop by in the morning. I think the police will be talking to you. That's what Mr. Lothrop said. Haley told him you had been with Banner last night."

"The police? Oh, no, please. Why do they always have to pop up in my life?"

"They're just questioning everybody who might know something. It's pretty sad back at the camp right now."

"Yeah, I bet it is. I should be there. I feel like I should be there, which is strange, because this morning all I wanted to do was run away."

"I blame myself," Leo says. "I just didn't notice how much pain she was in. I knew she got picked on and she could drive you crazy the way she cowered and skulked around the crafts hut, but I just didn't pay her enough attention."

"You!" I'm so surprised to hear this. "Leo, you pay attention to everybody. If you didn't even know what was going on in her head, then I don't know who would. And anyway, you're not to blame. I am. For real. She told me about her parents not liking her and stuff, and I went and told her to just show 'em. And look what she did. She showed them all right. She showed all of us."

Leo hung his head and shook it. "You know who's really hurting is Ashley Wilson. She's going to need a lot of help getting over this." He looks at me. "I guess we all played a part in her suicide." He pats my leg. "I really need to get back now. I should be there. You take care."

I tell Leo to be sure to ask Ziggy to come see me tomorrow sometime, and he says he will. He kisses my forehead, and then he leaves.

CHAPTER TWENTY-SEVEN

I FORGOT that my mother was even in the room when I was talking to Leo. I'm embarrassed that she heard us talking about Banner.

She comes over and sits down on the side of my bed. She has this really sad look in her eyes. "It sounds like you have had a really hard day, Elly-belly. So you were close to this girl? This Banner?"

I shrug. "I guess. She confided in me, and I tried to help her. I tried to get her to loosen up in these dance classes I've been teaching." I look at my mom, and she looks surprised. Back when I lived in Kenya, I wouldn't do anything to help out at the orphanage. I wouldn't go near the place. I was a real pain in the butt to my parents, so I understand my mom's surprise.

"I know, me, teaching dance, or me teaching anything—

what a laugh, huh? But Mom, I wasn't half bad, I don't think. I mean, I don't know much about real dance, but we just had fun in my class. The kids got some exercise and we had fun. Banner, I think, really loved my class."

Mom leans in and kisses my forehead the way Leo did, the way Ziggy did. "I'm proud of you, Eleanor. It sounds like you're really involved with those campers." She brushes back my hair with her hand.

I nod, and we sit together silently for a minute or so, and then I think about Emma Rose and I wonder why a nurse hasn't brought her in to see me yet.

"Leo said you heard about Emma Rose," I say.

"Who?" Mom looks puzzled. "Do you mean Banner?"

"No. Emma Rose—my baby."

Mom nods, and her face falls. She looks sad again.

"I want to see her. The nurse is supposed to bring her in."

"Elly, I don't think that's such a good idea, under the circumstances, do you? Maybe it's best if you don't see her." She takes a deep breath.

"Don't see her? But Mom, why?"

"Oh, honey, I'm so sorry. I'm just so sorry."

Mom looks as if Emma Rose had been born without a head.

"But I want to see her. I need to see her. The doctor says she's precious, and Leo says she's beautiful. I want to see her."

Mom pats my hand, and I pull it away.

"Let's talk first."

"What's there to talk about, Mom? I already know about Sarah. She doesn't want the baby anymore. She's left, hasn't she? Is she coming back?"

"You can understand how upset she is, can't you, El? She was counting on this baby. She's got a nursery at home, and she's bought all kinds of baby clothes. She was counting on it more than any of us realized."

"Well, it's her own fault. I only told her today that I wanted her to have it, and I told her that the Lothrops wanted the baby, too, and now look, neither of them want her. Right? The Lothrops have already had one brain-damaged child, and they don't want another one, right?"

My mother nods.

"It's like she's damaged goods or something. They were swarming all over me when they thought I was giving birth to the perfect child, but really, what child is ever perfect? Look at Lam. Look at me. Look at Sarah, even. She's not so perfect. Oh, no, I see her in a whole new light now. She couldn't even stay and tell me herself that she no longer wanted the baby. Everybody just ran away soon as they heard about Emma Rose. So, it's not my fault. I never led her on in any way, Mom."

Mom nods and she's listening, but she's staring out the window. The blinds are open now, and I don't remember seeing anyone open them. I see mountains and a blue sky and sunshine. "I think I may have led her on," my mom says, bringing me back to attention. "Your father and I were so sure you'd come around, and you did. You did, Elly. You did the right thing offering your sister your baby."

Somehow I don't think so. I don't think saying it's the right thing is the right thing to say. It makes me feel funny. Is it right to just hand over your baby to someone else?

My mom has tears in her eyes, and it looks like she's really struggling to keep from letting go, and I think maybe she's heartbroken as much as Sarah is.

I take her hand in mine. They're rough hands. My mom works hard in Kenya. She likes the hard work, though. She's never been one to sit still.

"I'm really sorry I blew it again, Mom. Maybe this baby is—maybe I'm being punished for all the horrible things I've done."

Mom's face changes, and she looks suddenly exasperated with me. "Come on, Eleanor, it doesn't work like that. It just happened, okay?" She wipes her eyes and goes and gets a tissue and blows her nose, and it's like blowing her nose has cleared her thinking, too, because her voice changes and she sounds all businesslike all of a sudden. "Now, we need to make a decision about what we want to do about the baby. I was thinking of adoption."

Mom studies my face and waits for my reaction.

"Adoption? You mean *you* want her?"

Mom's eyes widen with horror. "No! No, Elly, I can't do that."

"But you work with African children with AIDS all the time. Emma Rose just has a different kind of problem."

"No, Eleanor," she says, and the way she says it, I know she means *No way, José.* "Working with orphans is not the same as adopting an infant. I'm not up for the challenge of raising a child with Down syndrome. And it *is* a challenge."

"So, who adopts her, then? The Lothrops? Sarah? Who?"

Mom straightens her back and takes another deep breath. "Elly, I think we should give her to an adoption agency."

"What?" I try to sit up straighter, too, only my gut hurts, so I fall back against my pillows again. "No, Ma. No way. What if she never got adopted? What would happen to her then? She'd be all alone—no. Not my baby. I want to see her. I want to see Emma Rose."

"Now, Elly, listen to me—"

"No! I want to see her. Have you had her taken away or something? I want her." I'm wailing now. "Please. Please let me see her. I have a right to see her. Mom, please!"

"All *right*, Eleanor!" Mom says. "All right, but you need to understand. Raising a child on your own, or even with Lam's help, at your age, would be such an uphill struggle, but a child with Down syndrome, it's just about impossible. She's always going to need special care—special doctors to look after her heart and her lungs and her eyes, special schooling to keep her on track, and her growth will be limited. She might not be able to do all the things you do—all the things you take for granted—

reading and writing, and of course these specialists you'll need will cost lots of money. Think about it. Adoption is the best thing for her."

"Mom! I want to see her!"

Just as I say this, another mother is wheeled into the room. She's smiling, and her husband is walking beside her, holding her hand. "I'll bring your baby in in just a minute," the nurse says as she bustles around, helping the woman get herself settled.

I've stopped wailing and me and Mom just watch all this, and I know that that's the way it's supposed to be; a grown man and a grown woman, happily married, and happy about the birth of their perfectly made baby.

"Could you—could you bring me my baby, too?" I call out. The nurse looks at my mom instead of me, and my heart just stops. I'm so sure my mom has had the baby taken away already.

Mom smiles and nods, and the nurse nods back. "Okay, dear," she says, looking finally at me. "I'll be right in with her."

I can't wait. I just can't wait. A minute or two later, the nurse is back and she has a bundle in her arms, but it's the other woman's bundle. I'm just about ready to jump out of my skin, but then in walks another nurse with another bundle. My bundle.

The nurse walks toward me, and I stretch out my arms. She's carrying Emma Rose. She's bringing me my Emma Rose.

"Now, here we are," the nurse says. "A sweet baby girl."

I lift back the blanket and there she is, Emma Rose. She's

perfect. She's perfect! She's got the sweetest little face with happy-looking eyes. They're so happy looking I laugh, and Mom comes and sits beside me and she laughs, too. Oh, and she has these perfectly tiny little hands with tiny little fingernails, and I touch her hand and it's so soft and warm. "Hey," I say, "I know you. And you know me, don't you, baby cakes? We've known each other for months, haven't we? Yes, we have." I lift her face to mine and feel her breath on my cheek.

Ah, Emma Rose. You're my baby girl. You came from me. You belong right here with me. I'll never abandon you. No, I will never give you away. No way. How silly to think that I ever considered it. I'm so glad Sarah's gone. I'm so glad she doesn't want you, because she can't have you, and neither can Lam's parents. Nobody can have you. You need me, and I need you.

"Are you planning to breastfeed?" the nurse asks me, and I see my mother shake her head, but I jump in and say, "Yes. Yes, that's what's best for the baby. I read about that. It gives the baby all kinds of health protection and stuff, but is it the same for a Down syndrome baby?"

"Oh, yes. It can be even more important. Breastfeeding is good for the baby's physical and mental development. It can make a difference all its life, but with a D.S. baby it's a bit more difficult to do."

I can hardly take my eyes off of Emma Rose, but I glance at the nurse and ask her what she means.

"A Down syndrome baby doesn't have as well-developed

muscle tone, so she may have trouble sucking at first, but don't give up. You can supplement or use a breast pump for the first couple of weeks, and then I'm sure she'll be just fine on the nipple."

I think of how a couple of days ago if anyone had used sucking and nipple in the same sentence, it would be in some kind of dirty joke and I would be rolled over laughing, and now I'm listening to her like what she's saying is perfectly natural.

The nurse leaves, and I say right away, "Mom, I'm keeping her. I'm keeping Emma Rose. I have to. Look at her. She's perfect. Isn't she perfect?"

My mom shakes her head and tears up again. "Oh, Elly, do you always have to do everything the hard way? You just don't know what you're getting yourself into."

"But, Mom, look at her." I raise the baby up to her, and the baby makes this little tiny noise.

Mom takes the baby in her arms and smiles down at her. "She's precious. She is." She touches the baby's nose. And laughs.

"See? You love her already. So do I."

Mom stops laughing and tilts her head at me. "Of course I do. But honey, she needs more than what we can give her. You want the best for her. I know you do. Elly, think of your life. You're sixteen. You've got your own problems to deal with. Your husband got arrested today."

I look up, surprised.

"Yes, that's right. I know all about it," Mom says. "I also know you would have been arrested, too, if you weren't scheduled to have a baby this morning."

"But I was innocent. Really I was. Yeah, okay, I know I was considering it, but I wouldn't have done anything. I wouldn't have—I swear!"

"See, Elly? There's doubt. You're still getting yourself into trouble. Even caring for a normal baby is beyond you right now, but a child with Down syndrome? Honey, you need to consider her life; her *whole* life, not just this moment and how cute she is."

I look at my baby's round little head, the broad forehead, the happy eyes, the teeniest little nose and little red lips—I want her. I want to take care of her—feed her and bathe her and change her diapers and teach her how to walk and talk and read, because I know my little girl will learn to read. I want her so badly. I can't explain it—why I feel so strongly—but I do. I hear what my mom is saying, and I know she's right. I know it. I'm trouble. I want what's best for Emma Rose, but there's something, something inside me that's telling me that this is what I'm meant to do. As if my whole life up to this point was in preparation for having her and caring for her. I'm meant to be a mother to this child. I know it. I can feel it. I know I can do it.

"You have high school to finish, and then hopefully college to attend, and where will you live? How will you support yourself?"

I think of Ziggy. My sweet, loving Ziggy. He said he'd

take care of me and the baby. He's the only one who wants both of us.

"I'll find a way," I say. "And anyway, I can stay at the cabin till I find something better, or until you find a new home to rent."

"Oh, El, there's no cabin anymore. The Lothrops are out of the picture."

"Out of the picture? Totally? Because I didn't want Lam in the delivery room?"

"No." My mother gives me this pitying look and smoothes back my hair.

"What? I can't live there anymore because Emma Rose has Down syndrome?"

"Yes, that's right, sweetie. It's just too painful for the Lothrops. She told me a little of what they went through when they lost their first child. They're afraid of getting attached and then—"

"And then Emma Rose dies? But I've seen grown-up people with Down syndrome. My baby isn't going to die. No way."

Mom's eyes show worry, but she covers up by smiling at the baby and making cooing sounds.

"But Lam's her father! They're her grandparents. You're her grandparents. Really, I don't understand how you all can just reject her like this."

"Oh, El, it has nothing to do with rejection. It's about doing what's best for the baby."

"Well, okay, but I can live with you and Dad, can't I, until I find a job and a place of my own?"

Mom's whole face just sags. "Elly, I think you misunderstood my letter. We're not here to stay. We just came for the delivery, but we've got to go back to Kenya. So many people are depending on us—a whole community. It's where we belong."

"But, what about me? I'm depending on you, too."

Mom starts to say something, but then the nurse comes in and says it's time to take the baby back and that I need to rest now. I hate to let go of Emma Rose. I'm so afraid my mom's going to tell them to take her away and give her to an orphanage or something. Before she leaves I make her promise that she won't do anything, and she does. "She's your child, Elly. I won't do anything without your consent. But think it over. Pray about it. Listen to God. I think you'll realize adoption is the right thing to do."

She kisses me, and leaves.

Everybody's gone. It's quiet. Even on the other side of the room, where the other mother rests, it's quiet. I'm left alone with my thoughts.

My first thought is that my mom is always saying something like, "I think you'll see it's the right thing to do." She always knows what the right thing to do is, and I never do. Is it because she's a mother or because she's got an in with God, or just because she's always had her head screwed on straight? If I'm a mother to Emma Rose, will I suddenly know all the right things to do? Is that how it works?

Mom always thinks doing the right thing is so important. "Do the right thing, Elly," she says, or "I expect you to do the right thing," or "We always knew you'd do the right thing." How? How did she know? Did she really, or does she just say that as a kind of bribe, or as a way of persuading me to do what she wants me to do? Because always the right thing to do is the exact same thing as what she wants, and it's not usually what I want. I always seem to want the wrong thing, and now I want Emma Rose—oh, yes, I want her so badly, and that's the wrong thing to want. I'm supposed to want to give her away. At first the right thing was to give her to Sarah, but now that's not the right thing anymore. Emma Rose has Down syndrome, so now there's a new right thing. Now the right thing to do is to give her away to strangers and maybe never see her again. But that's just impossible. How could I do that? How could I risk nobody ever adopting her? If my own family doesn't want her, who's to say a stranger will? How could putting her up for adoption be a better choice for her than keeping her? And how could I stand it knowing that I abandoned my baby? I couldn't bear thinking of her being alone. I know about being alone. I know about loneliness, and no, I can't do that to Emma Rose. I remember Banner. How alone she must have felt to want to kill herself—how desperately alone.

Do the right thing. Do the right thing. I wish those words would get out of my head. Why don't I ever do the right thing? I did the wrong thing last night when I was in the break hut with Banner. Show 'em, I said, show 'em. That was so not the right thing to do. How do I live with that? How do I live with that kind of guilt? I see Banner in the lake with her hair spread out all around her head like a fan of light, a halo, and then she's on land and her eyes are open and she's staring up at the sky, looking toward heaven. That's someplace I'll never see, that's for sure, but I hope, if there is a heaven the way my parents think there is, that Banner is there.

My thoughts go round and round. I sleep some and cry some and think about my baby some and try to figure out what to do, and then I sleep some more. Then it's nighttime, and I eat dinner and I get to see my Emma Rose one more time. I try to breastfeed her, but it doesn't work. The nurse tells me that it's okay. Then the nurse shows me this contraption she calls a breast pump and teaches me how to use it so the baby can have my breast milk even if she can't take the breast. That's how the nurse talks. "Even if she can't take the breast." If Lam could only hear her, he'd die laughing.

Before she leaves, the nurse reminds me that the doctor will be in to see me in the morning.

I ask when I can get the catheter out of me because they forgot to take it out, and she says no, they didn't.

"We'll take it out tomorrow," she says on her way out the door. Then she pauses and adds, "If you're good." She winks and leaves, and I wonder if she's been talking to my mother.

CHAPTER TWENTY-EIGHT

I THOUGHT if I dreamed, I would dream about Emma Rose, my beautiful baby, but instead I dream about Banner. She's whispering something to me, only I can't hear her. I keep asking her to speak louder so I can hear, but she just whispers again. She puts the necklace she made around my neck and whispers something else, and still I can't hear her. I want to hear her. Why can't I hear her? "Speak up! Speak up, Banner. Tell me what you're trying to say."

I wake up all in a tangle in my bed, and my belly hurts where they cut me open. I'm crying again and I can't stop, but I try to be quiet about it so I don't wake the mother asleep on the other side of the curtain.

I get breakfast and painkillers, and the nurse tells me to get up and walk as much as I can today. She says after the doctor has seen me, they'll take the catheter out. I can't wait.

I ask to see Emma Rose. "Let's just let the doctor visit you first," she says.

"But the lady next door got to see her baby."

"That's different. She and her baby will be going home today. You've got two more days. Don't worry. Everything's fine."

The nurse pushes me back against my pillows so that I'll lie down and relax, but I don't feel relaxed. Shouldn't I be trying to feed Emma Rose again? I'm anxious to see the doctor. It seems nothing happens until I see him, so let's get the show on the road. Let's see him already. Where is he? It's six in the morning. The hospital is bustling with activity, so the doctor must be here somewhere. Let's see him. The nurse hands me the breast pump to use again so they can feed my baby with a bottle of my breast milk. I want to feed her. Why can't I at least feed her the bottle?

* * *

It's nine in the morning, and still no doctor and no Emma Rose—and I still have my damn catheter in. A new nurse is on duty now, a male nurse. I ask him when the doctor will be in to see me, and he says soon. "Well, what the hell does 'soon' mean?" I shout at him. "I've been waiting all morning."

The nurse whispers, and it reminds me of my dream. "Shhh," he says. "You're not his only patient, little one."

While he's saying this, a man, an old geezer with a little bit of white hair on a mostly bald head, comes in and looks around. He's short and wearing a pair of black slacks, a white shirt, and one of those beanie caps on his head—a Jewish hat thing.

He comes over to my bed and clasps his hands together and kind of bows a little bit. "Eleanor Crowe?"

"Yeah?" I pull my sheet and blanket up to my neck and slide down in my bed a little. He reminds me of an undertaker. I wonder if he's about to tell me Emma Rose died in her sleep. Please don't tell me that. Please!

"I'm Rabbi Yosef."

Rabbi? Oh, no! A rabbi. Oh, yeah, now I get it. When I filled out my admission forms, the nurse asked me what religion I was, and I thought it was none of her business, so I said Jewish just for the hell of it. Now I'm probably going to get arrested for impersonating a Jewish person. The rabbi's probably going to quiz me to see if I'm Jewish, then have the police haul me away as soon as he realizes I don't know beans about being Jewish. Well, these police can just stand in line with the rest of the force, because I'm about to get hauled away for pushing Banner Sorensen into suicide and probably as soon as I step foot out of the hospital the officer from Bethel who picked me up yesterday will be waiting to haul me off, too.

"I'm not Jewish," I say. "I lied."

The rabbi sits down. "You did, did you?"

"Yeah. Sorry. I didn't know what I was doing."

"Well, now that I'm here, maybe I can help you?"

"Help me? Help me how? I don't need a rabbi. I need a grief counselor. That's what I need."

The rabbi nods. He nods really slowly. Then he smiles. "I

am trained in grief counseling, Eleanor Crowe. Is there sorrow around the birth of your baby?"

"Okay, look, no offense. There was a little girl at the camp where I work, and she just died. She killed herself, and I need to sort out some thoughts, but if I talk to you, I don't want all this God stuff brought in, okay?"

"But God is already in it. I don't bring Him in. He is already here."

"See? Like that. Go easy on that kind of talk."

The rabbi raises his brows. "What happened, Eleanor? Tell me about the little girl who killed herself."

And so I do. I tell this geezer everything, including how I sometimes just wanted to kick Banner in the butt for being such a wimpy crybaby. I tell him about my talk with Banner in the break hut. I tell how she must have thought I meant show 'em by killing herself. By the time I'm through telling him everything, I'm in a pool of tears.

Rabbi Yosef hasn't said anything the whole time, but now he takes my hand and just holds it.

I grab a tissue off the little tray table I've got on the side of the bed and with my free hand blow my nose. I grab another and wipe my eyes. "I just never realized how desperate she was. I mean, to want to kill yourself, that's as desperate as it gets."

"You want to feel better about it."

"Yes."

"You want not to hurt so much."

"Yes," I say. "Yes, it hurts so much. It does."

"You want not to feel like it was your fault?"

"Right. Yes. That's right."

"Just let yourself hurt, Eleanor. It is a painful thing that's happened. You're supposed to hurt."

Okay, I didn't expect him to say that. I thought he'd tell me what my parents always tell me; that God will forgive me, no matter what.

Then he asks, "What does the pain feel like?"

"What? What do you mean?"

"Feel it. Feel the sadness. Feel the loss of this young girl. Feel the guilt."

"I do. I do feel all of that."

"Really feel it, Eleanor."

"Yeah, I do." I close my eyes and I tell myself to really feel it, as if I haven't been really feeling it already. This guy's a nut case.

Feel it. Feel it. I feel this spot in the middle of my chest, that's where it hurts the most. I feel all caved in there. I tell the rabbi this.

"Yes. Yes," he says. "Keep feeling it."

I try to keep feeling it, but it's weird about trying. The more I try, the more the feeling seems to just kind of dissolve away. I think about how guilty I feel.

I open my eyes. "I shouldn't try to get rid of my guilt," I say. "I am guilty. I should feel that. I don't want to not feel guilty, otherwise . . ."

I can't finish what I was about to say, because I don't know how to, but something is dawning on me.

"Yes, Eleanor. What would happen if you didn't feel guilty?"

"It would be like I didn't care, and I do care. I care a lot."

"And feeling guilty lets you know how much you care?"

"Yeah. That's right. I can't just go around feeling guilt-free. What if I did that? My mother would kill me. Everybody would kill me."

"So you feel guilty to keep people from being angry with you." He says these things like a statement, not a question, but I answer him like he's asking me.

"I feel guilty because it's the right way to feel." I put my hand over my mouth. I can't believe I just said that. "I mean, I feel guilty because I am guilty, because I do feel guilty, because it's the right . . ." I said it again. I look at the rabbi. "Shouldn't I feel guilty?"

"It's natural, sure," he says, nodding. "Go ahead, feel guilty. Feel as guilty as you can."

He's got some kind of game here, but I can't quite guess what it is. Somehow I figure I'm not going to feel guilty by the end of it, so I'm willing to play along. I close my eyes again and try to feel as guilty as I can. I think of Banner trusting me. I think of the way she leaned on my shoulder and looked up at me. I remember telling her to show 'em. How stupid could I be? I'm so stupid! Here it is. Here is the guilt. I feel it in my head and shoulders. My head feels like it's on fire, but the more I'm aware of this feeling, the more the feeling starts to leave, just like the painful feeling I had before. It's crazy. I get scared. I do. I feel really scared. I open my eyes. "But if I don't feel guilty for what happened to Banner, won't I feel guilty for not feeling guilty?"

"What does guilt do for you? What does it do for Banner?"

"Guilt tells you you've done something wrong."

The rabbi nods. "Good. Good. Then what?"

"What do you mean?" I wish this guy would just talk plainly or just give me some advice and leave. My head is starting to hurt.

"Well, why carry the guilt around with you? Once it's served its purpose, what use is it?"

"It's a reminder. It's a reminder of what I did wrong, so I won't do it again," I guess.

"You think you will do it again? Do you think the next time someone asks you for help, you will be able to help that person better because you feel guilty?"

"No. I might be able to help because I had that experience with Banner."

"So it's the learning experience that you need to remember. And I would think you would like to remember Banner, your friend."

"Yeah. I guess I don't need to hold on to the guilt. That's what you're saying."

The rabbi nods.

"That's cool."

"Remember Banner," he says.

"I will, always."

"Good. That's good."

I feel better. I feel lots better. I smile. "I thought you were going to tell me that God will forgive me, no matter what."

"Ah. Do you need me to say that?"

"No. I hear that all the time. It's just—you didn't mention God once. Is that allowed? I mean, aren't you supposed to because you're a rabbi? Won't you get in trouble?"

The rabbi stands and puts his hands on his back and arches it. "I think I'm safe," he says. "I'm sorry, but I have to go now."

"Will you come back to see me? I mean, could you?" I ask. "There's my baby. I have questions about my baby, and I don't know what to do. Maybe you could help me with that, too? I'm here for today and tomorrow and maybe the next day."

"I'll be back." He holds out his hand and I take it, and we shake. "It's been good talking to you, Eleanor Crowe."

"Thank you. You, too."

The rabbi leaves, and I lie in bed just thinking about everything for a while, and it's funny, he never talked about God, but I feel as if God was here, as if maybe I had been talking to God all along.

CHAPTER TWENTY-NINE

THE POLICE come to see me and question me about Banner. I tell them the truth—the whole truth—because now that I have Emma Rose, I need to stop lying all the time. I'm scared and I'm crying, and I expect them to tell me that they're going to arrest me, but they don't. They just sit there and take notes, and then when I'm through telling them everything, they pat my hand and leave. The end. Then, before I can recover from their visit, the doctor finally shows up. A nurse had removed my bandage earlier, and now he checks my belly where he cut me open and says it looks good. I can leave it uncovered. Then he tells me Emma Rose had some trouble breathing last night but that she's fine now. They ran some tests on her, but everything checked out okay. All I want to know is when can I see her, and all he says is, "Soon." He pats my leg. "Let's get that catheter out first, okay? And I expect to see you up and walking the halls today. Go slowly, and if you're too dizzy, sit down." He pats my leg again, and he's gone. His whole visit lasted all of two minutes.

A nurse comes in to remove the catheter. Ahhh! Then she brings me Emma Rose. My Emma Rose. I'm extra glad because my breasts are so engorged and leaking—again. They want Emma. She puts her warm mouth on my breast and she tries to suckle, but she's not strong enough. I feed Emma Rose with a bottle, and then I burp her and feel her warm head. It feels so alive. She's so alive. I hug her and kiss her and play with her tiny hands and feet.

I'm left alone to play with Emma Rose. Oh, I just love her. I want to show her off. I want to show the world my baby. I can't wait to see Ziggy. We have so much to talk about. We're in love. We're so in love, and now we have Emma Rose. I want him to know this. I'm not sure he knows that we're keeping her. Oh, I can't wait for Ziggy to see her. When he sees her, he's going to sweep both of us into his arms and he's going to say, "Come with me to Boston. I'll take care of you. I'll take care of you and Emma Rose."

I'm lying in bed with my baby in my arms, and I'm half awake and half asleep, dreaming of me and Ziggy and Emma Rose in a cute little apartment in Boston. My chest of drawers, the teal one with the painted flower bouquets and red glass knobs, is standing in the corner of our bedroom next to the crib. It's so wonderful and we're so happy.

Ziggy says something, but I don't quite hear him. "What?"

"You're beautiful," he says. I smile and open my eyes, but it's not Ziggy, it's Leo, and he's got his video camera and he's filming me.

I wave him away. "Leo, I look terrible. I just got my catheter out."

He turns the camera off for a second and smiles at me. "I'm not filming that end. Now, smile and show everybody Emma Rose." He lifts the camera again and turns it back on.

I remove the blanket from Emma Rose's head and lift her up. "This is my baby. This is my Emma Rose," I say. "Say hello, Emma Rose. Say hello to all the campers." I put her in my lap so she's sitting up, and I take her hand and wave it at the camera.

"You want to hold her?" I ask Leo.

"Sure."

"Be careful, though. She's brand-new. She's delicate."

"I've held plenty of babies before, Elly. Don't worry." He sets the camera on my bed and takes Emma Rose in his arms. She looks so teeny-tiny next to him.

"How have you held plenty of babies?" I ask. I swing my legs over the side of the bed and slowly stand up. I do feel a little dizzy, and my belly, where I was cut open, feels really heavy. I reach down and hold myself there, as if I still had a baby inside.

"I have eleven brothers and sisters. I'm the oldest."

"Eleven! That means your mother had twelve kids. Wow! Twelve kids. Poor lady. But no wonder you're so good with the campers. You're used to it."

"Not all of them were babies. We're all adopted. Some of

my brothers and sisters we got when they were older, like three and four. But we've had some babies, too."

"I'd think you'd be so sick of kids by now."

Leo smiles at Emma Rose and puts her against his chest and pats her back. "Ay-uh, you'd think."

His fingers are long and slender, and his hand covers her whole back, practically.

"Isn't she tiny?" I ask, and he nods.

We decide to take a walk, but just as we get to the door, the nurse is back to take Emma Rose away again. I can't wait till it's just me and Emma Rose and Ziggy alone, with no nurses trying to take her away.

Leo and I go for a walk down the hall and out to where the waiting room is. He tells me a bit about his life on the farm with his parents and brothers and sisters. They grow blueberries and make maple syrup. "I love maple sugaring time. We get a lot of kids who come to the farm and want maple-syrup snow."

"Yeah, my parents and sister and I used to go to a farm for that. I loved how they'd pour the maple syrup on the snow and we'd scoop it up, and the syrup would be all thick and sugary."

We get silent after that, and I'm wondering where Ziggy is and where my parents are. Yesterday, before the baby was born, everybody was hovering around all over me, but now it's just Leo.

"So," I say, "do you think Ziggy will be by soon? And have you seen Lam? Have you spoken to him? What's he saying about everything?"

"Lam's gone. He took off."

"Took off where?"

Leo rubs his chin, and I notice he's growing a beard. It's coming in reddish brown. Funny I hadn't noticed earlier. "I don't know," he says about Lam. "Probably a friend's house."

"Why did he leave?"

"I don't know, Elly. I really don't know his business. Lam and I have never been close." Leo sounds irritated.

"Sorry," I say. I put my hand on his, and he takes my hand and squeezes it.

"No, *I'm* sorry. I didn't get much sleep last night. There's lots going on at the camp. The Lothrops are trying to keep business as usual these last days of camp, but lots of kids have gone home already. The mood is pretty down right now. The Lothrops are asking the parents to bring their kids back for the final night when we'll do the video and talent show and pass out awards and badges to the campers. It will be good to end on a high note. I think I've got some good footage, too." He lifts his camera.

The talent show—I had forgotten all about it. "I was really hoping Banner would be in the talent show. I really only came up with the idea because of her. I wanted everybody to see her dance."

Leo squeezes my hand again. "I know. I remember you telling me that. You did your best, Elly."

Then we're silent again, and again I think of Ziggy.

"So, have you talked to Ziggy?"

Leo studies a really ugly picture on the wall. It's supposed to be an autumn scene, but the colors are so muddy it's just de-pressing. "Yeah, I talked to him. He says he's got a really busy schedule today. He's got some campers to deal with who are still having trouble with Banner's death. He doesn't feel right leav-ing them." He looks at me now, and he looks embarrassed, like he's embarrassed for Ziggy not being here.

"Oh, okay. Yeah. I'm being selfish. I know I am. I just don't know what's going on—at the camp, and with Ziggy. I wish I could leave and go back there with you. Of course I have Emma Rose to think of now, too. I can't leave until she's ready."

"So you plan to keep her, then? Your mother was saying something about adoption."

I look down at my hands. My fingernails are dirty, and I wonder how they got that way. I hate that I touched Emma Rose with dirty hands. I need a bath.

"Yeah, Mom says adoption is the right thing to do. 'Cause I can't give the baby everything she's going to need, like doctors and special teachers and money to pay for everything. I'll be a single parent, and that's hard enough with a normal child, but Emma Rose will need special care all her life—blah, blah, blah."

"She has a point there," Leo says. "Emma Rose may never be able to grow up and live on her own. You don't know yet, but that's a possibility."

I get to my feet and hold on to my belly again. "Of course you'd say that. You were adopted. Of course you'd say that." I feel pissed.

Leo stands, too, and he looks pissed right back, which is

a new one, because Leo never gets pissed. "For your information, I don't always think giving your child up for adoption is the best idea. Some of us get stuck in bad foster homes or horrible orphanages, and lots of kids never get adopted. It's not the perfect solution everyone thinks it is. And some of my brothers and sisters have problems, big problems, because of things that happened to them before my parents got them. And one of my brothers my parents got when he was three days old, and he's still messed up. So, no, I don't think just because I was adopted that you should put your baby up for adoption, too."

I touch Leo's arm. "I'm sorry. I didn't know. I'm sorry, Leo."

He lets out his breath and forces a smile. "I know you are. It just gets me sometimes. No offense, Elly, but girls get pregnant and figure it's no sweat, they'll just give it away. They'll just give it up for adoption. They figure some nice happy couple's going to take them the very next day and everything's going to be beautiful. But adoptive couples get divorced just like other couples, or they turn out to be abusive, or a foster parent abuses them. It's not perfect. It's not a perfect solution."

I think of the parenting magazines with all the pretty people and the nice sane advice they give for even the craziest problems. It all sounds so easy in the magazines.

"Nothing's perfect. Nobody's perfect," I say, and I think that maybe I expect life to be perfect, and Sarah and my parents to be perfect, and me to be perfect, but I'm so far from perfect it makes me hate myself a thousand times a day. Emma Rose isn't perfect, but she is to me. She's special to me. I accept her as she is. Why can't I accept myself?

"We just have to accept that life is perfectly imperfect," Leo says.

"My parents say that life only looks imperfect, but that's because we can't see the whole picture. Only God sees the whole picture. We see through a glass darkly."

Just then my mom and dad come into the room. They look annoyed. "We've been looking all over for you," Dad says. Mom walks over and kisses my cheek.

"I'm supposed to walk around today so I don't get blood clots in my legs," I say. Then I introduce my parents to Leo, but they remind me that they've already met.

I wonder what my dad thinks of Leo, who's dressed in these goofball golf shorts made out of patchy material in all different colors. Also he's not wearing his Hawaiian shirt anymore, just the WeightAway shirt, with all the signatures on the back. I notice that he and my dad are the same height and build—real stringy with broad shoulders.

Dad acts happy to see him again and he shakes his hand, so I figure he likes him. That's a first for my parents, actually liking one of my friends. We all talk a little bit, and Leo explains the back of his shirt. "The last week of camp, I wear it uncovered so the campers can see all the names and point out their own. They get a kick out of it." Leo shrugs, and Dad and Mom think it's a great way to encourage good deeds—one of their favorite topics. I smile. I'm happy to see the three of them together talking like adults and not the way my parents always were with Lam—like he was just this evil dude trying to lure their daughter into sinful deeds. I'm glad they came back, and I think that maybe, after they've gotten used to the idea, they'll want to stay in the States and help me raise Emma Rose.

"So, where have you guys been?" I ask them during the lull in the conversation. "I thought you'd be here early this morning. It feels like everybody's deserting me." I laugh, kind of, but it does feel like that.

"We've been exploring options for your baby and talking to a social worker."

I frown. As far as I'm concerned, there are no other options. I'm going to raise Emma Rose. "So you're really going back to Kenya, then?"

Mom and Dad exchange glances, and I know of course they will. That's their life's work. I get that, only I guess I kind of wish I was their life's work.

Leo says he's got to be going, and he gives me a hug. I thank him for coming, and I tell him how much it means to me. "You're a great friend, Leo."

"You, too, El," he says. "See you."

It doesn't take long once I'm left with my mom and dad to get right into a discussion about putting Emma Rose up for adoption. My mom has bought a book about caring for Down syndrome children.

"If you'll just read this, Eleanor, you'll see all the work that's involved. It's very, very difficult, even if you're an adult and you're married. Don't ruin your life. Don't ruin Emma Rose's. Do the right thing, El."

"Raising any child is difficult. It's the hardest thing you'll ever do in your life," my dad adds. "You're just not ready for the responsibility yet."

On and on, and blah, blah, blah.

I don't tell them about Ziggy. They'd probably think living in Boston with him was the wrong thing to do. But Ziggy wants me and the baby. He told me so, and I know he'll take real good care of us. I'll get a job, and he'll create music, and someday he'll become famous and we'll live out in Hollywood, and Emma Rose and I will be hanging out with movie stars and their kids. That would show my parents. I just need to talk to Ziggy, then we can come together to my parents and tell them our plans— our dreams. I've got dreams! For once I don't mind looking into the future, because now the future includes Emma Rose. It includes Emma Rose, Ziggy, and me—a family.

CHAPTER THIRTY

∽

ANOTHER DAY in the hospital goes by, and the only visitor besides my parents is Leo. Ziggy's helping with the talent show and still dealing with the grieving campers. Even Leo can't stay long, because he comes on his break, and that just lasts an hour, and it takes twenty minutes to get here from the camp. I feel sad and lonely and strange, and I don't know what the strangeness is, except I'm still hurting over Banner's death. Every time I hurt or feel guilty, I try to really feel it the way Rabbi Yosef said to do, and it helps for a while, but it comes back again, so I find I have to keep "feeling" it over and over, just to get through the day. The one bright spot is Emma Rose, but now that's gotten all smeared with sadness because my parents are getting to me, and maybe they're right. I've read through most of the book on Down syndrome my mom bought me, and yeah, it does sound hard, really hard. Emma Rose will need to have physical therapy and speech and language therapy and occupational therapy, and the book says I should sign her up right away for this—like right now! The sooner the better. The one good thing is that the state and my insurance will pay for this, although the book said a lot of parents of Down syndrome babies have difficulties with insurance companies.

I read that bonding with the baby is wicked important, and that I might not find out till later in my baby's life that she has something like epilepsy, which Down syndrome babies can have. And she needs an especially healthy diet, which can cost extra, so I need to read up on how to create healthy meals—and I can't even boil an egg. So I'm pulled in two directions. Do I find some couple all grown up with lots of money and happily married who wants a Down syndrome baby and give her to them, or do I keep her because I love her and I believe that when it comes down to it, nobody cares as much as I do about my baby? Nobody will take care of her any better than I would. I'll do whatever it takes, and I'll have Ziggy there to love me and help me. It will be the three of us together, a happy family. Yeah, if I could just talk to Ziggy and get straight with him what our plans are, then everything would be good, everything would be all right.

I know I'm blinded by my love for Emma Rose, so I decide to call Sarah. I feel I need to talk to her, even though I'm not sure what I'm going to say or why I'm really calling.

She picks up on the third ring.

"It's me," I say.

"Oh, Elly. What a disaster! Look, I'm sorry. I'm sorry I left so fast. I should have said goodbye, but you don't know. I've been such a wreck. I had my hopes so set—I just so wanted—I—I—What's wrong with us Crowe women, anyway? Down syndrome! Is that why I keep miscarrying? What will I do now? And my nursery. I can't even go past the door of that room. It's just devastating is what it is."

All of this comes pouring out of her. No hello, no how are you, no how's the baby.

"The doctor says it's nobody's fault."

"Of course he says that. But you don't really believe him, do you?"

"I don't know. Maybe I did do something wrong, or it's in the Crowe genes," I say. "Or maybe it's the Lothrops' side. Maybe they passed on some defective gene, or maybe it just happened, but who cares? She's beautiful, Sarah. Her name is Emma Rose. She smells so sweet, like sugar cookies, and she makes this cute little sound almost like a cat purring. I wish you had stayed. I wish you had seen her."

She huffs into the phone. "She's *brain damaged,* El. She has *Down syndrome.* Do you really expect me to want my first and possibly my *only* child to have Down syndrome?"

Sarah acts like I'm too dense to understand the words. "Yes, *I know* she has Down syndrome," I say. "So what? I'm thinking of keeping her myself."

"You? Are you insane?"

"Probably. I'm insanely in love with her, that's for sure."

"Come on, Eleanor, why are you always like this? If there's a hard way or a wrong way to do something, why do you always have to pick it?"

"Well, what do you think I should do with her?"

"Give her away. Put her in an institution of some sort. Let people who know what they're doing handle it. Really, El. Really, you're too much sometimes."

"Thanks, Sarah." I say this sincerely, not sarcastically, and I can tell by the tone of her voice that she's surprised by this.

"You're welcome, but for what?"

"For helping me make up my mind. For proving to me that I'm making the right decision. Have a nice life, Sarah, a nice safe, boring, perfect life."

I hang up before Sarah can say another word and smile to myself. Yeah, it's going to be hard, and expensive, and I can't cook, and I don't have a job yet, but I have Emma Rose and Ziggy. Sarah and Mom and Dad don't know that. I have Ziggy, and we'll manage just fine.

CHAPTER THIRTY-ONE

EMMA ROSE and I are supposed to be able to go home tomorrow morning, but I don't even know where home is anymore. My parents are staying in a hotel, and the Lothrops don't want me back at the cabin now that Lam's gone, and they're not interested in Emma Rose.

There's a memorial service for Banner at the camp tonight. Banner's parents are having the funeral in New Jersey tomorrow, so they won't be there or anything, but there will be candles and singing and people talking about Banner. I want to be there. I beg the doctor to let me leave the hospital early. "You said I might be able to leave today, anyway, remember?" I say. I tell him that I'm feeling great (with the help of Ibuprofen), and that this is really important. He finally agrees to discharge me in the evening under my parents' supervision, but not Emma Rose. I can't get her until tomorrow.

So now I'm free. I'm on my way to the service at the camp. My parents are driving me and attending the memorial service with me. I'm not allowed to drive for a while or have sex for six weeks (as if!), but I can take a full shower, and I'm excited about that. I feel like a total grunge. I'm also not allowed to lift anything heavier than Emma Rose.

When we get to the camp, it feels like I've been gone for three weeks instead of three days. A whole crew of kids come up to me and hug me, and they want to see Emma Rose, and I have to tell them that I had to leave her in the hospital. "But she's so beautiful. Wait till you see. She's perfect," I say.

They all say I look different now that I'm not so big, even though my stomach still sticks out a ways, but they look different, too. It's as if in the past three days the campers just dumped a ton of their weight into the lake or something. Maybe I just hadn't been noticing, but most of them have really lost a lot. One person who looks like she's gained some back is Ashley Wilson. She looks exhausted, too, and I figure she's feeling guilty for always picking on Banner. Now she can't ever take it back. Every awful thing she said will go with Banner to her grave. I feel so sorry for her, especially since I've picked on Ashley Wilson now and again just to get her back for the way she treated Banner.

My parents head off to the main cabin to meet with the Lothrops. Probably so the four of them can come up with some scheme to get me to give away Emma Rose. When are they going to figure out their schemes always backfire?

I go find Ashley Wilson and try to talk to her the way Rabbi Yosef talked to me. I don't think I explained it all that well, and she looks more miserable than ever. I'm afraid she might kill herself, too, because you never know how a person is really feeling. I know that now, so I give her a big hug and say, "God will forgive you no matter what," and she smiles at that and thanks me.

I look everywhere for Ziggy, but I don't see him until the memorial service begins. We're all gathered at the lake, and we're standing in a line waiting to get our candles lit. The old lady, Lam's grandmother, is in her wheelchair behind me. She bangs into me with her chair, and instead of saying sorry or excuse me when I turn around to make a face at her, she says, "Why don't you look where I'm going?"

"What? Me look where *you're* going? That's rich," I say, even more annoyed.

The old bat cackles and I think maybe she was trying to be funny, but I'm not sure, so I decide to ignore her.

Ziggy is one of two counselors lighting everybody's candles. We step up two at a time. I make sure I end up on Ziggy's side. I'm just so happy to see him that my heart is leaping for joy. As soon as it's my turn to step up to him, I get that zinging feeling, and we're not even touching each other. I smile and say hi. He looks so surprised to see me, and then he looks embarrassed and he stares at my candle when he says hi back.

I know he's ashamed because he hasn't had time to get to

the hospital, but I understand. He's trying to keep busy so he doesn't have to think about Banner. He and Leo and Jen tried to revive her, and they failed. He's sensitive, so I know that he's hurting.

"I'm keeping the baby," I whisper, excited to be telling him this news. "We'll talk after."

Ziggy nods but remains somber and looks past me to the next person in line.

Once all the candles are lighted, we stand in a semicircle around the far end of the lake and Mr. Lothrop leads us in a prayer. The wind is low, so most of the candles stay lit. The stars are out and they're twinkling, and I remember how Banner loved that. I recall how she said she wanted to live here in the winter with a stack of books to read. Tears spill down my face.

Ziggy leads us in singing "Today," which was Banner's favorite camp song, and by the time we're singing the lines *"I can't be contented with yesterday's glories, / I can't live on promises winter to spring. / Today is my moment and now is my story, / I'll laugh and I'll cry and I'll sing,"* everybody's weeping, even my parents.

Then it's time for people to get up and say something about Banner, and Mrs. Lothrop starts it by saying how polite Banner always was and how much she loved Rufus the cat. Then some of the girls in Banner's cabin talk about Banner's favorite book, *The Secret Garden,* and how Banner would say that someday she was going to have a secret garden just like the one Mary Lennox found. They tell about the day Banner did the splits both ways, and they say that was amazing. One little girl, maybe eight years old, steps forward, and she says, "I think Banner was very pretty and she had very pretty long hair."

Then Leo steps forward. He blows out his candle, so it's harder to see him really well, even though I'm standing pretty close to him.

"I have no idea what I'm about to say," he begins, "but I've been thinking a lot about what happened. I know we all have." He lowers his head and lets out his breath. His cheeks puff out when he does this. He takes another breath and looks out at all of us.

"Uh—I feel really guilty about Banner. I feel like I should have done more. I should have listened more and hugged her more. I should have taken her more seriously when she told me she was unhappy. I know that a lot of us feel this way. We feel responsible for what happened, and I think we should." Leo pauses and clears his throat. "We're all responsible for each other for lots of things. Most importantly, we depend on each other for companionship, for friendship. And I think sometimes we can take friendship for granted. I don't think Banner did, because she didn't have too many friends. She was a nice girl, but let's face it, she was a whiner."

I hear whispering when Leo says this, and I'm wondering if they're agreeing or they're just so shocked that he said something negative about Banner. Maybe it's both, because that's how I feel.

"Banner was so afraid, wasn't she? And maybe some of us

made fun of her because of this, but we didn't realize how much it would hurt."

Leo lowers his head and pinches the bridge of his nose to keep from crying.

He sniffs and takes a deep breath at the same time. Then he lifts his head.

"There are lots of Banners in this world, and we can't help ourselves—we pick on them, and we say things that we shouldn't, but these types of people just bring it out of us." Leo shakes his head. "I don't know what we can do about that, except remember Banner, and catch ourselves before we speak."

Leo pauses and relights his candle. He holds it up, and everybody else just automatically holds theirs up like Leo's about to make a toast.

"So I guess what I want to say is that we have to pay attention to one another. We have to have compassion for one another. I know that's sappy, but we do. And we have to remember everything we say matters, and sometimes a lot more than a person will let on. We have to know that! Banner taught us that. It's so easy to toss some words out there without any thought. And we just don't realize the damage those careless words can do. So, that's what I'm going to remember. I'm going to remember Banner at her best. Let's just all of us always remember Banner."

Okay, so I'm crying like crazy now, and my candle's out because I cried on it. Leo just said everything I was thinking, even though I didn't know I was thinking it until he said it.

We sing some more camp songs, but thankfully not *the*

camp song about leaving our weight on an old tired log. When it's time for everyone to go to their cabins, we climb in a single file up the hill with our candles, and we sing that old folk song "Kumbaya."

As kids drop out to go to their cabins and the boys troop downhill to theirs, the voices get quieter and quieter until there are just a few of us left outside still singing.

We sing one more verse and stop, and all is quiet. I can hear people moving about in the cabins, but all the lights stay off and nobody talks. No one wants to break the spell of the service.

CHAPTER THIRTY-TWO

I TELL my parents that I need to talk to Ziggy, and before I can run to find him, my parents stop me and hug me. "We're proud of you, Eleanor. The campers here really seem to look up to you."

This feels really good. Really, really good. "Thanks. They're great kids," I say.

I go to Ziggy's cabin and knock quietly on the door. One of the boys answers it and says Ziggy's not there.

I look for him in the break hut and haul myself all the way up the hill to the main cabin and check the boys' latrine even, but I can't find him. It's too dark to go all over the camp searching for him. I go to my cabin, the one I shared with Lam. I step inside. It still has that funky Lam smell. I just stand there and cry a moment. I cry for Banner, and I cry because I can't find Ziggy.

I look around. It's dark, and everything is in shadow. I see the moose head still sitting on the floor propped up by its left antler, and I cry some more because the pathetic head reminds me of Lam and the mess the two of us have made of everything.

I hear a few whispered voices of people walking by, but other than that it's quiet and cold. Yeah, it's really cold. I hug myself and shiver, and I feel spooked by the ghosts of Lam and me and our marriage. But then I hear Ziggy. I hear his voice! It's soft, but I hear it. He's talking to someone, and he's close. I hurry back outside, and I see him coming toward me. He has his arm around Jen, and his head is bent toward hers.

"Ziggy?" I say, and he and Jen both look up.

He doesn't smile. He just waves and keeps on talking and walking right past me—with Jen. I stand there too numb, too frightened, to take in what just happened. I tell myself to go after him, because what the hell is going on? But I don't. I can't move. I feel everything inside me crumbling. I'm shaking all over, and I can't breathe. I don't know how long I stand there not breathing, but it's either take a breath or pass out, so finally I take a big, loud, crying gulp of air, and then another and another, and slowly, slowly, I allow what just happened to register. I jam my fist in my mouth to keep from making that awful sound that's coming from my body, the gulping, crying, sucking sound, while the thoughts seep in. *Ziggy hasn't been too busy to come see me; he's been too scared. Too scared of Down syndrome. He doesn't want me anymore. He doesn't love me! He's just like all the others.*

He doesn't want Emma Rose, and if he *doesn't, then how can I take care of my baby? How can I do it on my own? I can't. I can't do it on my own.*

I start that loud gulping/crying noise again. I hurry back into the cabin and fall on the bed so I can bury my face in the mattress and really cry. After several minutes of weeping and pounding my fists into the bed, I find myself thinking again about Banner. Remember Banner, Leo said. Poor, sad, lonely Banner. At this moment I understand how alone and desperate she must have felt, because it's exactly how I'm feeling. Nobody's on my side. Nobody's going to help me keep my baby.

I know my parents are somewhere in the camp waiting for me, so eventually I wipe the tears off my face and get up to leave. Before I go, I walk over to the chest of drawers Ziggy bought me. I run my hand over the top of it. "It's a pretty chest. I'll keep it." I turn away and leave.

My parents are waiting for me in their rental car. I climb in the back seat. "I couldn't find him. Sorry I kept you waiting," I say, keeping my head down so they can't tell that I've been crying.

"That's all right," my mom says. "We had a nice talk with the Lothrops. They're agreed. The best thing to do would be to put the baby up for adoption."

The baby. Did she call my child "the baby" because if she said her name, Emma Rose, the baby would seem too much like a real person? Because she *is* a real person! And the baby is *my* baby. To lose her is to lose a part of my body, an arm or a leg. She grew inside of me, we shared the same heartbeat, and now my heart is being torn right out of me. That's what it feels like, but I don't say anything. I don't explain this. I know whatever I would say wouldn't matter and it would be too hurtful, because I'm hurting and I'm angry about Ziggy and about my parents always being right, and about the idea of having to give up my baby because I'm sixteen and I haven't graduated from high school and I don't have a job and my parents are going back to Kenya.

* * *

The next morning I feel gross all over. I'm bleeding, my breasts are sore and engorged, so I have to use the breast pump to express the milk, and my belly feels full and heavy and achy. It takes so long to get myself clean and showered, and then once I do, my breasts leak into my bra because I forgot to put the little pads in to soak up the milk. I change my bra and put the pads in and go down to breakfast in the hotel with my parents.

At breakfast, my dad pulls out a notepad, and on it he's written the name of an adoption agency. "We called them," my mom says. "They can come out today, and you can sign the forms and they'll take Emma Rose and find a nice mother and father for her."

"You know that, do you?" I say. I shove my plate of eggs away. I can't eat.

"What?" my mom asks. She looks irritated.

"Do you have a crystal ball in your purse or something, Mom? Because I want to know how you know that they'll find a *nice* mother and father for her. How do you know? Huh? How do you know this? Is it really that easy? Is it? To just hand over a live human being?"

My father stands up, because I'm getting loud and people are starting to look at us.

"Let's finish this conversation in the car, all right?"

"Yeah, whatever. I'm sure that's the *right* thing to do. And we must always do the *right* thing, mustn't we?" I throw down my napkin and get up. I'm in a foul mood. I spent the whole night trying to decide if Ziggy really was ignoring me or if maybe he just had something super important to say to Jen. I want to call the camp. I want them to put Ziggy on the phone. I want to give him one last chance. I don't want to give up on Emma Rose.

I follow my parents out to the car, and we pile in. Once inside, my mother says, "They screen the couples. Anybody can give birth, but parents who adopt have to go through a rigorous screening process."

"What you're really saying, Mom, is that anybody would be better than me."

"Eleanor, enough," my dad says, twisting around in his seat. "This is not a personal attack on you. You're right—your baby is a live human being and she has needs. She needs food and diapers and clothing and visits to the doctors and constant care, night and day, so if you're not there because you're working, then you need to pay someone to care for her. She's not one of your dolls that you can entertain yourself with for a few hours then toss aside when you feel like going shopping or going to a party. She's for real. This is for real. And we need a real solution, not one of your pie-in-the-sky fantasies."

"Well, thanks. Nice to know what you really think of me, folks." I say this because I'm hurt, but I know they're right. I hate that they are, because I'm desperate to keep my baby. I want my Emma Rose. And I don't just think I'm being stupidly stubborn about this or contrary because I hate that my parents are always right. This is something I feel deep in my bones. I do. I feel I'm the best person to care for my baby, and I don't care how insane that is. Emma Rose isn't even a week old, and already people are rejecting her—Sarah, the Lothrops, Ziggy, my parents. She could spend her whole life in an institution waiting for someone to adopt her, waiting for someone who will love her most especially, when here I am, I'm here, and I already love her. I need to be there to protect her, to make sure she knows she's loved, always. Otherwise—otherwise she could become one of the Banners of this world. We belong together; that's all there is to it.

My father starts the car, backs up, and heads for the hospital. It seems all I do these days is cry, but anyway, I sit in the back of the car and cry some more. I'm so miserable I just want to sink to the floor of the car and roll up into a ball and cry the whole world away. Instead, I stare out the window at the beginning of another sunny day in Vacationland, USA.

CHAPTER THIRTY-THREE

ON THE WAY to the hospital, I ask my mom for her phone and I call the camp. I get Mrs. Lothrop. I ask her if she could get Ziggy for me. "It's really, really important," I say. "Practically a matter of life or death."

Mrs. Lothrop sighs big, but then she tells me to hold on. I hear her open the cabin door and call out to a passing camper to go get Ziggy; he's wanted on the phone. "Tell him it's Eleanor Crowe," she adds.

While I'm waiting, I think about Ziggy. We love each other. He fought with Lam over me. He kissed me, and we both felt that zing-zing. I know we did. We had dreams about Boston and taking Emma Rose to concerts and museums. I just misunderstood what was going on last night, that's all. That's all.

We're pulling into the hospital by the time I hear the kid's voice in the background again. "Tell her Ziggy can't come to the phone."

"Did he say why?" Mrs. Lothrop asks.

"Uh-uh," the kid says.

Then Mrs. Lothrop is on the phone with me. "Eleanor, I'm sorry . . ."

"I heard," I say. "Thanks, anyway." I hand the phone back to my mother. I don't cry. I feel too numb to cry. I can't believe this is happening to me. I love my baby, and I have to give her up. That's it. It's over. I lose. Emma Rose loses, and now that's going to be her life—always losing. How nice that *losing* is the trait I've passed down to her.

I tell my mom to call the adoption people, and I get out of the car, because I don't want to hear the conversation.

I go into the hospital, and I see Rabbi Yosef walking toward the elevators carrying flowers. He was supposed to come back and talk to me. We were going to talk about the baby. I think that seeing him is a good sign, a hopeful sign, and I grab it. I hurry after him, holding on to my belly and hoping nothing tears. I call to him in the hallway.

He turns around and he recognizes me. He smiles and waves to me with his free hand. "Is this Eleanor Crowe I see?" he says.

I rush over to him. "Yes, it's me. Hi. We were—remember we were going to talk? I need to talk to you right away. It's an emergency. They're going to take my baby, and I don't want them to. They're taking her away and . . ."

Now I'm crying so I can't speak—what else is new?

The rabbi leads me to the elevator, and we get off at I-don't-know-what floor and walk to some empty meeting room, and he tells me to have a seat.

I pull a chair out from a table and sit, and he does, too. He sets the flowers on the table. They're a mix of red and yellow flowers. They smell really sweet, like Emma Rose does. I wish Emma Rose and I had gotten flowers, but nobody was happy to see her except me.

"I'm keeping you from seeing someone," I say.

"I have a few minutes for you, too, Eleanor. What is the emergency with your baby?"

"I—I had a baby, a beautiful baby girl, and she's—I call her Emma Rose. She has Down syndrome. My parents want me to give her up for adoption. They're talking to the agency right now! Someone will be coming today to take Emma Rose away!"

"I see," the rabbi says, nodding. He studies my face. He takes my hands in his and looks straight into my eyes. "You want to keep her," he says.

"Yes!"

"How will you keep her?"

"How?"

"Yes, where will you live? How will you pay for her expenses? How will you care for her?"

"That's what I don't know. All I know is I want her. I do."

"Wanting her isn't enough, of course. You must provide for her. So how will you do this?"

"I told you, I don't know." I feel exasperated. I want him to understand how badly I want Emma Rose. Can't he see it? Can't he see it in my eyes? He's looking right at me.

"When you have the answer to this question, you will know whether or not you should keep her. She can't live on air. What will you do for her, Eleanor? What are you willing to do for her?"

"Anything. Everything."

"Do you have a job?"

"No, but I'll get one."

"Are your parents able to help? Will you live with them? You're how old?"

"Sixteen. No, they're going back to Kenya. That's where they live now. But I'll get a job here and find a place to live and get somebody to look after Emma Rose while I work and—and, I'll do it all. I'll do everything."

"That is exactly what you *must* do. You must do everything for this baby, because she is totally helpless. And if you can't do all of these things, then you need to find someone who can. And Eleanor"—the rabbi pauses—"you need to do all of these things *before* you take the baby. A promise isn't good enough. You need a job and a place to live and someone to care for the baby while you work *now*, not later."

"But—but that's impossible!" I slap my hands in my lap. "I can't find a job in five seconds or an apartment just like that. I can't." I study the rabbi's face. He looks so—so sorry for me.

He knows. He knows that it's over. I have to give Emma Rose away. I burst into tears all over again and cry into my hands.

"I'm here," the rabbi says.

I lean forward and reach out for him to hug me, and he does. I cry my eyes out. It hurts so much. Losing Emma Rose hurts so much. I can't bear it.

The rabbi holds me and lets me cry on him. Then he releases me. "Eleanor, you're being paged," the rabbi says.

I stop crying and listen. "Eleanor Crowe, please report to the information desk on the first floor," a voice says.

"That's my parents. I've got to go. Thank you. I'm sorry I got your shirt wet. Thanks for talking to me." I stand, and so does the rabbi.

"You've got a good head on your shoulders, Eleanor. Your heart is ruling right now, and that makes it hard to see what you need to do, but you know. Deep inside you know what's best."

"I guess I do."

"God bless you, Eleanor."

"Yeah, I wish he or she would."

CHAPTER THIRTY-FOUR

MY PARENTS didn't want me to see Emma Rose again. "It will only hurt you, Elly," my mother said, and she was right, but I knew not saying goodbye would hurt more.

The social worker from the agency arrives, and she waits with us for the nurse to bring me Emma Rose. The woman's tiny, like me, with red hair that hangs all the way down to her butt. She tells me that I have ten days to change my mind. I don't need ten days, because my mind is exactly the same as it was the first second I set eyes on Emma Rose: I want her; I love her! But wanting her and being able to take care of her, as my parents and everybody keep pointing out to me, are two different things.

My mother sees the tears forming in my eyes as I prepare myself to say goodbye, and she turns to the social worker. "This is the right decision, isn't it?" she says. "Maybe you can help

Eleanor understand. She's so stubborn. A nice couple will adopt her, won't they? People who will love her and who can provide for her."

"Mom, I don't want to hear it. Okay? I've heard it all before."

"Actually," the social worker says, "except for your daughter's lack of a job and a place to live, she would make an excellent parent for Emma Rose."

"What?" the three of us say in unison.

I lift my head and wait for this woman to explain.

"I know she's very young and perhaps naive about what it's going to take to raise a Down syndrome child, but of course until we have a child of our own, we're all a bit naive. I'm sure you had a certain fantasy about how it was going to be raising Eleanor. It's never quite as we picture it."

My parents both blush when she says this, and I imagine they had a nice rosy picture of how it was going to be raising me. And then came the reality.

"As you've said to me a couple of times over the past few days, Mrs. Crowe, Eleanor is very stubborn. Emma Rose is going to need someone stubborn to be an advocate for her in the schools and with the medical professionals and in any activity Emma Rose may choose to pursue. From the things you told me when we talked earlier, Mr. Crowe, Eleanor has a lot of energy, which she will need in abundance if she were to raise Emma Rose. You said she's intelligent, and that helps. She *is* the child's mother, and she loves and wants her. With a child like Emma Rose, love obviously won't solve all her problems, but it will sure go a long way."

"But she's only sixteen! She's inexperienced. She needs to finish high school and go to college," Mom says, looking apoplectic.

"Of course, I know this," the woman says. "And single parents in general have a lower socioeconomic status than a two-parent family. No, it's not ideal. And it's certainly possible that we'll find a loving home for Emma Rose, but there are no guarantees. I just want you all to understand this. I want you all to consider both sides of the equation. There can be a lot of guilt feelings that crop up later when a child is given up for adoption, not just with the birth parents, but with the grandparents as well. I don't want you to let go without understanding this, because guilt can be seriously destructive." The woman takes a deep breath, and I think my dad's about to say something, but then the social worker speaks again.

"I know you've said that you have plans to return to Kenya, Mr. and Mrs. Crowe, but perhaps you'd reconsider and stay home to help Eleanor raise Emma Rose."

Okay, I cannot believe what I'm hearing. Someone on my side. A social worker on my side. "Thank you," I say, and I go over and shake her hand.

"You have ten days; just think about it," the woman says, looking over my head to my parents.

"I won't get Elly's hopes up like that," my mother says, her face turning ever-deepening shades of red as she speaks. "We've explained to her that we just do not feel equipped to deal with a Down syndrome child."

"We expect Eleanor to return to Kenya with us—just Eleanor."

Now I'm apoplectic!

"If we took both Elly and the baby in with us, we would end up becoming full-time parents of Emma Rose," my father says. "I believe we know Elly a bit better than you do."

"No! No, you don't," I say, and I'm fuming. "You just think you do. You've always thought you had me all figured out, but it's never who I am at all. You don't know me. You don't know that I love caring for other people. I'm good at it. I found that out this summer. I was always so jealous of you and those AIDS babies, I never went near them. But now I know I'm good with kids. I'm good at something. And it feels good having to think about someone other than myself all the time."

"Eleanor, let's not go into this now, all right?" my mother says. "If you need something to care for, you'll have plenty of opportunities in Kenya."

"But there's a child who needs me right here! How can I abandon her when I know exactly what that feels like?"

Before they can answer me, the nurse walks into the room and looks around at our angry faces, and the smile on her own face dissolves.

I rush over to Emma Rose and take her out of the nurse's arms. My mother says something; I don't know what because I'm not paying attention to any of them anymore. Then everybody leaves the room, and I'm alone with my baby one last time. I kiss her face and her arms and hands. I hold her tiny body close and smell her sweet head. My little sugar cookie. My Emma Rose.

I seriously consider running away with her, but where would I run? Nobody's taking her against my will. I can keep her, but what would I do with her? How would I keep her? That's what Rabbi Yosef asked, and the answer is, not very well without a job and a place to live.

I play with her hands and feet for the last time, and I talk to her and tell her I won't forget her, ever. I smooth down the little blond hairs that stick straight up on her head and kiss both of her cheeks again.

"You're going to grow up to be happy and smart and beautiful. Your new parents are going to love you and give you everything your heart desires. You're going to be loved by everybody who ever meets you. But remember, I loved you first, and I'll love you always."

I kiss her nose, and she makes this gurgling noise, then starts to cry like she knows I'm about to leave her. My breasts leak at the sound of her cry and it reminds me that we're bonded forever, no matter what happens.

It seems as if I have only five seconds with Emma Rose before my parents and the nurse return. The nurse lifts Emma

Rose out of my arms, and I feel my body trembling all over. I wait until Emma Rose is out of the room because I don't want her to hear me cry, but when she's gone I break down. "My baby. How can this be happening? Please. Mom, Dad, please. Please help me. Please! Please!"

Mom and Dad hold me and shush me and pat my head. Mom speaks softly in my ear. "It's going to be all right, shhh. We are helping you, Elly."

"No, you're not," I cry. "You're killing me. Don't you see? This is killing me."

Dad speaks in my other ear. "We're doing the best thing for everybody. In a few more years, you'll understand this. Shhh, it's going to be okay, pumpkin. Shhh."

I'm inconsolable. I want to die. It's all just too much. The hospital gives me some pills to calm me down and gives my parents some extra to take with them. Then with me still crying and hiccupping, and my parents shoving a bottle of water at me, trying to get me to drink it, they pile me into the back seat of the car and speed off.

* * *

We're on our way back to the hotel, and my parents are already talking to me about returning with them to Kenya. There's nothing keeping me here, they say, and time and distance will help with the healing. I don't think so. Nothing will help. A part of me has been torn away; just torn off of me. There is this big gaping hole that will never be filled or repaired—ever.

We pull into the hotel parking lot, and as we're getting out of the car, I see Leo coming out of the hotel.

"Leo?"

"Eleanor? Are you okay?"

I know I must look like a complete wreck, because I feel like one. The pills are working, though, so although I cry, I'm not the blathering, slobbering crazy person I was just a while ago. I tell him what happened, and I tell him about Ziggy, and he says how really sorry he is. He looks like he can barely keep from crying himself, and I wonder what it's like for him, since someone must have given him away. Does it help for him to know how much I want to keep this baby? How much I love her?

"I wish I could find you a job," he says. "I'm living in a dorm with two roommates or I'd . . ."

"I know, Leo." I hug him. "It's okay. It's over. I'm sure I would have made a terrible mother, anyway."

"You know that's not true," he says, and I can see he means it. This comforts me.

Leo invites me to the awards night and talent show, and I say I'm not up for it, but he convinces me because it's the last night of camp and the kids are all asking about me and they want me to be there.

"Okay," I say. "I need to tell them all goodbye, anyway, and I have to clear out the rest of my stuff. I'm going to miss those kids. They kind of grow on you, don't they?" I think about all the campers, all their different personalities, and my girls in cabin seven. I'm glad I got to play at being a cabin counselor for a while. I liked it a lot.

I sleep the whole afternoon and go out to dinner with my parents at the Bethel Inn Resort, this giant yellow clapboard inn in the center of town. Then we drive up to the camp. Just like the night before, a bunch of campers come up to greet me, and a couple of the little ones take my hand and drag me along to the main cabin. The place is decorated with the campers' artwork—drawings and paintings, and on tables around the room are their crafts, the little boats, the scarves and blankets or knitted things that will someday become scarves and blankets, the dulcimers, the clay bowls and mugs, and the necklaces.

I notice the campers are enjoying seeing their work on display. Lots of them have their parents with them, and I see them smiling as they lift something their child has made and examine it closer. I notice even my parents are enjoying the show. I feel good that I suggested this. The display was my idea. I wish I had Emma Rose with me. I'd carry her in my arms and talk to her. I'd tell her about each camper as we looked at the artwork. I want to show her. I want her here to see everything. I want to be around when she sees the new world she's entered, and when she learns how to speak and how to walk. I want to hear her call me Mama.

"Looks like they put just anybody's crap on display, don't it?"

I turn around to see who said this, and it's who else but the old bat sitting in her wheelchair holding up a lopsided mug one of the campers had made.

"Oh, yeah? And who made you judge and jury?" I say, totally irritated. "I think this mug has lots of personality."

"You do, do ya?" The lady sets the mug on the table and crosses her arms.

"Yeah. Perfection is overrated, if you ask me," I say.

"Ha!" the lady says, but before she can say anything else, my dad comes over and puts his arm around my shoulder. "This reminds me of all the art shows you and your sister were involved in at school, remember?"

"Yeah, and you could actually recognize all of Sarah's art, unlike mine." I notice my dulcimer isn't on display and I'm grateful, especially with that old bat behind me making judgments. Now I see where the MIL gets her personality.

I see the lady wheel off toward the refreshment table. I look around for Ziggy, but I don't see him. I don't see Lam, either.

Mr. Lothrop gets up onstage and speaks into the microphone, asking everyone to find a seat. Once we're seated and sort of quiet, he announces that they'll be handing out badges and awards first, then we'll have the talent show.

Leo had warned me that the talent show wasn't going to be all that long, because a lot of kids dropped out after Banner died. "But we'll do it again next year and have it on a separate day from the awards. The Lothrops liked your idea."

The badges and awards take a while, but it's fun for me to

see what the campers had been up to when they weren't in the crafts hut or in my dance class. After the serious awards, there are the goofy awards, like Camper Most Likely to Actually Cook and Eat Mashed Cauliflower at Home, and Camper with the Hottest New Body.

Then Elizabeth, one of the unholy four, goes up onstage. "Now for the counselor awards," she says. These are goofy, too. Lam gets Hottest Counselor Award, but he's not there to accept it, and Jen gets the Walk, Don't Run Award. Gren gets the Boy, Am I Embarrassed Award, and as usual, her face is bright red when she gets up to accept it. Leo gets Favorite Counselor Award for like the hundredth time, and Ziggy gets Counselor Most Likely to Be Seen in Hollywood. Ziggy goes up to accept the award, and when he climbs onstage he pulls a pair of sunglasses out of his pocket and puts them on. He takes the award and makes the peace sign and hops off again.

I wonder how he can be so cute and happy and all that when he has just destroyed my whole life. I bite down hard on my lips to keep from crying. I wonder what Emma Rose is doing right now. Where is she? Who has her? I can't stand to think of it.

Stop it. Stop thinking of her. Just stop!

I'm yelling at myself in my head, and then I hear my name called and I sit up.

"Eleanor Crowe, for Most Original Dulcimer!" Elizabeth announces.

Abby on the front row passes my dulcimer to Elizabeth, and Elizabeth holds it up. Everybody cheers and laughs, and I go to the stage to accept my award. When I get up close, I see that campers have autographed it. There are signatures all over, including Banner's. I'm so surprised. I take my misshapen dulcimer, and Elizabeth says, "To remember us by."

"Thanks," I say. I turn to leave, and Elizabeth tells me to wait.

"We have one more award for you," she says into the microphone. She holds up a handmade plaque. For Eleanor Crowe, the Counselor Most Like Our Mothers (But in a Good Way) Award."

She hands me the plaque while everybody cheers, and then when the cheers die down, a group of girls from the back sing out, "Yes, Mother!" and everybody laughs. I head back to my seat, and another group calls out, "We love you, Elly!" and I'm so touched and embarrassed and happy and miserable at the same time. I wave and laugh to show them I'm grateful, but really, of all the awards to get on the day I give my baby away. If they only knew. I sit down, and my parents and the kids behind me all pat me on the back.

I want Emma Rose. I want to be her mother. I should be her mother. I *am* her mother.

The talent show is lots of fun. Most of the performances are funny skits or singing, and of course, there are my dancers. I'm so proud of them. They look really good up there. They look so pulled together. In class they'd argue about whose idea they should use, and who gets to be in front for this part, and who gets to be in front for that part, but onstage they're all together, dancing like the whole thing came to them so easily. Of course I'm thinking about Banner, because her dance was special, and I wish again that everyone could see her. I feel for her necklace around my neck and hold the clay thumbprint with the heart on it in my hand. I press my thumb into the heart.

When the talent show is over, I think we're through, but then Leo gets onstage and announces that for the grand finale, as with every year, he will play the video montage.

The lights in the cabin are turned off, and everyone is talking and excited. The montage opens with the Camp Weight-Away sign and Mr. and Mrs. Lothrop greeting the campers. Then we see kids falling out of canoes at the lake, and parts of a swim meet, and Bo Winkler doing a belly flop—ouch! We see kids playing softball. Everybody in the lodge cheers at one point because there are like six shots in a row of Joe Trumbell missing the ball and finally he hits one. Joe stands up in the audience and raises his fists in the air. We see kids taking a shortcut through the woods in the morning running class, and in the cooking class Leo catches kids sneaking bites of food when the Lothrops aren't looking. There are scenes from cabin life, the weigh-ins, and a food fight in the dining hall, and shots of disgusting-looking globs of food. We see sick kids at the nurse's cabin, and all the different sports and classes, including my dance class. Leo has strung together several shots of me saying, "Who's going next?" over and over, and there's even a bit of footage where the MIL is standing behind the old bat in her wheelchair just outside the open doorway of the dance hut watching me with the girls. I don't remember them being there. I never saw them. I was so into what the girls were doing with their new dances that I never saw them. It makes me wonder how many other times those two were spying on me that I didn't know about. Leo captures me with my arm around little Bruce Whelan in the crafts hut, and sitting out on the porch of the hut talking with a group of knitters, and me working on my dulcimer, and I have my tongue stuck out to the side like a goofball. There's even one with Banner and me. Leo is shooting from behind us, and we're walking away with our arms around each other's waist. I don't remember that time, either. Then the screen goes blank, and I'm grateful that Leo didn't show the film he took of Emma Rose and me. I couldn't bear it. Not now. We all start to clap and cheer, but then the screen lights up and we see a shot inside the main cabin. There is Banner standing on the stage. Everybody gets really quiet.

Banner takes position in the middle of the room and poses as if she's about to dance. She's got her arms folded across her chest and she's facing sideways and her back is rounded and she's looking at the ground. She has one leg crossed behind the other, her foot pointed, and the top of it resting on the floor. Her leg is bent. "Okay, I'm ready," she says. Then we hear the music, this tragic *Madame Butterfly* music that Ziggy had made a copy of for her. Banner starts to move, but then she stops. She looks into the camera. "Wait," she says. "I forgot my dedication."

"Oh, right," Leo says. We don't see him; we just hear his voice.

Banner giggles and wipes at her eye with the back of her hand. "Okay, so, um, this is dedicated to Eleanor Crowe, because she's the best counselor ever, and I love her." She pauses. "Did I sound okay? I sounded stupid, didn't I? I should do it again."

"Banner, you're doing great. I know everyone would love to see you perform this for the talent show if we have one."

"I can't do it live. People will laugh at me. They always do. Anyway, I'm too fat to really dance." She pauses again and looks down for a minute. Then she looks back into the camera. "Eleanor is going to be so disappointed in me, isn't she? I should have done this for class, but I just couldn't." She bites down on her lip.

"She's proud of you. She thinks you're a good dancer. She told me so, and I know she would want everybody to see your dance, but she'll understand if you choose not to do it in front of everyone."

Banner nods and just stands there looking lost in thought.

"From the top?" Leo says, and she nods again and gets into position.

Yeah, I'm crying again, but so is everybody else. The whole audience is in tears, and the dance is so—so sad, her hurt comes right through the camera at us. She's just so tragic dancing around the room, but she's good, too. I mean you can't stop watching her. The expression in her eyes and her arm movements just hold you in a trance. She grabs at the air and you feel yourself being pulled into her neediness. She pushes away and you feel her anger. Her arms curve around her body and you feel her sorrow. I can see by the looks on the other campers' faces seated around me that they are feeling it, too. She lunges and turns and wraps her arms around herself, then reaches out to us as if she's begging for something, grasping, straining until it's too much and she falls to the floor. Then slowly she pulls herself up again, and she's spinning and flinging herself to the four corners of the room, searching for something, pausing in each corner, standing on tiptoe suspended, waiting, then falling back and spinning off in another direction, but none of them satisfy her, and she spins herself into the center and winds down until she's on the floor again all tucked and wrapped up inside herself.

The music fades and it's wicked quiet in the room, and I'm so touched by her dance and her dedication. Dear Banner. Poor, dear Banner. She really could have been a dancer when she grew up. I know she could have. What a waste of a beautiful life. What a loss for us all. I think this, and I think of myself. I don't want to waste my life. I want to make something of it. She dedicated the dance to me. I was important in her life. I'm not sure I've ever felt important to anybody. My parents have always made me feel that the AIDS orphans in Kenya are more important than I am. I've always felt guilty for even needing them at all when they have so many other kids needing them. But Banner, and some of the other campers, they needed *me*. I've been important to them. And I'm important to Emma Rose. Or I could be. I should be. I'm her mother. I created her. I want to make her the most important person in my life.

I stand up, and I feel my mother's hand on my back. I turn around. "I'll be back. I just have to—to get a breath of fresh air. I've just got to . . ."

I don't finish. I leave before the lights come back on.

CHAPTER THIRTY-FIVE

I GET OUTSIDE and I take several deep breaths. It's cool out and the air smells clean and icy and it reminds me of a winter's day snowboarding in the mountains. It's so pure and cool. There's a good breeze, and after a few minutes I get to feeling chilled. I decide to go for a walk. I step off the porch of the main cabin. I hear all the voices behind me, all those campers' voices, and all the counselors' voices. I love this place. I love living on the mountain, and the view to the lake, and all the pine trees, and the stone paths everywhere, and the cabins dotted about here and there, and all the kids, even the snotty and bratty ones. I never expected this. I never gave it a thought. All I thought about was myself and Lam. I hardly even thought about Emma Rose. Not until I met her. But now, as I walk along one of the paths, I feel like a whole world has opened up to me—a world beyond just myself. And I like it. It's better than just being me, and just thinking about who I am, and whether or not I'm being cool, and if Lam loves me.

I see a light on in my cabin, and I go over and open the door. I find Lam on the couch, leaning over my trunk/coffee table, sniffing cocaine.

"Great, really great, Lam," I say.

He holds out his rolled-up dollar bill to me. "You want? You're not pregnant anymore. You're free. You can have anything you want now. I've got some beer. It's kinda warm but—"

"What I want is our daughter," I say. "I want Emma Rose."

Lam leans back over the trunk and finishes his line. Then he blinks at me. "You shouldn't have named her," he says. "She's going to get a new name, anyway. Someone will rename her."

"I think I hate you."

"No, you don't." He smiles and flips his bangs out of his eyes. "That social worker called here. She said I have ten days to decide if I want the baby." He leans back on the couch.

"I want her," I say. I take a step farther into the room.

Lam spreads his arms out on the back of the sofa and stares at the ceiling. "Go ahead. I'm not stopping you. Figures we'd create a damaged baby, huh? I never thought of that happening, but I should have guessed."

"She's not damaged. She's perfect. Did you and your parents even look at her? Did you even meet your daughter? She's beautiful, just like we thought she'd be, and she does have your eyes and she does have my mouth, so there. She's us, you—you . . ."

I just want to kick him, but he's too stoned to care, so what's the use? I march past him and go to his ugly chest of drawers. I yank open the drawer and pull out all my clothes. "And by the way, this is the ugliest piece of furniture I've ever seen in my life!"

"Hey, don't knock it," Lam says. "I found it at the town dump. I got it for free."

"Town dump? Well, it smells like it, that's for sure. What a loser, Lam. You're such a loser."

Lam nods. "Yeah, so my parents keep telling me."

That makes me stop. I feel for Banner's necklace and press my thumb into her thumbprint. "Hey, look, I didn't mean it, Lam. You're okay. You just have to get off the stuff. You need to get clean. You're great. All the campers think you're so hot. And you know I'll always love you. You're my first love and the father of Emma Rose—you'll always be important to me. You're important, Lam. Your parents think so, too, and that's why they're so upset. They need you, even if you never take over this camp. They need you."

Lam acts like he hasn't heard me. He turns his head and checks out the skin around his thumb. "So I guess we ought to get a divorce and move on to the next exciting chapter of our lives," he says, sounding bored.

I don't know why it should, but it makes me sad to think of divorcing Lam. What a disaster our marriage has been from day one. What a total mess.

"Yeah, okay." I go over to the couch and dump a pile of my

clothes onto the seat. "I'm sorry how it turned out, Lam," I say. "I don't blame you, you know. It just was never right."

He turns his head and looks at me. "So, I guess it's you and Ziggy, huh?"

"No. No, it's me and nobody. Ziggy was never really interested in me. I was just some kind of fantasy trip for him." As I say this, I realize it's true. It's one of those truths I know deep inside before I realize I know it. It's only speaking it now that I understand.

"Sorry, El." Lam sniffs and runs his finger through his bangs to shove them out of his face. "So, I'll have my peeps get in touch with your peeps, okay? For the divorce?"

"Sure, Lam. Okay, well"—I look about the room—"I'll come by tomorrow and pick up everything, all right?"

"Okay by me," he says.

I go over and kiss him on the cheek, and Lam's hand brushes mine. We both smile, and I know we've forgiven one another. For what? For marrying, I suppose, and making such a mess of it all. Then I turn and leave.

CHAPTER THIRTY-SIX

I GET BACK to the main cabin, and everybody's hanging around having a snack of the usual carrot and celery sticks, apple slices, and iced Red Zinger, but the night is winding down. I find my parents and tell them I want to say goodbye to the campers. Then I go around saying goodbye and thanks, and I love you, and be good, and I'll miss you, and all that, and I mean every bit of what I'm saying. I want to keep all the campers with me. I want to see them grow up and find out what happens to them all. I want to come back next summer, but I doubt the soon-to-be-ex-ILs would be too thrilled to hear that.

It's a big tear-fest for everybody as we all go around saying our goodbyes. I look for Ziggy, but I can't find him. Finally I go over to Leo. I've saved him for last.

"Thanks for everything, Leo," I say. "You've been so good to me. You *are* the best counselor and the best kind of friend."

Leo hugs me. "We'll keep in touch, Elly, won't we?"

"Yeah, I'll let you know my address when I know it. I'll tell the Lothrops. Oh, and Leo, I haven't told anybody, but I'm going to keep my baby."

Leo looks surprised and maybe happy. He pulls me over into a corner so we can talk better. "Elly, how? That's wonderful. Are you sure?"

I laugh. "Yeah, I'm sure. I don't know how. I mean, I know it sounds impossible, but I've got ten days to get a job and find a place to live, and I'm going to do it. I am. If I can do that, then maybe my parents will realize I'm not just being contrary or stubborn. I'm serious about this. Tonight has reminded me of something I've only just realized this summer, that I'm really good with kids, and I like that I matter to these campers. I want to matter to Emma Rose, too. I want to give her a good life."

Leo looks worried.

"I know, I know, taking care of older campers for a little while and all isn't the same as caring for and—and providing for a brand-new baby. But so what? Everybody keeps telling me that Emma Rose will be too much work and I can't handle it and all that crap, but how do they know that? Why is everybody always so good at predicting *my* future? How do they know I can't handle it? I'm the only one who really knows what's in me. Anyway, the social worker believes in me. She does," I say, when I see Leo raise his brows.

"So I have to work hard. So what? I can do that when I put my mind to it. So it will be a struggle. So what? Emma Rose is worth it. So she has Down syndrome. Perfect! I think she's just perfect for me. And I'm going to be perfect for her."

"Okay, Elly, okay," Leo says. "I'm on your side. Let me know how I can help, all right?" He pulls one of his Sharpies out of his back pocket, and he asks me to sign his shirt and write down my cell phone number on it. Then he writes his on my hand, and it's time to say goodbye.

"Okay, well, if you know of any job that I can get where I can bring Emma Rose with me or anything like that, or if you find one, let me know."

"I'll scour the papers every day for the next ten days," Leo says. He smiles, but he looks concerned.

I don't blame him. It sounds impossible, but there has to be a way. There just has to be, because I know, I just know with everything I have, that I can give Emma Rose a good life.

* * *

So the days zoom by. My parents are making plans for me to go with them back to Kenya, and they're leaving before the ten days are up. They're leaving on day eight. Clearly they have no second thoughts about staying home.

We pick up all my stuff at the cabin and say our final goodbyes and thanks to the Lothrops. My mom says we ought to try to sell all the baby stuff, and that's when I tell them I'm planning on staying here and keeping the baby.

So, you can imagine the scene. Once again Elly is being stubborn and unreasonable. Once again I'm doing the wrong thing instead of the right thing. Once again my mom has shut down, and she's so calm it's scary, while my dad is pitching a fit. "Eleanor, we've been through all this before! How can you be so naive as to think that you could possibly handle a baby—any baby, all on your own? It's out of the question. You're coming with us to Kenya, and that's the end of it."

I kind of wish I were stoned, because it would be a lot easier to deal with my parents, but that part of my life is over. I have to think of Emma Rose. I'm living my life for Emma Rose now, and knowing this gives me courage and hope. I let my parents think what they want, but they see me every day poring over the help-wanted ads in the paper. The only kind of job I can get is at a McDonald's or KFC, or some part-time drug store job. I look at the ads for places to live, and even here in Rumford the few places that are available to rent are too expensive for me. I look at the cost of diapers and baby food, and it's ridiculous how much those things cost. I figure I'll have to buy cloth diapers and wash them by hand. But how will I have time for that, plus care for Emma Rose and get a job, and pay for gas and food and daycare, oh, and go to school? I go round and round and get nowhere, and the days keep flying by.

I call Leo, who's back at the University of Maine in Augusta doing his ceramics, and he says he's been looking but he hasn't found anything. I ask him if maybe his parents would like to be foster parents to Emma Rose until I can find something. I'm desperate and he knows it, because he can hear it in my voice, but he says no. "They're having some big trouble with Ted, my eleven-year-old brother. They've said an even dozen is it for them. I'm sorry, Elly."

"Does your mom need any help? Maybe I could live there and just kind of help out?"

"She couldn't pay you," Leo says. "But that's not a bad idea. Becoming a live-in nanny or something," he says, his voice brightening.

"Yeah, it's not. Now I just need to find someone in Rumford—ha, ha—who needs a live-in nanny, and who will hire me plus Emma Rose."

"I'll keep looking," Leo says.

Nothing happens. Nothing! I feel so desperate. There's nothing for me in the papers. Leo checks the Internet, and there's nothing there, either.

My parents want to take me to the agency to sign the forms giving up my rights to Emma Rose.

"We're leaving in the morning," they say. "Come on, Elly, you aren't going to find anything at this late date. You've said your goodbyes; it's time to let the baby go now."

"The baby? The baby? She's not *the* baby; she's *my* baby. She's *my* baby! She's your granddaughter. I don't get it. I don't get how you can turn your backs on her. How? How?"

"Calm down, Elly. Just calm down," my dad says, glancing around our hotel room as if he's expecting spies to be behind the doors or something.

"No, really! You've always been there for the orphans. You always have time for them, but when is it ever time for me?"

"We've given you everything, Elly, now, come on, enough of this." My dad looks tired. I know I'm being hard on him. I'm just so frustrated, though.

I try to calm down and speak in a normal tone of voice. "Okay, you gave me everything. You gave me everything Sarah got, everything but you—your time. Your attention."

This wakes my mother up. She glares at me from the bed, where she's been sitting with her arms crossed, not even looking at me. But I say this, and she's alert. I've accused her of doing something wrong. "Do you really think you've needed us more than those poor children?" she asks.

"Yeah, Mom. Yeah! And I know you've always made me feel guilty for feeling this way. I shouldn't need you, not when there are AIDS babies that need you more. Well, guess what? I did need you, and I do need you now. I need you now!"

I wipe at my eyes, where tears are threatening to spill out, and I think of Banner always wiping at tears even when they weren't there.

"Sarah's ten years older than I am. Sarah was almost all grown up before you ever even went to Kenya. She was nineteen and I was just nine when I lost my parents to the AIDS babies."

"Come on, let's not be dramatic, Eleanor," Dad says. He gets up from the chair he's been sitting in and goes to stand in front of the window overlooking the Androscoggin River. He looks thin and old. I've never thought of him as looking old before, but the wrinkly skin on his elbows looks like something off an elephant.

I close my eyes. "Why can't you do this for me? Why can't you stay home for me? Why can't you help me raise my baby? Why are you being like this?" I open my eyes and glare at my mother. "Is it because I did wrong? I wasn't supposed to get pregnant. I've been a bad girl. That's it, isn't it?"

I can see by the look in my mom's eyes that I've nailed it. I've totally nailed it.

"Oh, yeah. You don't reward a bad girl by helping her fix her mistake, right? Well, this mistake is a human being! Don't punish her because of me. Do it for Emma Rose. If you can't do it for me, do it for her."

"Maybe you're right, Elly," my mother says in this eerily calm, monotone voice. "Maybe there is a bit of punishment in our decision. Why should we constantly pay for and be punished by your mistakes? We're tired of it. You obviously have no idea what you've put us through over the years. Still, if that's all it was, a punishment, then we'd get past it and do the right thing. But Elly, to put it as plainly as we can, we don't want to parent a Down syndrome child. Even part-time. We have our work. We need to do what we feel is right for us. Working with the orphans in Kenya is our calling."

"Yeah, well, I believe Emma Rose is mine. She needs me,

and I want to be there for her. I'm as committed to raising her as you are to your orphans."

I might as well have saved my breath. My parents aren't budging. I guess I should have known they wouldn't, but I had to try one more time. They tell me that it's time to go to lunch, and after that we'll go to the agency and sign the papers.

I refuse to go to lunch with my parents. I'm way too depressed. While they're gone I pack my bags for Kenya, but my mind is still racing. There has to be something.

I'm in the bathroom washing the tears off my face when my cell phone rings, and it's Leo.

"I've found a job I think you might be interested in."

"Oh, yeah?" I say, without much hope. "What is it?"

"It's in Andover, not too far away, and it's a live-in position, so it's just what you were looking for."

"Yeah? What would I have to do? Never mind, I'll do it. Whatever it is. What's the number? What's the address?"

Leo gives me all the information, and I thank him and we hang up. I start dialing the number, but then I stop. How could I possibly explain myself over the telephone? "Hi, I'm sixteen and I have a Down syndrome baby and I want to live in your house and take care of you." Right, that would go over well. I don't know why I think it will go over any better in person, but I figure it's my only chance, so I go for it. I leave a note for my parents and take Rambo, the old hunk-a-junk car we're supposed to turn over to a junk man today, and I drive to Andover.

It's a beautiful drive with mountains and fields all along the way. I speed along Route 5, and I slow as I get into Andover. I see Church Street. That's the address Leo gave me. I find the house. It's like a picture-book house, white with green shutters. I see a car parked in the front. I pull into the driveway and get out. I'm shaking. I know this is my only chance. I have to get this job.

I ring the doorbell and wait. While I'm waiting, I check out the yard. The grass is overgrown, and there are flowers, but the weeds that have grown up everywhere are choking them. There's an old swing set that's rusty and lopsided, but I can imagine Emma Rose on it. I could get some Rust-Oleum and paint it, and straighten it somehow, and then I could push Emma Rose on the swing, and catch her when she goes down the slide.

I wonder about the kids I'll be taking care of in this house. What kind of parents would let their kids swing on a falling-down set like that one? Or are the kids older now? Why would I need to take care of older kids? I'm so nervous now my teeth start to chatter. What am I walking into?

There's no answer, so I push the doorbell again, but I don't hear a ring, so then I knock.

Finally the door opens, and there's a lady standing in front of me with her hair in goo, and she's got on latex doctor's gloves that have goo all over them, too. Then I realize it's not a lady, it's the MIL! It's Mrs. Lothrop!

"Mrs. Lothrop? What are you doing here?"

"*I'm* visiting my mother. What are *you* doing here?"

"I—I don't know. Leo told me to come. I—I guess he made a mistake or something."

I swear I'm going to kill Leo the next time I see him. What kind of joke is this?

"Leo? I don't understand?" the MIL says.

"I'm looking for a job. A live-in position. Leo gave me this address." My heart has sunk all the way through the ground. I didn't know I could feel any lower than I already felt, but this disappointment is too much. Mrs. Lothrop of all people.

The MIL is dabbing at her forehead trying to keep her goop from running. "My mother's looking for a live-in nurse, but you aren't a nurse," she says. "And I don't know how Leo could have known about it, because I haven't advertised for the position yet. And anyway, my mother's in a wheelchair. She needs to be lifted in and out of it. She needs to be bathed and someone to cook her meals."

"I can do that! I can cook and clean and I'm stronger than I look. And, don't worry, I'm not quitting school. I plan to study at home and get my GED."

Leo suggested this idea, and I thought it was a good one. I could stay home with Emma Rose if I studied online instead of going to school.

"Please, Mrs. Lothrop, I'm desperate. I've got to keep Emma Rose. She's your granddaughter. Did you even look at her? Did you see her and touch her and smell her little head?"

The MIL closes her eyes and backs away from me, waving

her hand in front of her face. "No! No, I won't go through that again." She opens her eyes and draws her brows together. "Eleanor, don't set yourself up for that kind of pain. Believe me, let the agency place her with a good home. Let her go. I'm telling you it will be far less painful than having to do it later."

I stand there with my mouth hanging open. Less painful? She has no idea what I'm going through.

"But she's not going to die. Just because your child died, it doesn't mean Emma Rose will."

The MIL has closed her eyes again, and I realize it's over.

She starts to shut the door, but she pauses a second. "I'm sorry, Eleanor. You'd better go on now," she says. "Goodbye." Then she closes the door in my face.

I can't move. I've just lost Emma Rose—again. The tears roll down my face. I think about having to go to Kenya. I think about helping at the orphanage. How can I work with those children, knowing someone else is taking care of my baby? Maybe Emma Rose will never be adopted. Maybe she'll live out her life in an orphanage. How ironic would that be? No, I can't go to Kenya. I won't.

The door opens again, and I feel hopeful—pathetically hopeful.

"Could you get off my doorstep now?" the MIL says.

"Oh, sorry." I try to move, but it's just too much for me. If I leave, I've lost everything. If I stay on her doorstep, it's not over. Mrs. Lothrop stands there in all her goop waiting for me to go. I can't lose my baby. I stare at the woman's face, and her nose looks pinched and her lips are set in this straight line. She looks so angry, and I see my parents' faces in hers, and all my teachers' faces, and all the other faces in my life of people who have never believed in me, and I just fall apart, right there on her doorstep. I sink down to the little concrete slab and burst into tears. "It can't be over. Please, it can't be. If you'd just go see her."

"What the hell is going on here?" I hear the old lady say.

"I've got it, Ma," the MIL says.

"Get out of the way and let me see already."

I hear the sound of the wheelchair motor, then there she is, the old bat peering at me from behind the MIL—great.

I know I'm acting like a baby, but I can't stop crying. I try. I wipe away my tears, but new ones spill down on top of the old and splat onto the concrete. Well, who cares, anyway?

"What the hell have you done to this girl?" the old lady asks.

"Nothing, Ma. She thinks she wants the job. She wants to take care of you, and I told her we were looking for a nurse."

The old lady rolls her chair into the back of the MIL's legs, and the MIL steps aside to make room for her in the doorway. "No, honey, *you're* looking for a nurse. I'm looking for this little bitty right here."

"What?" the MIL and I both say at the same time.

I wipe my face and nose on the sleeve of my T-shirt and stand up. "You're looking for me?"

"Ma, you can't be serious."

The woman draws her head back and takes a deep breath. Her chest puffs out with indignation. "Like hell I can't! When Leo told me what was going on with this little bitty, I was ashamed. So ashamed of all of you. This is the mother of my great-granddaughter! This is the mother of your grandchild! She and that baby need a place to live, and if she thinks she can put up with an ornery old fool like me, and look after me, then I aim to have her live right here!" She pounds her chair, then points her finger at me. "I've been watching you."

"I know," I say. "I know, and I'll do better. I'll be better. Whatever you want. Can I really stay here? I'll take care of you. I will. I'm stronger than I look and I'll—"

"Ma, enough! Leave her alone. This isn't funny," the MIL says. Her eyes dart from me to the old bat. She looks totally rattled.

Then I wonder if this really is some kind of a joke. I wouldn't put it past the old bat. Was she testing me at camp? All those batty things she said to me. Were they tests? Could I possibly have passed?

"Who's joking? I want her to be my nurse. I want her and my great-granddaughter to come live right here."

"Out of the question, Ma. Forget it. It's not going to happen!" The MIL's arms are flailing, and goo is running down the side of her face. "No! I can't—I can't handle it. You know what we went through with our little Amanda. How could you even think of it? And I don't want to be worrying about you and Eleanor and her baby up here while we're living down the mountain all winter."

"So don't worry. Who's asking you to? And it's about time you stop thinking of yourself and your twenty-year-old pain over the loss of Amanda, and start looking at what's right in front of you. You've got an opportunity to love and be blessed all over again, and here you are ready to slam the door in opportunity's face. I've never been so ashamed of you in my life!"

"But Ma—"

"'But Ma,' nothin'! The three of us are going to have a blast, aren't we, Little Bitty?"

I nod. "Yeah, sure. If this—isn't a joke."

"When can you start?" the old lady asks, and right on top of her, Mrs. Lothrop shouts, "Ma! No!"

The old bat rams her chair into her daughter's shins. "It's my money, and my life, and I can't think of anything better for an aging old fool than to have a house with a baby in it and a fresh-mouthed young teenager to boss me around. It'll be a gasser! Now, come on in. Let's you and me get acquainted."

I look at the MIL, and wait.

She scowls at me for like three minutes, and I can see her mind trying to process the idea of me back in her life just when she thought she had gotten rid of me. Finally she sighs and shakes her head. "Well"—she backs away from the door—"I guess—I guess—come on in. You can stay here on a trial basis only."

"I can't believe it." I'm grinning my face off, I'm so happy.

"Really?" I squeal, and Mrs. Lothrop rolls her eyes and steps aside to let me in.

"You might as well come on in and see what you're in for."

The old lady has turned her wheelchair around so it's facing the living room. She rolls forward and calls behind her. "Come on, Little Bitty, let me show you the lay of the house and the little boot box where you'll be staying when you're not slaving away." She chuckles at her own joke. The old bat has a weird sense of humor.

"Okay, first of all," I say, trotting along behind her, feeling suddenly, and fantastically, on top of the world, "I don't want to be called Little Bitty. And second of all, you've got to act nice around my baby, and no swearing, because I'm going to raise her right. I'm going to do the right thing by her. And third of all, no more ramming into people with this chair of yours. It's not a bumper car, you know."

"Yeah, yeah, whatever you say, Li'l Bit."

"That's right, Old Bat, whatever I say."

The old bat cackles.